**"I'm having a hard
Christmas trees grow**

Hope stepped away from the corner where she'd been leaning against the wall, watching them.

"Other than hunting our plastic one out of storage, I have not had a real tree-hunting experience, but I think you and the kids should go by yourselves."

What? She was still upset with him?

Maddie took Hope's hand and tugged her even closer to Ben. She wanted her to come, too. For an entirely different reason, he was sure.

Ben started to reach out to take Hope's hand himself. He wanted to pull her out the door. Make her come, because he needed her to be there. He was taking the kids to get a tree because a crazy voice in his head was telling him it was the right thing to do. Whether it was going to be a good thing, he didn't know for sure. What if being in that tree lot proved too hard to take and he ruined the night for his kids? He wanted her there when he helped the kids hang all the ornaments Zoe had collected over the years. How could he get through that without Hope there to pick up the pieces if he broke down?

But maybe she didn't want to pick up the pieces.

Dear Reader,

Silence is something that—as a mother of three boys and an outrageous number of pets—I've begged for at times. Anything for a little bit of soothing peace and quiet in which to work, think (and actually be able to hear my thoughts) and decompress. But, as a mother, I also know firsthand how frustrating and destructive silence can be, especially for a child.

Although my kids have come a long way, two of them struggled with being able to cope with and express overwhelming emotions when they were younger. As a result, they'd shut down. The teacher calls, school visits, hours of trying to get them to open up...I'll never forget any of it.

It's heartbreaking for a parent not to be able to get through to their child. For my kids, the silence would last from endless minutes to hours. But for Maddie, the young girl in this story, it has gone on for months... triggered by the tragic loss of a parent. I'm so grateful that my kids didn't have the same diagnosis or trigger as Maddie, but nonetheless, it still comes down to internal suffering. An inability to cope. A cry for help. And whether it's a child or adult withdrawing, silence can be a dark, stressful and lonely place...until love and trust finally break through.

I hope you enjoy this story of how two people suffering on opposite sides of the world discover each other, rediscover the power of love and family and, together, show a little girl that it's okay to be happy again.

My door is always open at rulasinara.com, where you can find links to my blog, all the places I hang out and more, so feel free to drop by!

Rula Sinara

HEARTWARMING

After the Silence

———

Rula Sinara

Recycling programs
for this product may
not exist in your area.

ISBN-13: 978-0-373-36718-4

After the Silence

www.Harlequin.com

Printed in U.S.A.

Rula Sinara lives in Virginia's countryside with her husband, three boys and zany but endearing pets. When she's not writing or doing mom stuff, she loves organic gardening, attracting wildlife to her yard (cool bugs included) or watching romantic movies. She also enjoys interviewing fellow authors and is a special contributor for *Happy Ever After* on USATODAY.com. Her door is always open at rulasinara.com or awritersrush.blogspot.com.

Books by Rula Sinara

HARLEQUIN HEARTWARMING

The Promise of Rain

To check out Rula's books,
visit her author page on Harlequin.com.

To each of you who has helped a child
to heal and rediscover joy.

Acknowledgments

Infinite thanks to my author sisters for their support
and shared stories of surviving deadlines when
life throws a few curve*boulders*...and to my reader
friends for your generous and beautiful words about
my first book in this series, *The Promise of Rain*. You
all kept me going.

And, as always, thank you, Victoria Curran, for your
patience, incredible insight and for encouraging me
to be cruel to my characters. Plain and simple, you
make me a better writer. I'm blessed to have such a
gifted editor and teacher to guide me.

PROLOGUE

ZOE CORALLIS HELD her breath as the door to the baby's room clicked shut. She counted five seconds before daring to tiptoe away, cleared a good five feet before exhaling, then scurried to the kitchen.

"Mommy, I finished copying down my spelling words and the oven just beeped," Maddie said, jumping off the kitchen stool and stuffing her notebook into her brown-and-pink gingham backpack. "Did you want to check them?"

Zoe chuckled as she turned off the oven timer before it could ring and wake up Ryan. Maddie, knowing full well there wouldn't be homework checks this afternoon, already had her backpack zipped up.

"I trust you, sweetie," she said as she pulled two round pans of Ben's favorite banana cake out of the oven and set them on the stovetop to cool. She dipped her head, teaming up with the effervescent light spilling through the window, and scanned the counter for rogue crumbs. Spotless.

"Is he almost here?" Maddie asked.

Zoe glanced at the oven clock for the hundredth time since morning. Three-fifty. Which meant the cream-cheese frosting and strawberries weren't going to make it onto the cake until after Ben arrived, and she'd wanted everything perfect and ready. After ten months of hell, he deserved to come home to peace and quiet. And Zoe knew how much having the house calm and clean helped him recover from experiences he never discussed and she didn't dare imagine.

Zoe held Maddie's cheeks and kissed her pert little nose. "Almost." She gave Maddie's two dark braids a playful tug, then took her backpack from her hand. "I'll put this away. Do me a huge favor and go help Chad pick up his toys so Daddy doesn't trip on them."

"Okay." Maddie tucked her stool under the counter, then cupped her hands against her chest. "Can we tell him about the puppy yet?" she whispered. Chad was too young to be trusted with a secret, and Maddie was nearing bursting point, not being able to share their plans to raise a puppy. Zoe was so exhausted today that she had fleeting second thoughts about the yearlong commitment—raising a puppy for a service-and-guide-dog-training organization that was known for helping veterans—but seeing her daughter's face beaming reaffirmed her decision. Maddie loved animals, and the experience would not only be great for the kids, it would be great for Ben, too. Her gift to him. A way to serve…from home.

"Let's give Daddy a day to settle in before we tell him. Think you can keep it hush until tomorrow morning?" With the pup scheduled to arrive in five days, they'd definitely need to tell Ben as soon as possible. Breakfast time would be good. Maddie scrunched her face as if she'd sucked on a lemon and dropped her arms.

"Fine. I'll survive," she said with a dramatic sigh.

Zoe watched her daughter skip into the family room off the kitchen and half listened to her coaxing her four-year-old brother to clean up rather than play. He protested. Loudly. Peace and quiet were near impossible on a good day. She sure hoped the antibiotics for

Ryan's ear infection would kick in so he'd sleep through tonight. That, or Ben was going to need earplugs. Zoe rubbed her forehead. With no caffeine because of nursing and no more than three hours of sleep last night, she knew anticipation was the only thing keeping her from crashing. She felt guilty for not taking the kids to get Ben, but with a sick baby and the wait time involved, it just wasn't possible. It wasn't his first homecoming, but it felt like it. Every time he made it home safely, she couldn't shake the niggling fear that they'd used up their good luck. Zoe's eyes burned. She'd give her life to know that Ben would be safe and sound forever.

She swallowed hard and reached for the baby monitor perched on the counter by the fridge, and made sure Chad hadn't fiddled with the volume setting. She would not break down. Not in front of the kids, and certainly not in front of Ben. He'd be dealing with jet lag and exhaustion. He didn't need her falling apart at the sight of him, too. Not when she wanted so badly to convince him not to reenlist—again—and that this was the place to be.

Home.

And changing her shirt would be a good

move. Even she, immune as she was, could smell the sour tang of baby burp on her shoulder.

"Maddie. Chad. I'll be right back. Hide the toy box behind the sofa when you're done."

"Daddy!" The creak of the front door, thud of a duffel bag hitting the floor and Chad's squeal sent an explosion of everything pure, wonderful and fated surging through Zoe and lodging in her throat. The sight of him standing in the doorway did her in.

"Ben." She could barely hear her own voice over the wail from the baby monitor.

His lips curved into the crooked smile that had charmed her from day one. Zoe held back for the kids and thanked her stars when Ryan's cry through the monitor mellowed to a gurgle, then silence. She watched as Ben knelt down to hug Chad, then held one free arm out to a suddenly shy Maddie. Chad was young enough to get excited over the *idea* of Daddy, but Maddie's uncertainty broke Zoe's heart. At nine, she was realizing just how much of a stranger her dad really was. Seeing her finally wrap her arms around him set Zoe's tears in action. He stood up, and in seconds Zoe ambushed him, legs around his waist. Her lips met his in a long, warm kiss. She ran her hands along the stubble that shaded his face and kissed his neck, letting herself get enveloped in the strength, warmth and scent that was only his.

"I missed you. Oh, man, I missed you," she whispered.

"I missed you, too," he said, nuzzling her hair and holding her firmly against his chest. He didn't let go. Zoe loved that he didn't let go—in spite of the fact that the aroma of baby burp couldn't have escaped his keen marine senses.

"Something smells good," he said.

Zoe laughed and pulled back.

"I need to change my shirt."

"Me, too. I'll be right behind you. I need to set my bags in the bedroom."

Zoe stroked his cheek again. "By the way, I'm making your favorite cake, and as soon as I change, I need to run to Bentley's to pick up dinner."

Ben flattened his hand against his heart.

"You're the best. With extra cheese?"

"Made to order just for you," Zoe said. Ben loved her home-cooked meals, but ordering his favorite burger from the same pub where they'd gone on their very first date had become a homecoming tradition. Thank goodness Maddie had reminded her this morning. Lack of sleep nurtured brain fog.

Zoe fingered his collar, then rested her hands on his shoulders. Whatever had been bugging him, they were finally face-to-face. They'd sort it out. She knew he worried about money. But once he met his son, nothing else would matter.

She hoped.

"Ryan is sleeping, barely, but you have to come see him. Mom says he looks like me, but I don't know. I think he has your nose."

"Poor kid," Ben said, ruffling Chad's hair before picking up his oversize duffel and following Zoe toward the bedroom hallway to the right of the kitchen.

"Poor kid has an ear infection. He might be cranky when he wakes up, but I won't take long. Maddie can help you."

"Yep, he likes me," Maddie said, looking at Zoe for confirmation.

"How could he not? You're the greatest big sis and helper *ever*," Zoe said, letting Ben enter the master bedroom ahead of her. Maddie looked expectantly at her father for approval, but he just set his bag near the foot of the bed and looked around the room without a word, as if he'd entered a hotel room and needed to get his bearings. It happened whenever he came home. And by the time they'd find a new rhythm and his awkward, withdrawn silences would subside, he'd get ready to head out again.

But not this time. Zoe needed to convince him that he'd served enough and that she needed him here with her. The kids needed their dad.

Zoe rubbed Maddie's shoulder and gave her an encouraging smile.

"Do me a favor. Go touch a finger to one of the cakes and see if it's cool enough to frost. You can start on it while I pick up dinner."

"Okay!" Maddie ran down the hall, the hurt of her dad not responding seemingly forgotten.

Chad scrambled up the side of the bed and started jumping.

"Get down, buddy, before you fall," Ben said, scooping him by the waist and setting him on the floor.

Zoe slipped into their small walk-in closet and quickly changed. She couldn't help feeling a little nervous and self-conscious around him. The last time he'd seen her she'd barely begun showing, but Ryan was only four weeks old and, as slim as she was, she was still battling the remains of belly flab and stretch marks. She stepped out just as Ben pulled an army-green cap from his bag and put it on Chad's head.

"I'll be back in fifteen minutes," she said.

"No, wait," he said. "I can go. You stay in case the baby wakes up." *The baby. Not Ryan.*

"Ben, you'll be fine. He was up all night, so I don't think he'll wake up for a while. Just go take a peek at him."

Ben started to protest, and Zoe put her fingertips to his mouth, then ran her thumb along his bottom lip in promise. "Go meet your son. Spend a little time with the kids. They go to bed pretty early. You'll survive."

Ben covered her hand with his, then let her slip away.

SOME THINGS WERE not meant to be miniature.

Ben cocked his head and looked at his swaddled son. Poor thing really did have his nose. *Don't worry, bud, you'll grow into it.*

He was actually a cute little thing, *little* being a scary word. With the same caution he'd use to handle a live grenade, he reached down and laid his hand against Ryan's chest. The pulsing of that tiny infant heart against his callused palm blew him away. Innocence. It killed him that he had taken part in bringing another innocent child into a world ravaged with so many evils and dangers…but he had. And it was his duty to make sure his family was provided for and no harm came to them.

Wow. Kid number three. Ben swiped his palm down his face. Higher bills, expenses and college tuition…which meant no way could he give up his steady pay and bene- fits. Not yet. He was more valuable to them on duty anyway. Whenever he was home, his time was dedicated to fun and relaxation with Zoe and the kids. If he had to tackle child rearing on a daily basis, he'd probably just mess up what Zoe had going. She was the most amazing wife a marine—any man, for that matter—could have. The most incredi- ble, patient woman and mother he knew. And they had a system. His career meant they'd be safe and provided for and she…she held down the fort and made it all worthwhile.

It worked for them, and she seemed happy enough.

He hadn't had any doubts about her happiness until she'd recently begun talking, via Skype, about how relieved she was that his duty was ending, and she wouldn't have to live day to day worrying about the infamous knock on the door. He'd let it go. Arguing over his decision to reenlist wasn't something he'd wanted to get into on a computer screen. Especially not with her pregnancy hormones out of whack. The way he figured things, he didn't have an option. Not with a growing family.

The doorbell rang, and Ben froze, expecting the baby to wake up. He pulled his hand away, careful not to cause any air turbulence. Put a real grenade in his palm and he'd deal with it. A crying infant with a loaded diaper? Now, that was a weapon he had no intention of handling.

"Daddy, the door!"

His breath caught, both from fear that she'd wake the baby and from the sound of *Daddy* from his daughter's lips. He rushed out of the room, intent on forestalling the next ring of the bell.

"Mommy says to leave the door answering to her," Maddie explained from behind a disaster of frosting and what he hoped was cake. Chad, perched on a stool next to her, was licking white goop off his hands.

Oh, boy. Zoe'll be back soon. Zoe'll be back soon.

"Make sure your brother doesn't fall," Ben said, pointing at Chad for emphasis. Man. At least they knew not to open the door to strangers.

Ben reached the front door and swung it wide, not in the mood for visitors, but half expecting Zoe's parents. Grandma could handle the goop.

The ground rippled beneath his feet when he saw the uniforms. His adrenaline jacked into high gear.

He was overreacting. Maybe this time PTSD had won out. They were probably just door-to-door fund-raising. They still did that, right? He scratched impatiently at his forehead, irritated with himself for going into battle mode.

"Yes, officers?"

"Sir, is this the home of Zoe Corallis?"

Is this the home of Zoe Corallis?

An icy cold bled across his chest. He shook his head, refusing to listen to what instinct told him they were going to say. This wasn't right. This was supposed to be home.

Ben's chest heaved, and his knuckles whitened against the door frame. The officer's words blistered in his ears. *Is this the home of Zoe Corallis? Car accident... We're sorry.*

"No. No." He shook his head emphatically, his words sounding like military orders even to himself. He fisted his shirt, where Zoe's touch still lingered.

"Maddie, take Chad to Ryan's room and stay there until I say." He turned to be sure they obeyed and was met with stunned looks. "Now! Go!"

Maddie helped her brother down and they disappeared like frightened prey. Ben braced his hands against the door frame, trying to process what was happening, then, like the friends he'd seen pelleted with shrapnel, he buckled and hit the floor.

Zoe.

CHAPTER ONE

Dear Diary,
They said writing to you would help.
I'm not sure. I can't tell anyone what I
did. Not even you. If anyone finds out,
I could go to jail…or hell.

HOPE ALWANGA STRIPPED off her bloody gloves
and gown, then rushed from the room, but
there was no escaping the merciless, cop-
pery smell that had penetrated her sinuses.
She pressed the crook of her elbow to her
nose to shield against the added assault from
the sweaty, desperate crowd still waiting to
be seen and made her way to the back of
the emergency room. A steady stream of patients was expected at any of Nairobi's public hospitals—she saw it as added experience
during her internship year—but this? This
was pure chaos. And she'd been forced to do
procedures she'd never done before.

She needed a minute to sit. Just one.

She collapsed onto a stool near a half-empty medical supply closet, leaned her head back against the wall and closed her eyes.

"Go home."

"No," she said, jerking her head up and pushing off the stool. The floor tilted, and her hands shot out reflexively for balance. "I'm fine. I just needed a second."

Zamir, her supervising doctor, put a gentle hand on her shoulder and urged her back onto the stool.

"Take that second and then go home. That's an order," he said.

"I haven't eaten anything. That's all it is." That and no sleep.

"Don't argue with your superior."

Hope rolled her eyes. Zamir could never nail a harsh tone when it came to her. He was closer in age to her much-older brother, and, given that he'd grown up as a family friend, he often teetered between his role as her supervising medical officer and a caring friend. A lot. Only, he knew full well that Hope wasn't interested in anything but focusing on her education and career. Hope brushed his hand aside and stood, taking a deep, readying breath.

"You need me here. We've lost two patients already this morning, and there has been no news of the rest of the staff coming back. I'm not going anywhere."

For two days now, they'd been running on bare threads. It was bad enough that, under normal circumstances, Nairobi's public hospitals were grossly underequipped. Only months into her internship, she'd already witnessed patients either dying or being turned away due to lack of medical equipment and supplies alone. Even children. God, the children broke her heart. Now, to add insult to an already critical situation, delayed government paychecks had spurred a strike by the majority of their medical staff. As an intern, her pay was barely worth counting anyway, but she wasn't here for money. She was here to help, but this…this was like asking a gnat to save a drowning shrew.

She turned to head back toward the main area. Failure wasn't an option. Not for an Alwanga.

"Hope, don't be stubborn," Zamir said, stepping in front of her. "You need to get some sleep or you'll be useless. You'll start to make mistakes. I can't have that happen. Stay and I'll write you up."

Hope stopped dead in her tracks, then looked right at him. Her pulse drummed at the base of her throat.

"That man did not die because of me," she said, pointing down the hall toward the patient they'd just lost. "I did everything—"

"I didn't mean him," Zamir said, shaking his head and holding up his palms. "You were brilliant in there. Hope, that man had been thrown from a *boda-boda*. He didn't have a chance. Not with what we have here. But I need you to get some rest before I end up having to resuscitate *you*. Or before you *do* make a human mistake."

Hope pressed her lips together and cringed at the mental image of Zamir resuscitating her. He'd love that, wouldn't he? Zamir to the rescue. Always looking out for her. That was exactly why her parents loved him so much.

But he was right. Anyone who dared hitch a ride on Kenya's motorcycle-styled taxis, manned by an array of notoriously reckless drivers, was gambling with death. She'd done what she could, stepping in to assist Zamir in the absence of more experienced doctors and nurses. But her trained immunity to the stench of violent death had failed her today. The lack of sleep really was doing a number on her senses, and the last cup of lukewarm coffee she'd guzzled hadn't done much to help. She ran both hands back over her chin-length waves. She still wasn't used to the texture after her mom insisted she have it relaxed a few weeks ago. "Fine," she said. "Just for a few hours."

"Don't come back until tomorrow. I'll find someone to help. Maybe the strike will be over by then," he said, twisting his lips. Neither of them was holding out hope on that count. Even if it did end, the suffering and loss would have still happened. The supplies and equipment needed to better serve the majority of locals too poor to seek help from private hospitals or doctors—such as her parents—would still be an issue.

Hope nodded and walked away, too tired to argue anymore. What was the point? After finishing up her year here, she'd be moving on to her master of medicine in orthopedics before joining her parents' private practice.

That had always been the plan. All she was doing right now was rolling a boulder uphill.

She grabbed her things, made a quick call to Jamal, their family driver, for pickup and fled the building. A well-dented *matatu* packed with passengers revved its engine and missed her by two feet as it sped away from the curb. She gasped, then coughed out a lungful of exhaust fumes. And there was the reason she didn't drive. One had to have a little daredevil and adrenaline addict in them to navigate the streets of Nairobi. Being a passenger was scary enough, but she trusted Jamal. He'd been her family's driver since she was an infant, hired right after her parents had employed his wife as a house-keeper and cook, because at the time, with Hope's medical needs and heart surgery, they'd needed the extra help.

She made her way to where she spotted Jamal waiting. The October sunshine cleansing her face made up for the emergency room "aromas" and exhaust fumes. Boy, was she glad their family home was outside the city. Although lately, she hadn't spent much time there.

"Jambo," she said, climbing in with the

oversize woven shoulder bag she carried her life in: clinical books, notes, wallet, a few toiletries and probably a few items lost at the bottom that she'd forgotten about entirely.

"*Jambo*, Hope," Jamal said, closing her door, then making his way around to the driver's seat.

She quickly pulled off her socks and shoes and slipped her achy feet into the sandals she kept tucked under the front seat. She sighed and leaned back.

"Home?" Jamal asked.

"No, I need to stop at the university first. Then Chuki's, then home." She wouldn't be able to truly relax until she dropped off inhaler samples for Chuki's little sister. Her friend's family had been struggling financially for a while now, and the least Hope could do was to try to help out. Especially with the strike going on.

Jamal glanced at her through the rearview mirror before turning his focus on the road.

"You look pale. Dalila told me to tell you she's making some fresh *mandazi* just for you. She said not to tell your parents. She'll have stew ready by the time they come home," he said, winking at her through the rearview mirror.

"Mmm." Hope closed her eyes and savored the mere idea of a warm homemade doughnut. Her only vice. Her stomach growled, and she pressed her hand against it. "Dalila is an angel," she said, barely lifting her heavy eyelids.

"I know," he said, grinning.

Hope gave in to sleep as she smiled back. Not much of a nap, given that the campus building where her brother's research lab was located wasn't far enough for the solid dose of REM sleep she needed. She woke up at Jamal's prompting and dragged her groggy self toward the building and up the stairs to her brother's genetics lab.

"Jambo," she said, closing the door behind her and hanging her bag on the hook meant for his lab coat. She glanced over her shoulder, pretending not to notice the annoyed look on her brother Dr. Simba David Alwanga's face. "Dr. Alwanga" to all his staff and colleagues—especially the ladies—but family always used his middle name, David. Hope, however, had called him Simba ever since she could talk, and she was the only

person who could get away with it. He hated the fact that he shared a name with an animated movie character. She loved it.

"*Jambo*. No sandals in the lab. You know that," he said.

She did know. Standard lab safety called for closed-toe shoes, something she'd gotten in the habit of wearing during medical school, especially when working with patients and blades or needles.

"Sorry, but I couldn't stand it anymore. Every cell on me needed to breathe," she said, collapsing onto the swivel stool in front of the counter across from where he was labeling petri dishes. "Besides, I'm not staying long. Please tell me you got some."

The corners of his mouth quirked up.

"I promised, didn't I?" he said, still labeling and setting the dishes in organized rows.

She shook her head and chuckled at his smugness. Even as his sister, she had to admit he was a good-looking guy, on top of having a phenomenal reputation in the research world and a natural charisma women seemed to find irresistible. That actually worried her a bit. She had a hard time imagining him settling down, but at the same time, she didn't want him trapped by some woman who only cared about his name and success. Men could be so blind.

"I do appreciate the fruits of your effortless *labor*, dear brother, but one of these days you're going to meet your match, and she's going to laugh at your smooth-talking ways."

He flicked the on switch for the sterile hood that occupied a good five feet of the narrow lab's right wall, set his tray of dishes under it, then leaned back against the counter and folded his arms.

"Smooth talking? It's this face and the brains behind it," he said.

Hope rolled her eyes. She knew he was kidding for her benefit. Mostly. It took about two seconds for his eyes to narrow.

"You look terrible," he said.

"Did you really just compliment your looks, then insult mine? Just give me the samples," she said, hoping to deflect his concern.

"Hope, trust me, not even mud could mask your beauty—"

"Oh, for heaven's sake, tell me you haven't tried that one in public," she said, tossing her head.

"—but you really do look pale. And yes, *that one* got you these," he added, pulling two sample-size boxes out of his lab coat pocket and handing them to her.

"Thank you!" Hope jumped off the stool, took the boxes and gave Simba a quick hug. "I'll leave you to work."

"Not so fast." He guided her back to the stool and made her sit. So much for a quick exit. Hope knew when she was in for another lecture. A part of her understood the good place it was coming from.

As the youngest, she was stuck with the position of the family baby. Considering how "delicate" she'd been as a real baby, Hope was used to her every breath being scrutinized or worried over. Yes, it was love, but it was also irritating at times. At twenty-five, she knew how to get things done. So far, she'd been successful with every step of the career that her parents had carefully outlined with her. It was just that, as a woman, it seemed as if she always had to work harder for the same success and accolades as her male peers. Even her brother. So yes, she was tired.

"I know I look tired. I am. I just left hell,

but I'm headed home right after dropping these off, so I'll be fine. Jamal is waiting for me. Okay?"

Simba rolled another stool near hers and sat down. He pressed his lips together and looked off to the side before turning to her. There was no trace of his fun demeanor left. This was all lion king.

"Listen to me, Hope. This isn't just about today. I've noticed you going downhill for months now."

"I'm an intern at a public hospital. What do you expect?"

"I expect you to have good days and bad days. But be honest. You're miserable, Hope. Your face is like an open book. I see determination and exhaustion, but never joy. I see no peace in you."

Hope licked her lips and looked away, blinking several times to fight the burn of tears. He was right. Everyone always said that she had such an expressive face. Kind of a curse at times. No emotional privacy.

"Sometimes I feel as though I need to be autoclaved. It's expected."

"Sometimes you simply need a break. You're making yourself sick and I'm worried," he continued. "When was the last time you visited this friend of yours? Do you even still have other friends?" He pointed to the boxes Hope held.

He didn't really know Chuki, and she wasn't surprised that he couldn't recall her name. The women that caught his eye were in related fields…and not from Chuki's side of town. But he was right. It had been almost two months since she'd seen Chuki in person, and even that visit had been no more than thirty minutes. She shrugged. She couldn't do this now.

"Exactly. You care about her, yet you hardly see her. Do you know why I'm successful at what I do?" her brother asked. "Because I love this." He waved a hand at the lab. "This is my passion, Hope. I went after it because I wanted to. It satisfied me. Hard work? Yes, but there has to be balance."

Hope straightened and took a deep breath.

"That's enough, Simba. You can't tell me what I want and don't want to do."

"No, but I can tell you that your health comes first. Your happiness comes first. Can *you* tell me that if you had one wish on earth, it would be to join Mama and Baba's practice?" He sliced his hand through the air. "Do you even have a wish?"

The door to the lab swung open and Simba's friend and colleague Dr. Jack Harper stepped in. *Yes. A buffer.*

"Hey, you two slackers. Stop sitting around and get to work," Jack teased as he carried two racks of sample-filled vials to the far end of the lab near the centrifuge. He set them down and pulled a pipette out of a drawer. Simba gave her a "this isn't over" look and went back to his work.

"Jack. I didn't know you were going to be here today!" Hope said, perching her sandals on the bottom rung of the stool and swiveling it gently left and right. "How is everyone at Busara? How is little Pippa?"

"They're great. And Pippa... That *little* monkey is growing fast." His eyes sparkled like only a proud father's could. "Anna and Niara told me to say hi to you and to tell you they'd be around for some supplies soon," Jack said.

"Tell them I can't wait." She resisted the urge to ask when exactly "soon" would be. She really wanted to see them, but her brain tensed from the mere idea of how the logistics would work with her current schedule. Unless, maybe, if the strike ended.

Hope had met Jack and Anna a little over a year ago, when her brother was helping them sort out US citizenship and paternity paperwork for their daughter, Pippa, whom Anna had been raising in secret at Busara, her remote elephant research and rescue camp in the Serengeti. Anna had brought along her devoted friend Niara, and Hope had had a wonderful time taking Niara and her little boy shopping, while Anna and Jack had dealt with the embassy. At the time, Hope had almost been done with medical school. Jack, Anna and Pippa had come to dinner at their home a few times since then, after Jack had moved to Kenya and started collaborating with Simba, flying from Busara to Nairobi a few days a week. They'd all grown even closer as friends when Jack was crushed by the death of his sister in the States six months ago. He wasn't the biggest talker, but whenever he mentioned something about his niece and nephews back home, it was clear to Hope that they meant a lot to him.

"Sandals?" Jack asked, raising one brow at

Simba, as if surprised he hadn't chased his sister out of the room yet.

"Not you, too. You're more paranoid than my brother," Hope said, hopping off the stool to get her bag. The room spun, and she took a step back, sending the stool rolling to her left. She dropped the sample boxes and grabbed the edge of the counter to regain her balance, but Simba was already holding her by the arm and Jack was over in seconds with a backed chair from the small adjoining office.

"Are you preg—" Jack asked, picking up the inhaler samples.

"No!" Hope and Simba said simultaneously, glaring at him in disbelief. Then Simba looked at Hope with scary-wide eyes.

"No!" she confirmed. Talk about an impossibility.

"Pretend I didn't open my mouth," Jack said with raised palms. He handed her the boxes.

"I just got up too quickly. I'll be fine now."

"That's it," Simba said. "You're taking medical leave. Some time off."

"Have you lost your mind? I can't. Zamir needs me at the hospital. Half his staff are gone."

"Zamir called me today, worried sick. I'm not the only one who's noticed you withering away."

Hope felt the rush of blood heat her face.

"He didn't," she said.

"He did. I know I'll have his backing on this. He'll sign whatever is needed. The internship will still be there, Hope. If that's what you want. But you need to pause."

Hope rubbed her hands down her face. No. This was impossible. People would ask questions and spread rumors that she'd failed somehow. She'd embarrass her parents. She'd disappoint them, and she couldn't do that after all they'd sacrificed to save her life and to give her nothing but the best. Being where she was in her life wasn't just hard work, it was a privilege. It was the grand plan. And taking off would be the equivalent of being ungrateful…or worse, incapable. At least that was what people would think.

Simba was right, though. Doctors really did make awful patients, because if she was honest with herself about how she'd been feeling lately, she'd be surprised if her adrenal glands hadn't shriveled up.

God knew, she wanted to help people.

She really did. But lately all she was feeling was frustrated and depleted. She didn't dare admit to her family how many times the idea of escaping all their expectations and all her responsibilities had crossed her mind. Kicking back. Partying. Traveling places she'd seen in movies or read about in books. Freedom. How selfish was that? Witnessing poverty and disease everyday and then yearning for something different than the life she had? Some wishes were better left unspoken.

She closed her eyes and a tear escaped. She swiped it away.

"Um, can I get you something?" Jack asked, rubbing the back of his neck. Hope cleared her throat. She needed to get home. This was all too embarrassing.

"No, no. Thank you, Jack. Simba is making a big deal out of nothing." She scowled at her brother. "And you're embarrassing me here. Why don't you walk me downstairs, Simba? You can buy your little sister a snack to eat in the car."

He couldn't say no to getting food in her system. She really didn't want to argue in front of Jack, nor did she want to pass out before getting to the car. Jack slipped over to his vials and grabbed a pair of sterile gloves from a box, granting them a little privacy.

Simba paced in front of her like…well…like a lion.

"Hope, I know you're worried about what people will think. What Mama and Baba will say. I wasn't born yesterday. I'll handle them. Don't worry. No one will judge."

Hope sighed. "Look. I'll take a weekend or a week and stare at the walls at home. Will that make you happy?"

She waited for her brother to say something. The hum of the sterile hood and the occasional clink of Jack's tubes were the only sounds in the lab. Simba scratched his forehead, then looked around the lab as though in search of a scientific reason to nix her suggestion. He drew back his shoulders and braced his hands on his hips.

"No. This isn't about a few nights of sleep. This is about you not killing yourself and having regrets. I know our parents mean well, but the fact is, they're from a different generation. Even I have a decade on you and can see that. You're my sister. I want you happy. I want you to have perspective. Choices. Which is why—" he hesitated, scrubbing his jaw and exchanging glances with Jack "—I think you should take a few months and go to America."

The chair grated the floor as Hope stood, the bolt of shock keeping her on her feet this time.

"What? Jack, tell him he needs an MRI."

Jack held his sterile gloved palms up.

"I'm not getting in the middle. A wise friend once told Anna and me his favorite saying—'when two elephants fight, it is the grass that gets trampled.' In this lab, that would be me."

"Something tells me you're already in the middle. America? Really?"

Hope knew her brother had come through for Jack when Jack had discovered the daughter he didn't know he had was being raised in Kenya's wilderness. Had Simba cashed in on a favor?

"I'm helping you here, Hope," Simba said. "Haven't you always wanted to visit America? I've heard you talking to Anna. This is the perfect time. The perfect chance. Jack's family needs some help."

Jack tipped his head in agreement as he loaded the centrifuge.

"Don't feel obligated or anything, but when Alwanga here told me you needed to get away, it did make sense," Jack said. "Ben, my brother-in-law, could use help with the kids."

Hope gripped the sides of her head, then grabbed her purse off the hook and turned back to face the crazy men. There'd be no fainting. Her blood had hit boiling point.

"You expect me to go from medicine to childcare? A nanny? That's your idea of a getaway? A break?" she said, pointing at both of them.

"Whoa. Not really a nanny. Not in the official hired sense. Let's not complicate visas here," Jack said.

"He's right. More of an exchange," Simba said.

"Yeah. You all are like my family here in Kenya. Mine can be like yours while you're in America. I think a visitor would be good for them right now. A distraction."

Hope raised a brow.

"Okay, so *distraction* might be a bad choice of word, but you know what I mean." Jack looked between Simba and Hope. "I should keep my mouth shut now."

Hope closed her eyes. She did know what he meant. His parents had lost a child. His niece and nephews, their mother. And their father—Ben—had lost a wife. She sucked in her bottom lip. Was her brain so foggy that what they were suggesting had merit? An escape while saving face? She felt Simba's hand close around her shoulder. His voice deepened, and his words came slowly and reassuringly.

"You help out, and in return, you have a place to stay, people I trust around you, so that I don't have to worry about you alone in a foreign country. It works," Simba said.

Hope wrapped her arms around herself.

"What if Chuki's sister needs medicine when I'm gone?"

Simba sighed loudly.

"I'll take it. Give her my number here in case there's an emergency. Maybe I can convince the pulmonary doctor I got the samples from to see her once at no charge. If you go."

Hope studied the braided leather of her sandals.

"I'll sleep on it. But don't go buying plane tickets or anything," she said. She gave Jack a tired smile for his well-intentioned role of *trampled grass.* "Or making promises of help. We have another wise saying in Kenya. 'Thunder is not yet rain.'"

CHAPTER TWO

Dear Diary,
I had a bad dream again last night. This time, I couldn't remember her face. I woke up so scared. I hate sleeping.

IF BEN HAD to listen one more time to the mechanical grind of "Frosty the Snowman" coming from the holiday jack-in-the-box Grandma Nina had gotten Ryan yesterday, he was going to explode. He scrubbed his hands across his short, prickly hair and dropped his fists against the kitchen table. A tangerine tumbled off the edge of the centered fruit basket and rolled onto the chair next to him. This was pointless. Who in the blasted universe could think through all that noise?

The laptop screen switched to screen-saver mode. He'd been staring at it that long without touching a key. He shoved his chair back and marched into the family room, where

Chad, kneeling on the carpet in front of Ryan's bouncy seat, was gearing up to crank that Jack Snowman again. Maddie was curled up against a sofa pillow watching some show starring rainbow-colored ponies that was set loud enough to drown her brothers out. The place looked as though toys had attacked by air, land and sea. And a friend of the *real* Jack was flying in today.

That was likely the reason he was irritable. That and the phone call from Maddie's teacher letting him know that Maddie needed to be picked up at the nurse's office and asking if he could return after school let out for a conference—especially since he'd missed the routine parent-teacher conferences scheduled at the beginning of the month. All in one day. The teacher meeting meant that he'd have to head straight to the airport from the school. Which had forced him to call Nina to see if she wouldn't mind coming over to watch the kids. She'd jumped at the opportunity. Zoe's mom had her heart in the right place, but he was about to get bombarded with the implied "you're doing this all wrong" and "we know what your kids need more than you do" from all angles—his mother-in-law and the school.

With his bad luck, this Hope person would add her two cents to the pot.

He'd blasted the idea of anyone living in his house to help. He was managing just fine. Most of the time. Even now, the idea of having a stranger underfoot, on top of everything else, didn't sit well. However, Jack had made an effective point. Having live-in help would mean that he could focus more on developing his security-business plan. Plus, his mother-in-law would back off a little—or, as Jack put it, "worry less"—and see that he had everything under control. Maybe she'd get used to not hovering. Likewise, Ben wouldn't keep enabling the situation by having to call her for emergencies. He'd resisted a few weeks ago, when Ryan had come down with another ear infection on parent-teacher conference day, a decision that was biting him today. In any case, if this Hope got on his nerves, then he could have her stay at his in-laws and keep them occupied from over there. Nina loved guests. Either way, he'd have more control…and some quiet time to sort things out in terms of work.

"Hey, guys," Ben called over the exasperating ruckus. No reaction. He put two fingers between his lips and blew.

Maddie turned her cheek against the pillow and frowned at him before taking her time to pause her video. Chad stopped midcrank and looked up, and Ryan stared wide-eyed with his little hands securing his feet tight against his belly. Ben took the snowman from Chad, stuffed it into the box and snapped the lid with the sense of relief one got from defusing a bomb. This stay-at-home-dad stuff was really messing with his mind.

"That's better. Mads, keep that down, would you?"

She aimed the remote at her brothers and pretended to lower *their* volume. Silent sarcasm. A bit of silence was exactly what he wanted, except from Maddie. He'd change a hundred stench-drenched diapers if it meant she'd say something. Anything, other than the sounds of crying or the shrill, closed-mouth scream she did when she'd been pushed too far.

He had no doubt the parent-teacher conference he had to leave for in a few hours was going to be about just that. Again. The school nurse had shown him Maddie's handwritten note. One word: *headache*. They all knew there was more to it. Frustration twisted the muscles in his shoulders, and he cranked his neck to the side.

"Yeah, I get it," he said to Maddie. "Chad, pick up some of these toys before Grandma gets here. A dime a dunk."

He was not above bribery. After Zoe was killed, one of the school moms had stopped to check on him in the parking lot and had begun spewing advice. She'd assured him that bribery was a parent's secret weapon. Everyone used it. Not everyone admitted to it.

Chad immediately began tossing toys into the giant wicker basket by the couch. Unfortunately, each dunk came with a creative sound effect, and his four-year-old had gifted lungs. Maddie slammed a second pillow over her ear as she zoned out in front of the TV.

Ben grabbed a chewable and slobber-proof picture book, gave it to Ryan and set his bouncy seat near Maddie. Yes, he'd resorted to the television babysitter a couple of times, but all those colors had to have some visual-stimulation benefits. Right?

"I'll tell you what, man. How about you

help me inflate a bed? You can push the button on the pump motor. It's really loud."

A superhero landed headfirst on the floor near the basket. Ouch.

"How loud?" Chad asked, wrapping one knee around the other as though he was holding it in.

"Jet-fighter loud." Anything loud served as bribery with this kid.

"Like this?" The ensuing screech from Chad had Maddie pounding the pillow on her ear, Ryan whimpering and Ben wincing. It wasn't going to take long for this Hope person to flee to Nina's house.

"How about you go use the bathroom and meet me in your room to find out?"

"Okay!"

At least getting Chad in a different room would give Maddie some peace.

The doorbell rang, sending Ben's nerves prickling up his spine like a row of merciless fire ants, a reaction that hadn't subsided since Zoe's death.

He rolled his shoulders and went to let Nina in. He'd specifically told her he'd leave the door unlocked, but apparently she'd forgotten.

He found her standing there with a big cardboard box in her hands.

"I'm sorry, Ben. I had to use my elbow on the doorbell. This box is a little heavy," Nina said as she bustled past him. His nose twitched from an ambush of fruity hairspray.

Ben took the box from her and escaped to the kitchen. Nina made a beeline for the baby, after hanging her coat on the wooden rack by the door.

"So what's in the box?" Ben said, closing his laptop and stacking his notes on top, then setting them in the cabinet under the microwave. Zoe's mother did not need to see any of it.

"Oh, just some holiday decorations Zoe had stored in our basement because your garage was getting too full. I put a tin of chocolate-chip cookies on top. Go ahead and pull it out so you don't forget," she said. She unclipped Ryan and hugged him close to her shoulder, then slathered him with kisses and singsong words Ben couldn't make out.

He pulled a red tin decorated with elves and snowflakes out of the box, noted the rest of the contents and quickly slapped the flaps of cardboard back in place.

"Not happening," he said.

"Shh. Maddie's asleep on the couch," Nina said, turning off the TV and walking into the kitchen with Ryan in her arms. Her lips tightened. "Zoe's favorite thing to do was to decorate the weekend after Thanksgiving. That's in just over a week."

"It's not happening this year, Nina, so feel free to keep the decorations." He carried the box back to the entryway and set it under the coatrack so that it wouldn't be forgotten. She followed him.

"Let the kids have some fun, Ben. It could cheer Maddie up."

He looked at the half-tidied living room.

"I'd say they're having plenty of fun already. And no, I don't think it'll cheer Maddie up. We're not decorating this year. They can enjoy the decorations at your house. But not here."

"You told me yourself that Maddie's counselor said to make as few changes as possible so as not to stress her more. Not letting her go through the holidays like she always did would be a mistake. One that she might not recover from."

A direct hit. Nina and Zoe's father, Eric,

were known in the community for opening their hearts and home to others. Years ago they'd adopted Zoe's younger brother Jack after he'd lost his parents to drug overdoses. And they'd even accepted Ben—albeit reluctantly—when Zoe had brought him home from college and announced that they were getting married. Ben had always wondered if Nina harbored a nugget of resentment toward him, believing he'd triggered Zoe's decision to quit college to raise Maddie. Even if had really been Zoe's call. Nina was a fiercely protective woman, and ever since Zoe died, she'd directed those energies at her grandkids. As if they didn't have a dad, or at least one whose parenting methods and choices she agreed with.

He got the message loud and clear every time. She'd been around his kids over the years more than he had. She knew them better. He looked back toward the bedroom hallway. Empty. Chad had either taken himself to do number two in the bathroom, or was trying to pull the inflatable bed out of its box. As long as no little ears were sticking around the corner...

"Nina. You know how grateful I am for

all you've done over the years—being there
for Zoe and the kids, being here for us, helping me, especially with Ryan, over the past
seven months. But with all due respect, this
is my home, and they have a father. No decorating this year."

"But Zoe would—"

"Exactly. This was *her* thing. She decorated for Christmas. And she's not here. Out
of respect for her, it's not happening. What
my kids need is to get through the rest of
this year without any more pressure or sympathy or attention that does nothing but remind them of losing their mother. The stuff
in this box will only emphasize what they
don't have anymore."

Nina's chin and brow rose simultaneously,
and she turned her back to him. She carried
Ryan, who was half-asleep and drooling like
a pro on her shoulder, and laid him on his
back in the playpen occupying the corner of
the family room. End of conversation. Good.

Ben glanced at his watch. He hurried to
check on Chad and found him on the potty
buck naked and humming. Or was that moan-
ing? And at what age was he going to stop
stripping every time he used the bathroom?

"Daddy, I think I'm conti-pasted." *Constipated.* Ben knelt down and rubbed Chad's back. He should have known the packet of gummy lizards he'd given him in the car on the way to picking up Maddie had been a bad bribe.

"Uh, how about giving it a few more minutes? Here." Ben picked a book from a stack of Chad's favorites, which he kept in the bathroom for "encouragement." "Read this. I have to go, but Grandma is here. Call out to her if no torpedoes launch. But not too loudly. Maddie's napping."

"Okay," Chad said, taking the book.

Ben slipped into his room and grabbed his sweatshirt. Nina had picked up all the remaining toys and was checking Maddie's backpack at the kitchen table.

"She hasn't done her homework yet?" Nina asked, looking up from the student agenda.

"No. She can do it when she gets up, if she feels up to it."

"But she was watching a video," Nina said, putting the homework agenda back inside and propping the bag on a chair. Ben closed his eyes briefly and exhaled.

"She had a headache. Chad's on the toilet. I really have to go." He grabbed his wallet and keys. If he was going to make his appointment with the teacher, he needed to leave now.

"You go. I have everything covered. I really don't mind helping. Especially since I guess I won't get to help as much with Jack's friend around."

Oh, for crying out loud.

"You'll be busy cooking for Thanksgiving and then the holidays. You wouldn't want to deprive everyone, would you? Don't worry, you'll still see the kids," he said, opening the front door.

"I hope so. Of course, you'll bring them for Thanksgiving, then. Right? Even with losing Zoe, and with what Maddie is going through, there's a lot to be thankful for."

Ben's temples started to pound, and his knuckles whitened against the doorknob. Everyone mourned in their own way, but being thankful was pushing it. She had to be in denial.

"Nina, I'll bring them, but I'm not thankful for the drunk who killed my wife, and I'm not thankful for what my daughter is going through."

"But you should be thankful that you're here with your children and that they didn't lose both parents. Be thankful that Zoe wasn't still pregnant with Ryan when she was in that car." Her eyes glistened and her voice hitched. "Ben, *I* need you all there to get through it," she whispered.

Ben felt sucker punched. What if Zoe *had* still been pregnant? Bile burned his chest, and he swallowed the emotions churning with it. He nodded as he let go of the door. "Thanks for watching the kids," he said. "Lock the door. It'll be a couple of hours before I make it back."

"Don't worry. I'll be here when you come home." He could hear the door click shut behind him.

I'll be here when you come home.

How many times had Zoe said those words over the years?

He double paced to the Expedition hogging the small driveway. After Zoe's death, he'd bought a year-old model because of cost, but he wanted the equivalent of a tank to haul his kids around in.

At least maybe he could keep the rest of his family safe.

BEN SCANNED THE report card preview before him. It looked like a Fortune 500 company stock sheet. Numbers, letters, categories and subcategories. What happened to just giving students As, Bs and Cs? Or Fs… He quickly searched the columns, relieved when no Fs jumped at him.

Ms. Serval crossed her legs again and kept fiddling with her necklace. Did teachers really dress up that much for a school day? He wore his worst jeans just to get through a day with three kids. She had eighteen. Ben pretended not to notice when she flicked her hair back over her shoulder and leaned forward to pass him another sheet of paper, and tried not to pass out from her tear-gas perfume. Maybe that was what had triggered Maddie's headache. What he really wanted was for the woman to turn off the background music in the classroom. It was driving him insane, but he didn't dare give her a reason to get up and walk in front of him. Not in his precariously low position on the child-size chair he was in.

"What's an N?" he asked.

"That stands for Needs Improvement," said Ms. Serval.

"In class participation? Seriously? After

our meeting at the start of the year with the school counselor, knowing what's going on, did you really find it necessary to give her an N on her report card? I'm sure there are ways to show participation that don't involve raising your hand and speaking."

Ms. Serval pulled back and gave her skirt a tug.

"Well, she's doing great academically, really, Mr. Corallis. I wanted you to have a chance to see her interim grades, since you missed the scheduled conference."

"The office gave you my message about my youngest getting sick, right?"

"Yes, of course. I completely understand and sent you an email about rescheduling."

She had? Crap. He had a vague recollection of one that he'd planned to get back to. And forgot.

"Please understand, the whole report card is computer based now," she said, redirecting the conversation. "We have to input a grade or letter, and there are criteria we have to follow to be fair. I couldn't put anything else, given the situation. I do understand the reason and I understand that she's getting therapy for her selective mutism and to help her heal from her—your—loss. But it's more than that. Lately, she acts as though she doesn't care. As though she's not paying attention. Zoning out in the afternoons. And once this week, when I tried to correct something on her paper, she simply crossed her arms and sat at her desk staring at her paper for almost an hour. She refused to respond to anything I said. By working, of course. I don't mean verbally."

"An hour?" he asked, adjusting his balance on the chair. Why had she let Maddie sit there that long without calling Mrs. Eggers, the school counselor, or him, for that matter? Ms. Serval gathered the report-card papers, then clasped her hands.

"Not quite an hour," she said, tipping her chin, "but I was doing what I could. Mrs. Eggers wasn't here that day. She covers other schools certain days of the week. I had to keep seventeen other students on task, Mr. Corallis. I tried to get her attention as I kept teaching, and hoped she'd come around on her own. It was so close to the end of the day that I didn't want to encourage the behavior by letting her go home early."

"I don't think she was trying to be difficult or manipulative."

"I didn't mean to imply that at all."

Then, maybe he needed a hearing aid. Ms. Serval scratched her cheek.

"It's just that we're almost through the first quarter and I'm worried that if she withdraws more, as opposed to showing improvement, it'll take its toll on the rest of her school year. I realize you've been taking her to a therapist and thought you could share these observations. I'll be honest. I spoke to Mrs. Eggers, and she mentioned the option of putting her in Special Ed if things got worse."

"No." Ben couldn't help it, but the mention of taking Maddie out of a regular classroom so early in the school year felt like a threat. "I'm sure that would be appropriate and helpful for a lot of kids, but Maddie isn't learning disabled. Nor is she autistic. This is different. She belongs in a regular class with her peers," he said, standing up. Ms. Serval quickly followed suit.

"I agree...if she doesn't regress. Which is why I thought that maybe more interaction with kids casually, outside school, might help. This is just a suggestion. Actually an idea her art teacher gave me. A lot of children respond to art, and I teach an art club at the community center on weekends. I'd be more than happy to work outside school hours with her. If you think she won't be comfortable with a group, I wouldn't mind coming over and spending time with her. Her brothers could even join us if they wanted."

Wow. Ben's neck itched. Zoe had been an avid artist and photographer and used to tell him how much she enjoyed volunteering her skills at the school. No doubt Ms. Serval knew that. What he didn't feel like sharing at this moment was that they were between therapists. He'd stopped taking Maddie to the one she'd been seeing and was still in the process of finding someone who'd do a better job of connecting with her. Even with medical coverage, nothing was free, and he'd expected her to show improvement at the couple hundred an hour the therapist charged.

He hadn't bothered with *family* counseling, in spite of everyone bringing it up. He figured the boys were still young, and he... Well, he'd survived loss before. He'd pulled through that year in college, when his mother, who'd single-handedly raised him down in Virginia on nothing but waitressing jobs, had passed away from an undiagnosed tumor. That was when Zoe, a photography student, had come up to him in the library and asked if she could take candid shots for a project. She'd said that he had a distant look she wanted to capture. Everything had changed after that moment. It was then that he decided to join the marines. He'd needed to prove himself. Make something of that latchkey child his mom had sacrificed for. And for Zoe.

He'd survived.

But he hadn't been a kid at the time, and with the changes Maddie's teacher had noted over the past few weeks, he had to wonder if the sessions had indeed been doing any good at all. Or had the changes for worse occurred because he'd been devoting more time to his computer lately?

"Thanks, but I've already arranged for help outside school." Not exactly the kind she was talking about, but not exactly a lie, either. He didn't have details beyond the fact that Hope was a medical intern, so for all he knew she could be specializing in pediatric psychiatry.

"Let's see how she does over the next month or so. After the holidays."

"Of course. Oh…" Ms. Serval picked up a blue folder and textbook from the corner of her desk and handed them to him. "I put together the work she missed today and some of the worksheets we'll be doing tomorrow, just in case it turns out she's coming down with something. Thanks so much for coming in here today. Maddie really is a sweetheart. I'm so sorry for all you're going through." She reached out, so he shook her hand. It felt limp.

"Thank you, ma'am," Ben said. Then he escaped for the peace and quiet of his SUV.

A solid night's sleep would be better, but that would have to wait until he made it home and got the kids to bed. Hopefully Ryan would have a good night, but that was about as predictable as peace in a war zone. He swore as he put the gear in Reverse. He'd never inflated the guest bed in Chad's room. If Chad fell asleep early… Well…if any kid could sleep through the pump noise…

He pulled into the airport parking lot at 1700 hours and found a spot two lanes and six cars north of the target entrance. The sun was setting, and the edge of the cold front they were expecting had definitely arrived. He scribbled *Hope* on the back of a sheet of paper he ripped from a notepad he kept in the console for whenever Maddie forgot hers, and headed for baggage claim thirteen. He stopped briefly to check the monitors in case changes had been made since he'd called to check on the flight earlier that afternoon. Thirteen it was.

The hustle and bustle of people headed their own way, doing their own thing, was nice. Like being camouflaged in a crowd. He needed a few minutes of feeling invisible today, but traffic had made him later than he'd hoped.

He waited for a passenger shuttle car to drive by and then crossed over to the carousel. He crumpled the paper in his hand. Hope was hard to miss. Other passengers had already left with their luggage, save for a family of four and a man in a suit on his cell phone. The slender woman he was certain was Hope stood about five-five or six and wore a bright orange scarf that framed her face like a headband, holding back a mass of dark curls. She wore flat sandals, one of those flowing ankle-length skirts in a bright pattern and an orange sleeveless top. As a marine, he was trained to register details. If she didn't have a sweater on her, she was in for a surprise. She stayed close to two green suitcases as she scanned the opposite direction, while alternating between fidgeting with one of her big hoop earrings and gripping an oversize woven purse against her side.

"Hope Alwanga?"

"Yes," she breathed, her hand pressed against her chest. No doubt she was relieved she hadn't been forgotten, alone in a foreign airport.

"Ben Corallis." He extended his hand, and she shook it firmly. Her full lips spread into a bright smile.

"Ben. It's so wonderful to meet you. Jack speaks so highly of his family."

Ben nodded, releasing her hand slowly, then stuffed his into the front pockets of his jeans.

"We miss him around here." Jack was one of the few guys he'd hung around with whenever he was on leave. He wished he still lived here. "These your only bags?" he asked, in case the airline had lost any.

"Yes."

"You don't happen to have a sweater you want to pull out of one of these before we hit the road, do you? It's a little chilly out," he said. He wasn't offering his sweatshirt. No one wore his favorite marine sweatshirt. Either Jack should have warned her about the weather or she should have checked her destination weather on the internet.

"Oh, I have one here." She reached into her shoulder sack and dug out a wad of cloth so small, he knew it wouldn't be warm enough. She set her bag between her feet while she slipped it on. Thin as an old undershirt. "I could use some cool, fresh air, actually," she said.

"First time in a plane, huh?"

"Yes," she said, closing her warm brown eyes briefly. "I'm going to try to forget that I have to do this again in order to get home."

He picked up her luggage as she slung her bag back onto her shoulder.

"I can get one of those," she offered.

Not likely, unless she was packing solid

muscle in those thin arms. Her suitcases felt like a few elephants had stowed away.

"I have them," Ben said. "Car's this way." He headed toward the glass doors closest to where he'd parked and heard a gasp behind him when the second set of doors opened, letting in a gust of wind. He looked over his shoulder. She slapped her hands down on her skirt to keep it from blowing and hunched her shoulders. Welcome to a Pennsylvanian cold front.

He glanced at the parking lot and gave in. He really wanted to get home, but she was Jack's friend and his guest. He backed up enough for the doors to close.

"Go back in and I'll bring the car around. Just keep an eye out for a silver Expedition," he said, wondering belatedly if she knew what an Expedition looked like.

"No, no. I'm fine. It just took me by surprise." She fisted the sides of her skirt so it wouldn't blow. "Lead the way."

Well, okay, then. Ben headed out. Dark had settled, and the wind chill was pretty uncomfortable, even for him. And this was only November. She wasn't going to last three months. He let her into the car before loading her bags into the back, then jogged around to the driver's side and got in. Hope's laugh caught him off guard. He'd have expected the cold to have irritated her more than the plane trip.

"I'd say I got my fresh air," she said, rubbing her arms.

That was one way to think of it.

"I guess you did. Seat belt," he said, nodding toward her shoulder strap and waiting for her to buckle up.

He cranked the heat as soon as the engine was running. The dash read forty-three degrees. Likely in the thirties with the wind factor. He backed out of the parking spot and hit the road.

"Just wait till our first negative temperature day," he said. "Fahrenheit," he added, knowing she'd be used to Celsius. He'd spent enough time overseas to do the conversions in his head. "It feels close to two or three degrees Celsius out there."

Her eyes widened.

"Wow. Twelve is cold in Nairobi. We're actually warming up this time of year. My brother won't believe that I braved this in sandals," she said, grinning.

"Might have been more tolerable a few hours ago." She was enjoying this? First-time trip. New country. Maybe adrenaline was warming her up.

"Jack suggested that I wait and buy a few warm items here, since nothing in our stores was suitable for your winters," she said.

"Makes sense," he said. He tapped his thumbs against the steering wheel, unsure of what else to say. He couldn't talk about the weather the entire way home. How was this supposed to work for months? He hated gray areas, and he wasn't quite sure how to treat her. Child-care helper or family friend?

The silver bracelets on her wrist sounded like wind chimes every time she reached up to touch her earring. She rubbed her hands in her lap and looked out the window. There wasn't much she could see from the freeway in the dark. He looked at the dash clock, wishing the airport was closer to his house.

"Thank you," she said, breaking the awkward silence. "I'm…I'm sorry for your loss, and I'm grateful for being invited into your home. I'll do what I can to help while I'm here."

Ben scratched his jaw, then settled his

hand back on the wheel. He couldn't really take credit for inviting her, though Jack had insisted that Ben would be doing both him and his friend's sister a huge favor. Jack had never asked him for anything before. He'd said her family wanted to be sure she'd be safe…with good people. Her brother did take the phone and speak to him briefly during one of the calls. Sounded like a sharp guy. Joked about keeping her safe, especially from men. Despite his tone, Ben knew he wasn't joking. He couldn't blame him. Not that he'd ever admit it out loud, but Hope Alwanga could easily land a job as a fashion model and never make it back to her medical career. She'd be turning a head or two during her stay.

"Jack told me you're in medicine. Pediatrics?" he asked, refocusing.

"No. Well, yes, a few young patients at the emergency room I'm interning in right now, but mostly adults. Eventually, I'll join my parents' orthopedic practice. They work a lot with professional athletes."

Whew. She came from a family of docs. And money, or so it sounded, if they were working with athletes. And she was here, of all places, to help out with his kids? He'd been told that she was stressed, but stable, and needed a break…but, shoot, a break to him would be the Bahamas.

"So you must have a lot of little nieces or nephews," he said. "Younger siblings?" *Some sort of experience with watching kids?*

"No. I'm the youngest. It's just my older brother, Simba—Jack's friend—and me. I can't wait to meet your children, though."

This time Ben laughed.

Forget a few months. Hope wasn't going to last a day in his house.

CHAPTER THREE

Dear Diary,
Sometimes I close my eyes so that everyone will leave me alone. But I'm not really asleep. I hear everything. They fight because of me.

HOPE HAD WORKED with enough patients to know how to read body language, an important skill, given that many "cushioned" or omitted facts in their medical history or medication compliance out of sheer embarrassment. The hesitations. The flinches. Nervous laughter. Jack and Simba had assured her that she'd be doing Ben a favor and that he'd jumped at their idea of having her stay at his place and help with his kids for three months. But he sounded much more skeptical than enthusiastic. She wasn't so sure the man wanted her in his house any more than she wanted to be in anyone's way.

Oh, but this? She leaned her head back against the seat and looked out the window. Simba was so right. She needed this break. The good parts and the not so good, like over twenty-four hours of planes and layovers. She could have done without that. But she'd never in her life felt so free. This was spectacular. Ever since they'd exited the freeway, she'd been entranced by the dazzling lights that trimmed shops and street lamps. It was like a fairy tale. A scene out of a movie. Sure, a few places in Nairobi would set out some decorations at Christmas, but these were lights on steroids by comparison. She'd never seen anything like it.

"We're here," Ben said, startling her. He turned left onto a street lined with houses separated only by a few meters. Even in the dark, the glow from windows and entry lights revealed a well-manicured neighborhood.

"Oh. My. Gosh," she said, gaping at the house he approached. Forget fairy tale. After reading about it in stories, she now knew what "Santa's workshop" really meant. And she was going to get to live in it. Her pulse picked up. Chuki wasn't going to believe this.

The house looked as if all the colors of a

Masai village had been brought to life and showered with Serengeti stars. A sleigh with St. Nicholas—or Santa Claus dressed the American way. Giant wrapped gifts held by elves in green hats. Trees made of nothing but white lights. Even the roofline and windows sparkled.

"Christmas is celebrated quite early here," she said. "Your children are so lucky."

"Not celebrated yet, just decorated. The commercial side of things. Thanksgiving comes first in the US," he said, turning left into the driveway *across* from Santa's workshop. He shoved the gear into Park and turned off the ignition. "*This* is my house." He sank back in the driver's seat. Hope looked through the windshield.

No lights. Nothing. Save for a lit doorway. Hope quickly stamped out the hint of disappointment she had no right to feel. She smiled.

"It's beautiful." She unbuckled her seat belt and put her hand on the door.

"Wait a sec," Ben said, squinting from the reflection of lights in the car mirror. "I don't know if Jack told you, but my daughter... Maddie... She doesn't—"

"I know," Hope said, placing her hand on his arm. It was a reflex. Reassurance. Sympathy. Her bedside manner. But her fingers warmed, and she pulled back when he stared at her hand. "Don't worry. I'm aware and understand," she said, hoping the words explained her touch.

"Okay." He got out and went around back. Hope cringed when the rush of cold came through his open door. She took a deep breath, then exited, hurrying up the flagstone path. Her teeth chattered as she rubbed her arms and waited for him, but she didn't mind too much. She had a great view of the display across the street from here.

The front door swung open before he made it. A woman in beige pants and a blue tunic-length sweater scanned her from head to toe.

"You must be freezing," she said, ushering her in. "I'm Ben's mother-in-law. You can call me Nina."

"Nice to meet you, Nina," Hope said, shaking her hand. "I'm Hope."

"Yes, I think either Jack or Ben mentioned it. It's a lovely name. Is it short for anything?"

Hope raised her forehead and shrugged with a smile.

"No, just Hope." She knew what Nina meant by the question. She was expecting a more ethnic name. Her mother was of Luo descent and had decided to combine their common practice of giving their children both a Western name and a Luo name, based on the events of the day of birth. She'd been named only *Hope*, because it was what her parents were clinging to when she was diagnosed with a hole in her heart as a baby.

"Has anyone ever told you that you look just like that beautiful actress... What's her name? She won an award... Lupita something," she said, waving her finger, trying to make the connection.

"I know who you mean. I've been told we look like sisters, and I'm thinking of cutting my hair very short like hers. It seems so much easier."

"You'd be twins for sure. Come on into the living room," Nina said just as Ben pushed through the door, maneuvering one suitcase inside and setting it against the wall. He took a stack of what looked like mail out from under his arm and set it on a wooden console, then quickly retrieved the second suitcase from where he'd left it on the front landing and kicked the door shut with his heel.

"I take it you've met," he said, looking up as he took his keys out of the pocket of his jeans and set them next to the mail.

"Of course we met," Nina said, brushing her hand through the air. "Unfortunately, I need to run or Eric is going to get grouchy. I spoiled that man, and now he can't even fix his own dinner. Listen, Ben. I made sure Maddie's homework got done, so you're set for tomorrow morning. No sign of a fever or anything, but I sent her to take a shower. Chad was on the potty for quite a while before he went. I made a pot of vegetable minestrone for dinner, and everyone has eaten—"

"I'd ordered pizza before leaving and told them to have it here at five-thirty. Wasn't it delivered?" Ben asked. Nina cocked her head and tucked her graying chin-length hair behind her ear. Hope felt like a third wheel all of a sudden, not sure if she should sit on the sofa or keep standing. She desperately needed to use the restroom, but the insistent line of Nina's mouth and twitch at Ben's temple kept her from interrupting.

"I put the pizza boxes in the fridge. I really

didn't mind cooking," Nina said, grabbing her purse. "Oh, Chad said that you promised he could help with inflating that bed, so we went ahead and took care of it. He's playing on it right now, and Ryan is sleeping. He drank his entire bottle beforehand."

"Great," Ben said, cranking his neck to the side and back. "You took care of everything perfectly. I better walk you to your car before Eric wonders what happened to you."

"Well, maybe I should take a few minutes and go over some kid things with Hope and—"

"Nina. I'll take it from here," he said, putting his hand on Nina's back to guide her out. "I'll be right back, Hope. Make yourself at... comfortable."

Not at home.

"I really need to use the restroom, if you don't mind," she said, slipping the tote handles off her shoulder.

"First door on your left is a powder room," Ben said.

"Nice meeting you, Hope," Nina called as Ben followed her out the front door. As the door closed, Hope overheard her telling Ben that she was hurt that he wouldn't be needing her anymore. Clearly there were under-currents here she hadn't anticipated.

But all she cared about right now was pee-ing.

BEN LOCKED THE door behind him, rubbed his face with his hands, then exhaled. Why did he let everything Nina did or said get to him? He toed off his sneakers and turned. Hope was staring at him. For the next three months, the only place he could be alone in his house was going to be his bedroom.

"I, um, don't know what you'd like me to do," she said.

"Oh." He patted his jeans. What *did* he need her to do? He'd never had a houseguest or a live-in anything. Granted, he'd spent most of his married life deployed. "You prob-ably want to settle in, right? Or are you hun-gry?" He was starving as if there was no tomorrow. No way soup was going to cut it for him. The mere thought of vegetable soup annoyed him. It was the way Nina had said it. As if he was to blame for Chad being plugged up and Maddie not feeling well. As if he fed them takeout three meals a day. They were veggie pizzas, for crying out loud. A complete meal. He'd eaten his fair share of restaurant leftovers growing up and he was doing just fine. Then again, maybe it was a good thing there was healthy soup to offer Hope. Her being in medicine and all.

"I'm famished," she said. "I'd love a shower, too, whenever you are all done with the bathroom."

"Let me check on the kids real quick. If my daughter isn't using it, it's yours. I have my own in my room." He glanced around the place, from living room to kitchen. "Sit wherever you like. I'll be right back."

Ben hurried down the hall. Things might not feel so weird if the kids came out. Buffers. He could hear Maddie still puttering in the bathroom at the end of the hall. He cracked open Ryan's door. Sound asleep, but the telltale gurgling sound of congestion wasn't good. *Please get through the night, buddy.*

"Chad?" He crossed the hall and pushed open Chad's door. The kid had a slightly bigger room than Ryan and Maddie, but Maddie liked the way hers overlooked the backyard and had a window seat. It made sense to set up the inflatable bed in Chad's room for that reason. Plus, he wasn't sure how Maddie would take to a stranger in her room, and nights would get awkward if he went in to check on Ryan and Hope was sleeping there. This way, maybe they could alternate night calls if Ryan was teething or had another ear infection. But even with its extra room, he couldn't see how those two suitcases were going to fit. He hadn't even thought about emptying a few of Chad's dresser drawers, but maybe tomorrow he'd clear the top two that Chad couldn't get into.

"Daddy!" Chad leaped up from zooming cars along the inflated mattress set in a corner of the room. He hugged Ben's leg. "I want to sleep on that tonight."

"Sorry, bud, but remember what I told you about having a visitor? She won't be able to fit in your car bed."

"But I like this one," he said, throwing himself on it and spreading his arms and legs.

"Come say hi. We'll talk about this later."

"But—"

"Now, Chad. You can have a snack if you're still hungry. Come on."

Chad rolled off the bed and stomped past

Ben. Hope was sitting at the breakfast table, digging in her bag.

"Hope, this is Chad." *Good luck with him.*

"Hi, Chad," she said, beaming. She set her bag aside. "How old are you?"

Chad twisted his body around Ben's right leg and then looped around the left in a figure-eight. Ben picked him up and set him on his feet.

"Say hello to Miss Hope."

"Hello, Miss Hope. Could you sweep on my car bed?"

Hope kept smiling but gave Ben an inquisitive look.

"I don't have a guest room. There's an inflated mattress in Chad's room he's taken to. The novelty will wear off soon. I'm sorry it's not a real bed."

"It's no problem." She leaned her arms on her lap and brought her face closer to Chad's level. "I think your bed is special just for you, but I don't mind if you want to take naps on mine in the afternoons."

"Good luck with that." Ben chuckled. Her smile widened. She had a really nice smile.

"Are you living with us because my mommy's body broke?" Chad asked.

Ben's chest cramped. Hope's smile faded, and the corners of her eyes creased in sympathy.

"I'm only visiting for a while and helping out because everyone who lives in a house should help out. Right?" Chad grimaced. If she got him to nap and help out more with his own cleanup, she'd be a miracle worker, Ben thought. "And then I'll go back to my home on the other side of the world," she said.

Ben nodded and knelt down by Chad. He appreciated that Hope had set the stage, making sure his son knew she'd be leaving. In a planned way. Not unexpected, the way their mom left. The idea of his kids actually getting attached to her hadn't crossed his mind when her visit was arranged. It was just a few months. But what if they did grow to like her and then lost her? He cursed to himself. Given the new situation, he realized that he really did need to find a new therapist for Maddie.

"Is that where my mommy is? Are you going to trade places again, so my mommy will come back from the other side of the world?"

Hope pressed her fingers against her lips, and her eyes glistened.

"I'm sorry. I said the wrong thing," she said, shaking her head at Ben.

"No, it's not you," he said. God knew, Chad had a way of turning anything Ben said upside down, inside out and backward. He'd been told and had read on the internet about how kids Chad's age and younger perceived death. How literal they were about everything. Chad often asked when Zoe would be coming back, a question that upset Maddie every time. Ben had started keeping a doorknob pick on his dresser after she began locking her bedroom door when Chad wouldn't stop asking about their mom.

He ruffled Chad's hair.

"Hey, buddy. Remember that I told you mommy's not coming back? She's not on the other side of the world. She died and went to heaven."

Chad's shoulders rose and sank. "Okay. Can I have some pizza? Grandma said it would conti-paste me, even if I pooed the size of a dinosaur when you were gone."

"Then, I'd say you earned a piece. Grab a seat. You can have a slice, then it's bedtime."

Hope's lips parted as Chad climbed onto the chair next to hers. She was either speechless at how fast Chad switched gears or afraid to say anything more to the kid.

"Let me help you with the pizza," she said.

"I'm assuming you'd prefer hot soup. Especially after freezing out there. Nina is a great cook. I'm sure it's excellent. And healthy. So don't let the fact that we're eating pizza sway you," he said, pulling two pizza boxes out of the fridge. He didn't mind cold pizza for breakfast, but this was dinner. He wanted them hot. He opened a cabinet and grabbed a microwaveable dish.

"My parents always insist on home cooking. It's probably why I suffer from fast-food rebellion. And for the first time, my parents are too far to hover." Hope stood at the end of the counter, sucking in her lower lip and gazing at the slices he was placing on a dish.

"You want pizza?" he asked. She was around twenty-five, wasn't she? And her parents still hovered? His mom had never had time to hover, though he imagined that Zoe's parents probably had.

Hope crinkled her nose. "I just traveled clear across the planet. Doesn't that count for earning it?" she said, winking at Chad. "I love pizza. You wouldn't deny me my first slice on American soil, would you?"

Ben grinned. "You can have as much as you want."

He took the pot on the stove and popped it into the fridge, then started the microwave.

"I'm going to check on Maddie. Help yourself when it's ready, just make sure it's not too hot before Chad digs in," Ben said.

The bathroom door was ajar, and the light was off in it. He knocked on Maddie's door. No answer.

"Hey, Mads. There's pizza if you want. I'm coming in, okay?" He tried giving her privacy, since she was a girl, but sometimes it was tough not knowing whether to let himself in or not. He opened the door slowly, giving her time to shove the door shut if she was dressing. "Mads?"

She was already in bed with her eyes closed. Her bedside lamp was on, but he knew she didn't like the room totally dark. He touched her forehead. It felt okay. He walked over to her closet, turned the light on, then left its door open. He clicked the lamp off so the light wouldn't be on her face all night. Homework done or not, he was going to let her stay home tomorrow.

CHAPTER FOUR

Dear Diary,
I wish I didn't ever have to go to school
again. Sara keeps talking about her
new puppy. Daddy said no to the one
Mommy got. It was supposed to be a
present for him staying home. I think
he wants to go away.

HOPE COULD NOW add jet lag to her list of
worldly experiences. She needed caffeine.
The last time she'd made her own coffee,
she'd used a French press, not a drip machine
like Ben had, but she knew how to follow
instructions. She set up the filter and coffee
grounds she'd found in the cabinet overhead,
then turned on the coffeemaker. To her relief,
it gurgled and started to fill. Thank goodness
Ben didn't mind ordering take-out food. Actual cooking was beyond her abilities.

She padded quietly to where one of her

suitcases still sat against the wall by the entry. Ben had carried the one that had her clothes and necessities in it to Chad's room last night. This one would get emptied today. It was mostly filled with gifts Anna and Jack had asked her to take to the kids for them. What weighed it down were the medical texts her father told her she should take along, so that her brain didn't atrophy.

She got down on her knees, unlocked the suitcase and leaned the upper half back against the wall. Cooing came from a white baby monitor set on the end table next to the couch. Did Ben have another unit in his room? Or did he forget this one here last night?

A blur of orange caught her eye as something—or someone—scurried from the hall and disappeared into the kitchen. Two big eyes spied on her from behind the counter. Hope pretended not to notice and instead began taking gift-wrapped items out and carefully setting them down on the carpet next to her.

"Hmm. I think this present is for the baby, and this one, I was told, had to make it into the hands of the older boy." She rummaged as if she'd lost something. "Did I forget the present Jack and Anna said was for their niece?"

A little girl Hope knew had to be Maddie inched closer. The pumpkin-dotted hem of her orange nightgown skimmed the floor, and she hugged a stuffed monkey to her chest. Tangled hair framed her delicate face.

"I see I'm not the only one up early," Hope said. "Good morning. I'm Hope, one of your uncle Jack and auntie Anna's friends. You must be Maddie."

The girl gave an almost imperceptible nod.

"I had better find the present they sent you, then. They'd never forgive me." Hope pulled out the package she knew was Maddie's and held it out. Maddie got down on the carpet, set her monkey aside and began to unwrap. Her eyes lit up at the wooden keepsake box carved with elephants.

"You like it?" Hope asked. Maddie gave her a silent yes.

The cooing from the monitor turned into a staccato cry. Hope was going to assume that Ben forgot the monitor. They hadn't really gone over how things would work. How much she'd help versus getting out on her own to enjoy her time here.

"I'll tell you what," she said to Maddie. "Those over there are for your brothers, but this—" she held up a larger wrapped package "—has more gifts for all of you in it. Why don't you open it and take first pick while I go get Ryan?"

Maddie took the second package that Hope knew contained carved wooden African safari animal ornaments. She'd carefully wrapped each one so they wouldn't break on the trip. She got up and hurried to the baby's room. Ben's door across the hall from it was closed.

Ryan had muffled his cry with two slobbery fists in the mouth. There was no mistaking he was Ben's son. The likeness was almost funny.

"Hi there," she cooed as she picked him up from the crib. She'd told Ben she didn't have much experience with kids, but she had some. She'd picked up babies before. Ryan felt wet. Diaper changes were another thing, but she'd done plenty on dolls. And you didn't make it through medical school and half an internship without enough experience and sense to handle something as fundamental to life as baby care. She laid Ryan on a padded changing table to the right of the crib and gave the shelf underneath it a quick scan for essentials. Wipes and a diaper. How hard could it be? He squealed his encouragement.

"Shh, shh. Let's get you cleaned up and leave your father sleeping."

She undid the tape strips and opened the diaper.

"No! Oh! No, no, noooo!"

A geyser shot up, barely missing her face. She jerked away while trying to blindly slap the diaper back over him, but he twisted and rolled his legs up, sending the stream right over his head. "Hold still!" She kept one hand on his chest to keep him on the table and grabbed a clean diaper with the other. She tried covering him, but he threw his legs back down, redirecting his spray at the wall and upholstered recliner in the corner of the room before his tank was finally emptied. "Oh, heaven."

Her pulse raced. She looked at the chair and then at Ryan. If that chair was the one Zoe had used for all her pregnancies...

Ryan smiled.

Hope wanted to cry. She felt Ben watching her even before the fresh-showered scent of men's soap and shampoo reached her. He didn't say anything, and she didn't dare turn around.

His arm brushed hers as he reached around her to take over diaper duty.

"You can go wash your hands. I'll finish," he said. She stepped away from the changing table.

"I'll pay to have the chair cleaned," she said. "I'm so sorry. He just—"

"Hey," Ben said, looking at her over his shoulder. "Trust me. This isn't the worst thing that can happen in life."

BY THE END of Hope's first full day in his house, Ben had surrendered to Nina's help. And early this morning, he'd dropped Hope and the kids off at Nina and Eric's, then doubled back to get some work done. Saturday made a good day for them to go shopping and for him to regroup.

Hope had done well enough playing with the kids yesterday. He'd also managed to give her some out-of-reach storage space in the bedroom and bathroom—a high priority for him. Safety before comfort. He'd made it clear that Chad could spin danger out of anything, including her toiletry bag. But taking her shopping for cold-weather clothing staples was better left to another woman. And as much as Ben hated Nina telling him how to do things, he figured a bit of training from Nina would benefit Hope. It would also help Nina realize that Hope wasn't a threat.

Hope had been overly upset by the diaper incident and didn't stop apologizing until Ben pulled out the spray he still had from when Zoe had bought puppy supplies.

He'd discovered her plans to raise a service puppy while he was still in shock from her death. There was no way he could take that responsibility on at the time. Her friend Brie had taken on the puppy as her way of honoring Zoe, angry that he wasn't keeping it. He was the only one with a right to be angry. The last time he'd dealt with Brie was when he'd had his friend Cooper pass a box of dog supplies on to her.

The pee spray he'd discovered later in the cleaning closet. He found out early on that it worked just as well on neutralizing human baby pee.

As for Hope, the incident had triggered a slew of confessions. Like blurting out that she couldn't cook. Clearly she was used to having high expectations put on her—not unlike a marine—but who said he expected her to cook? Or did he? He had to admit that the coffee she made yesterday morning could have spurred hair growth on Ryan's chest. Just having someone play with the kids a few hours helped, but shoot, he was starting to wonder who was helping out whom more.

He reached for the sheet he'd printed out, then propped his phone with his shoulder.

"I'm telling you, man. I've hashed out the numbers, but I need you in on this."

Cooper Reaves had joined the marines when Ben had, only he'd gotten a medal and medical discharge after a roadside bombing left him with shards of metal embedded in his left calf. He'd been lucky to get away alive.

"How many times do I have to tell you I can't help? Not interested, Ben. There's no reason you can't go at it alone," Cooper said.

Ben heard the clink of glassware through the phone and wondered if his buddy was hitting the bottle again—at 0900 hours.

"Why don't I come over and show you what I think'll work." *And check up on you.*

"Why don't you not? You have enough going on. Take care of those kids. You want to start a security company, go for it. That's not my future."

"Then, what is? Fishing from a rocking chair?"

"Doesn't sound too bad. Nice and peaceful. Maybe I'll write a book. One of those war thrillers. Semiautobiographical. I'll be set for life." *Clank*.

Ben squeezed his temples and sat back, tossing the paper on the table.

"You're a technical guru, Coop. A computer genius. I trust you. No way I'm going into business with someone I don't know. I do the on-site consults. Camera placement, weaknesses, guards and all that. You take care of computer security and setup. Once it's up and running, a lot of the work can be done from home." Which was what he really wanted. A way to support his family, but also be able to be in command and control his schedule...and to be where he could keep an eye on everyone and make sure they were safe.

"Ben, I said I'm sorry, but you're on your own."

"What's in the glass?"

"What?" Incredulous laughter followed. "You think I'm slammed?" A few choice curses followed that. Not anything Ben wasn't used to hearing in the past, but here he caught himself automatically scanning the room for mini-ears, even with the kids gone. "Orange juice, man. Freaking orange juice. But hey, a guy doesn't agree with you, so he must be out-of-his-mind drunk. Right?"

Ben pushed off the table and punched the wall as he headed out the back porch door for a breather.

"No. I didn't mean it like that. Ignore what I said. Okay? Just think about what I'm telling you. This could work for both of us. Just think about it," Ben said.

"Yeah. Listen, man. I gotta run." Coop hung up.

Ben stuffed his phone into the pocket of his jeans. Coop wasn't being himself. Ben had dropped him off at a few of his therapy appointments, so he knew Coop was going, but he still wasn't the guy he'd known all these years. Then again, he wasn't, either. They'd all changed. Everything had changed.

Golden leaves showered down with a sudden breeze, mingling on the ground with those of the already bare red maples. "Fall confetti," Zoe used to call it.

He couldn't recall the last time he'd actually been in town to see it in person. She always took pictures of the kids in the yard, surrounded by pumpkins and leaf piles, and sent them to him. Now there were no pumpkins. No potted mums. His eyes burned, and he clenched his jaw, rolling every drop of emotion into anger. Fall confetti. The celebration of death.

He took a deep breath of fresh air and wished he could deny the calm it infused him with. The crisp scent of cold laced with a distinct smoky warmth puffing from someone's fireplace had been missing from those photos. A reminder that he hadn't been here. No real memories. This had been her favorite time of year, and not once had he truly shared it with her.

The morning sun faded under a canopy of blue-gray clouds.

He stepped down off the wooden porch, grabbed Chad's plastic tricycle by the handlebars and put it under the right side of the porch where all the yard toys were supposed to be, then went back inside. The change in the air took about a second to register. That smell.

He groaned. Ryan's crib sheets. Those diapers, touted as able to withstand an attack from down under, had lost the battle this morning. Ben had walked in on the natural disaster of disasters. Avalanche. Flood. You name it. He had a battery backup alarm on the house sump pump in the basement. If only there were overflow alarms that could be connected to diapers—now, that was a security system idea that would make a killing. He'd managed to disinfect Ryan and get everyone out of the house earlier, but in his desperation for more coffee and a minute to focus on work, he'd forgotten there was still a cleanup waiting.

His keys on the console urged him to defect.

"Suck it up, marine," he muttered, and headed for the baby's room.

HOPE HOPPED OUT of Eric Harper's car and opened the back door. Maddie was already helping Chad unlatch his car seat buckle.

It took two tries for Hope to get Ryan's backward-facing infant seat to detach from its base. Nina had shown her how to work it. She said that they kept the extra seats in their car because moving the seat base had become a pain early on, and Ben was afraid that they wouldn't secure it in place correctly. She eased Ryan's seat out of the car. These things were rather hard to carry and walk with at the same time.

"Thank you for the ride, Eric," she said. "If you wait until I take Ryan in, I can come back and get those." Ben's father-in-law had already pulled her three shopping bags out of the trunk. Maddie reached in and grabbed one particular bag. She opened it and handed Chad the coloring book he'd chosen, and then pulled out hers and a box of crayons. Maddie and Chad ran up the walkway together.

"Nonsense," Eric said, closing the trunk with one hand and waving her on. "After you."

The day had warmed slightly—at least the wind wasn't as strong—but she hurried to get Ryan inside. Eric followed more slowly, favoring his right leg. He seemed otherwise fit, save for a slight paunch that wasn't too noticeable with his height. He hadn't gone shopping with her and Nina, but Nina had driven back to their house, wanting Hope and the kids to stay for dinner. Hope had thanked her profusely for a great day and all her help, but said that she really needed to get home.

The word *home* had slipped from her. She hadn't meant it in the literal sense, but she hadn't missed Nina's flinch. She'd quickly clarified that she wanted to get the *kids* home, and that, since they were already strapped in the car, it would be easier than another round of in and out. Eric had offered to drive and give Nina a break.

Maddie had already rung the doorbell, and Ben stood to the side in jeans and bare feet as they ran in. He watched as she neared the door. At first she thought he was looking at his son, or beyond her to Eric, but when she glanced up a second time, his eyes were focused directly on her. His jaw twitched, and he turned his attention abruptly to Eric.

"Hi," Hope said as she passed Ben. He kept looking toward Eric.

"Yeah, hi," he said, practically under his breath. "Hey, Eric," he called out. "How's the knee doing?" Hope set Ryan's carrier near the couch and returned to the door. Ben stepped out barefoot onto the stone, took the bags from Eric and shook his hand.

"Well, you know how old war injuries can be. Good days and bad. I haven't been cycling as much since…well, you know…and the weather's gotten colder. Probably why it's being a pain," Eric said.

"I hear ya. My shoulder acts up on occasion. You take care of yourself. Thanks for dropping off the kids."

Just the kids? If he didn't want her here, all he needed to do was say so.

"Thanks again for your help, Eric," she said from behind Ben. "It was so nice to meet you." Ben turned, and she took the bags he was holding.

"You, too, Hope. Come around with the kids whenever you like." Eric looked at her, then directly at Ben, before waving and walking back to his car. Hope set the bags by the hallway and went to see if Ryan was still sleeping in his seat. Maddie and Chad were both coloring at the coffee table.

Ben had one hand still pressed against the front door and his back was turned to her. What was going on?

"Is everything all right?" Hope asked, approaching him so the kids wouldn't hear if something serious had happened. He turned and rubbed his hands on his jeans.

"Everything is fine," he said with a frown. He cleared his throat. "I wasn't expecting you back. I was planning to come and pick you guys up."

"Ah, yes. But we were already in the car and—"

"Next time, if I'm around, I feel better with them in *my* car."

"Of course. Next time. It's just that… It had been…" How did she explain without insulting anyone? "I thought it best to get the kids home before they became irritable."

One corner of his mouth turned up.

"You'd had enough of someone, didn't you?" Ben said, lowering his voice.

Hope licked her lips. He knew. She dropped her chin and tried hard not to smile.

"Maybe just a little," she said, peering at him from under her lashes. "I know she means well, and she did teach me a lot." She placed her hand over her heart. "But, bless her, I needed to breathe."

Ben chuckled. "She can smother."

"Yes, and some things she was pointing out were… Well, let's just say my education counts for something." Hope didn't want to bash the woman. Not really. But venting a little felt good, and Ben wasn't just anyone. He'd known Nina longer than she had.

"I get taught the obvious by her all the time. Tests a man's patience," he said, shaking his head and folding his arms.

"I'm sure she means well," they said simultaneously, then laughed.

Their eyes met and things got quiet. He looked at her the same way he had when she was carrying Ryan to the door. Intense. Perplexed.

"You look nice," he said.

Her cheeks warmed. She looked at the new boots and hooded down jacket she'd bought and put on before leaving the store.

"Credit goes to Maddie," she said loud enough for the kids to hear. She went to Maddie and put her hand on her shoulder. "Your daughter here has excellent taste. I couldn't have shopped without her. She chose pink for the jacket. Right?" Hope asked. She was rewarded with a smile. Maddie looked proudly at her dad.

"Great choice, Mads," he said.

Maddie held up her arm and turned her wrist to make the silver bangle Hope had given her in the car ripple with reflections.

"Don't forget what I told you about that," Hope said, fingering the two left on her own wrist. "My grandmother used to tell me that these bracelets were magical and could brighten any day."

Maddie's smile was so worth it. Hope had been about her age when her late grandmother had given her the bangles. It was her first grown-up gift, and she still remembered how special it had made her feel at the time. It felt right giving Maddie one.

"That was nice of you, giving her that," Ben said.

"My pleasure," she said, winking at Maddie. The girl surprised her by getting up and giving her a hug, then she ran back to coloring the jungle-themed pages she'd chosen when Hope had insisted on buying them something.

When the kids hadn't been paying attention today, Nina had told her that, before her silence, Maddie had always talked about working with animals like her aunt did in

Kenya. Zoe had promised her that someday she'd get to visit her little cousin Pippa at Busara, Anna and Jack's home, as well as the rescue camp for orphaned baby elephants. No wonder the stuffed monkey seemed to be her favorite toy.

Ben went to the kitchen table and began putting away papers and a laptop. So they'd interrupted his work when they arrived. Maybe she should have stuck it out at Eric and Nina's a little longer. She yawned. No way she would have lasted. She was exhausted. But, oh, was Simba right.

Despite the plane, diaper-change incident and not being able to quite peg Nina, being here, as far away from everyone and everything that had defined her up until now, was so…so…liberating. Exhilarating. A fresh page or chapter, even if she'd eventually reach The End and return to real life.

She'd just spent the day playing with kids, learning new things and shopping without that nagging voice in the back of her head warning her that someone might die on her watch or that she still hadn't read the latest article on ortho surgery her parents had handed her or that she'd fail everyone who mattered. Here, she could let go of all of that. Here, her parents had no say. Had Simba simply been worried about her health, or had cutting the umbilical cord for her been his intention all along?

She took off the jacket and slung it on the back of the armchair next to the couch, then sat down to unzip her new boots. She set them by the door and returned to unbuckle Ryan. He was still asleep, but if he didn't wake up, he'd be awake all night. She picked him up and nuzzled his wispy hair. He smelled and felt incredible in an all-encompassing way.

She'd never had the opportunity to hold a baby that closely. The few she'd handled were in medical settings. With patients, there were boundaries. A certain level of necessary detachment. This was different. So personal. She didn't want to put him down. Was this what women meant when they said babies were contagious? Was this why many of the women in her medical school class had dropped out after the first year or two to have families? Babies—children—were so small, yet they had such a powerful pull.

She looked at the pictures set on the built-in shelves that flanked the small fireplace. Most were of the children. Maddie looked a lot like her mother, and Chad was the spitting image of Ben, right down to the crew cut hair. There was one family photo, but Ryan wasn't in it, and there was one close-up of Zoe. She looked really happy.

Hope's heart broke for her, being in a place where she couldn't hold her children…and for Maddie and Chad no longer being able to cuddle with their mama, and Ryan because he'd have no memories of her, and for Ben. She bit her lower lip to stop her eyes and nose from stinging. She sat in the armchair and leaned back with Ryan against her chest and his head on her shoulder. His tiny fingers curled, and he clung to her sweater without waking. Chad held up a picture of a dinosaur colored in scribbles of at least fifteen different shades.

"Beautiful," she whispered before being lulled to sleep by baby magic.

BEN NEEDED TO stop looking at Hope, but something about her kept drawing him in.

It was disconcerting. There was a comfort

and warmth about her that confused him…if such a paradox was even possible.

He closed the cabinet in which he kept his laptop and papers, and looked past the kitchen counter and into the living room. He was checking on his kids, that was all. He wasn't looking at the way Ryan fit so perfectly in Hope's arms, or how her delicate hand cradled his head against her, or how at peace she looked.

He scrubbed his hand several times across his crew cut and opened the fridge, scanning its contents like a blind man. Watching her coming up the walkway earlier—coming home—had thrown him off balance. He hated that feeling. He had plans. He'd been killing himself to stay in control of his life— the kids' lives—since Zoe died. Only half a year. It wasn't enough. Even if he'd been gone almost a year the day he'd come home from duty. *The* day. What was wrong with him? He shut the fridge and went to his room.

He'd only known Hope a few days, but this wasn't about physical attraction. There were plenty of attractive women around. God help him, he'd discovered that being a widower was like having a girl magnet stuck on your back. Hope was different. Or maybe his darned subconscious felt safe because it knew she'd be leaving. He lay on his bed, propping two pillows behind him. A framed photo of Zoe faced him from on top of his dresser.

Never once had he betrayed her. In all the endless months that they were apart, he had never came close. Never looked at another woman. Not that way. And he knew plenty of military men who'd done more than look. So why did he feel guilty? Why did seeing Zoe's father walking behind Hope make him feel as if he'd betrayed all of them? But he had, hadn't he?

Zoe wasn't here.

CHAPTER FIVE

Dear Diary,
Last night I had a nightmare. I was feeding Auntie Anna's elephants, but then suddenly Chad and Ryan turned into elephants, and I started to cry. But Miss Hope came and pointed to a herd and kept telling me Mommy was there. Then Daddy turned into a crocodile and scared everyone away. I'm really never sleeping again.

HOPE PEDALED FASTER through the light drizzle. The morning had gone quite efficiently between both Ben and her. She'd managed to clean up and feed Ryan and Chad while Ben had packed Maddie's lunchbox and waited for the bus with her outside. He'd been in a rush to get to an appointment he'd made to check out a potential psychologist for Maddie, and then he'd mentioned something about getting his car inspected. Hope had planned to take the boys for a walk and had just about had them ready to go when Nina had popped by, insisting that she take the kids back to her place. Their house was only two miles from the university campus where Jack used to work, and the theater department was showing a production she thought Hope would like. After all, she'd pointed out that Hope was entitled to some time to enjoy America.

The sun that had warmed up the morning had disappeared by the time she'd exited the auditorium. Eric was supposed to drop her off while Nina watched the boys and pick her up after she'd had the chance to watch the show, see the campus and explore the nearby shopping strip, which included a gift shop and bookstore. Hope had insisted she could walk and that she needed the exercise, but Eric had said walking two miles would take too long if the weather turned.

He'd ended up loaning her a bike and helmet. Several bikes rested against the wall in their garage. He'd pointed out the one he used to ride, then hesitated before choosing one for her and giving her directions.

The path was easy, especially with so many signs. The roads here were laid out like a grid for the most part and so neat. Even the gutters along the edge looked clean.

She licked the drops of rain off her lips and pedaled around a corner. The darkened sky ahead reminded her of the rebellious rolls of dark thunderclouds that always brought the promise of rain and a break in the heat after the drought season back home. Rain cleansed. It was a good omen. She lifted her face and smiled as she waited for the light at an intersection. It was amazing that everyone actually obeyed traffic rules here. Well, at least from what she'd witnessed. Rules had been broken when Zoe was killed.

The light turned green. Every single shop she passed, as well as the towering parking lot lights, was decorated in giant mirrored glittering green and red balls. It was truly wondrous. Almost as incredible as the house across the street from Ben. All these lights and decorations a whole month ahead? Unbelievable. Mesmerizing. And it probably cost a fortune in electricity.

A raindrop that felt like the size of a fig hit the back of her neck and trickled down and around her collarbone as she leaned forward to pick up speed.

"No, not yet," she muttered, as if the clouds would listen. Her front wheel hit some loose gravel the exact moment that she let go of the handlebar and reached up to swipe another big one that had landed on her eyelid. She swerved straight into a parking lot and squeezed the brake, stopping just two feet from a parked Jeep. She gasped, and it took her a few seconds to steady her breathing.

She looked around for somewhere to take shelter until the heaviest of the rain passed. She jumped off the bike, and rolled it quickly toward the only building in the parking lot, a single-story place covered in wood shingles. The sign over the wood-and-stained-glass front door said Bentley's: Music, Food and Spirits. She latched the bike under the front overhang, hung her helmet on the handlebar and ran inside just as the sky let loose.

Safe. Hope caught her breath and brushed some of the drops that beaded on her wool sweater.

"I'll be right with you," said a young woman with long red hair pulled into a low ponytail. "Feel free to pick a seat."

"Thank you," Hope said. The woman disappeared behind a swinging door with a... dog? Hope froze. Dogs bit and chased.

The stray who'd chased her when she was eleven and some of the patient injuries she'd treated proved so. What in the world was a dog doing in a restaurant? Maybe that was why business looked to be slow. Empty wooden tables and chairs grounded the center of the room. The place was relatively empty but for a couple eating burgers near the bar area, and a single man. He sat at a corner table poking his straw at an empty glass of ice cubes before pouring a green bottle she recognized as mineral water. They seemed unfazed by the presence of a dog. It *was* after lunch, so maybe it wasn't the dog's presence that cleared the place.

You know you're overreacting. There are good dogs just like there are good and bad people. Get over it and sit down.

An earsplitting crack of thunder and a flicker of lights had her jumping from her spot. *Think logically. Being out there on a bike would be much more dangerous than a dog on a leash.* The built-in benches under the windows overlooking the parking lot seemed a tiny bit more secure than the central tables, unless she got cornered. She slipped into the booth nearest the door. Rain beat the window next to her with no sign of letting up.

"Sorry about that. First time here?" The lady who'd greeted her appeared by her table, along with the cream-colored dog, who sat obediently on command, with his leash clipped to her belt. She set a menu in front of Hope and pulled out a pen and pad. The dog stared straight at Hope as if he, too, expected an answer to the question. Hope shifted closer to the window.

"Oh, uh, yes. First time here, and in town," Hope said, frowning at the dog.

"Oh? Where from?"

"Kenya."

"Really? Cool. I have always wanted to go on a safari there. One of these days, maybe. A girl can dream, right? I'm Brie, by the way. I own this place, and this guy here," she said, tapping a hook on her belt to emphasize the dog had a leash on, "is Wolf."

His name wasn't one bit reassuring.

"Hi, I'm Hope. Uh, about the dog... I'm really uncomfortable around them," Hope said, holding the edge of the table.

"I assure you he doesn't have an aggressive hair on him. In fact, he's the best puppy I've raised so far. Aren't you, boy? I do apologize for not having his blue vest on. I had a mustard-container malfunction just before you stepped in, so it's drying off. I foster puppies for a guide-dog program, so he's not just any dog. Of course, I don't let just any animals in here. I keep a notice near the door outside."

"I—"

A deafening clap of thunder had them both cringing.

"I think I ran in here too fast to read anything," Hope said, hoping the obvious storm explained her dilemma. She'd heard of programs like the one Brie mentioned. They didn't really have one available for patients with visual disabilities in Kenya. Usually, if someone needed assistance, a child relative would take them around. It certainly wasn't the best way, but the closest guide dog program was in South Africa.

Brie's lips flattened. "Of course. I understand. Give me just a moment." She took Wolf back to the side of the bar counter, told him to sit and stay, then connected the end of his leash to a hook. She dipped behind the bar and returned with a glass of water and a napkin, then set them down on the table.

"I started raising pups for the program a long time ago, but then I stopped about a year ago, after taking over Bentley's from my uncle," Brie explained. "Then a friend finally took the plunge and agreed to foster. I had convinced her it would be a great experience for her family. But—" Brie's nose turned red. She scratched at her throat. "She died. Wolf had been assigned to her."

"I'm sorry," Hope said. What else could she say? She could tell Brie still hurt and felt terrible for her loss—she couldn't imagine losing her only close friend, Chuki—and guilty for not being a dog person. Although, really, that guilt wasn't going to make her run over and give the dog a hug. And although she'd missed lunch, none of this was helping her appetite. She glanced at the menu. She hadn't intended to order. All she wanted was for the rain to end so she could leave.

"Thank you," Brie said. "We're trying to make the best of it. For the most part, the exposure here is good for his training. My uncle still helps out to give me a break, and my aunt watches Wolf during our busiest hours."

She really talked a lot.

"Oh, and since it's your first time in town," she went on, "I should mention that we have a live band here Friday and Saturday nights, so if you're looking for some fun…"

Hope stared past her at Wolf, who was now lying on the floor in his spot. Brie smiled.

"He goes home early on those nights. I can't handle training him and keeping up with guests and loud music."

"Okay. I'll try to remember that," Hope said, fiddling with her dangling earring.

"Great. So what can I get for you? I've been talking a lot." *No kidding.* "You must me starving by now."

Was that an apology? Or just a hint that shelter from the rain wasn't a free deal here? She opened the menu. It was a lot to look at.

"The American Burger Bust is our special. It's really good," Brie said, glancing over her shoulder, directly at the man sitting on his own. She tucked a strand of hair behind her ear.

Hope wasn't a fool. Whatever the kitchen had a surplus of after lunch was going to be the best thing on the menu until it was gone. But a burger did sound good. Pizza and burgers: two things she'd wanted to try in America because Jack had told her they didn't taste quite the same in Nairobi, even in the restaurants serving American fare.

She looked at the prices. She'd converted some Kenyan shillings to US dollars so that she'd have cash on hand, but she had a long way to go before thinking in dollars felt normal. And the prices here were steep—and no bargaining them down—not that money was an issue for her, but more than eighty-seven shillings to get a dollar? She'd never bothered with credit cards in Nairobi. The fees weren't worth it, considering that the open Masai marketplace and most of the kiosks with art or handmade jewelry didn't take them. Anytime she was at a professional meeting or a gathering at one of the well-known restaurants or hotels, she was usually with family or some higher-up hosting a group from the hospital, and she never had to pay.

"I'll take the burger," she said, noting from the sound alone that it was still raining hard. "Also, do you have a phone I could use?" Boy, did she miss her cell phone. She'd figured, after finding out from her carrier that it wouldn't work in the US, that she'd survive a few months. But survival was relative, and habits were a funny thing.

"There's a pay phone right by the restrooms." She pointed to the far corner.

"Thank you." Hope removed the small leather satchel she'd slung across her shoulder and chest so that she could ride. She fished out a slip of paper she'd listed phone numbers on, then slid out of the booth and went to call Nina to let her know she was okay. Just in time, too. Worried about the storm, Nina and Eric had been about to call Ben for help in tracking her down. Hope reassured them, and headed to her booth, hesitating only to make sure Wolf wasn't on the loose.

She sat back down at her booth and eyed the menu Brie had left. She flipped to the backside and knew immediately she was doomed. Desserts with descriptions that were probably raising her blood sugar by simply reading them. Caramel flan, Guinness ice cream, a double devil chocolate cake, Irish coffee cake, mousse pie with Baileys Irish cream and cheesecake. Heaven help her, that was a dessert for every day of the week—and no one to bother her about what she should and shouldn't be eating. The only ones that sounded familiar were the flan, chocolate cake and cheesecake.

She turned the menu so that she couldn't see the list and pushed it away, chuckling to herself. She was so bad. She knew better. Her heart had healed long ago, but it was something her parents never really got over. Kind of like her fear of dogs. She'd pace herself. A greasy burger today and dessert another day. She'd only be here for three months anyway. She'd be good when she returned to Kenya. She'd even tell Dalila not to indulge her, even if she begged. Having a high metabolism was terrible for willpower.

She watched Brie carry a bottle of orange soda over to the man in the corner while balancing a dish on her other hand. She set it down in front of him, whisked his old bottle away and, smoothing her apron, asked if he needed anything else. She blushed. Wolf, who'd been so obedient, stretched his neck and began licking the man's leg, whimpering when Brie ordered him to sit. Maybe Wolf was actually a girl, too.

"I'm so sorry," Brie said.

"It's fine," he replied, eyeing Wolf, but not once looking at her.

Hope turned away as Brie approached her table.

"Here you go," she said, setting down a hot plate with a massive pile of fries next to the burger. The portion size blew her away. How big would a dessert be?

"Can I get you anything else?"

"It says here that you deliver?"

"Yes, we do." Good to know, given her cooking skills. "It does depend on how far, though."

"Lancaster Street."

Brie's face fell, and any sign of blushing at the man in the corner faded away. She studied the rain sweeping across the parking lot outside the window, as if trying to recall their delivery area, but the way she kept swallowing and curling her lips told Hope it was more.

"Yes," Brie finally said quietly. "We deliver there."

Passing Campus Drive on his way to Maddie's elementary school had become routine over the past few weeks. The call he'd gotten from the principal's office was becoming an expected frustration, too. Enough so that he'd contemplated pulling her out and finding someone who could homeschool her, since the other public school within driving distance was overcrowded, and he couldn't come close to affording private school.

He quickly banished the thought. It'd be easier for him, maybe. No more school visits, but it would mean tearing Maddie away from the classmates she'd known since kindergarten. And without familiar friends around, she'd have even less reason to come out of her shell. Besides, the one person Maddie seemed to like and connect with was her school counselor, and the last private counselor Ben had checked out didn't have enough experience with mutism. Plus, his overall personality wasn't...maternal enough.

Rain sloshed across his windshield as he switched his wipers to a higher speed. He stopped at the light, wishing he'd made it through. He hated the way his stomach tightened, as though his soul was being sucked into a black hole, every time he passed that intersection...and Bentley's. Today that feeling felt tenfold. Maybe it was because of

Maddie, or maybe the depressing weather, but somehow, ever since Hope had arrived, he couldn't stop hearing Zoe's voice in his head in a way that was more real, more frequent than it had been since the first weeks after her death. An unsettled feeling washed through him. Then something purple caught his eye through the sheets of rain. Something unmistakable, yet impossible.

Zoe's bike and helmet. At Bentley's.

Nausea roiled in his gut, and he sucked in a breath as his cell phone rang. He glanced at the light to make sure it was red and then at the caller ID. The school.

"Corallis here," he answered, glad he'd charged his Bluetooth. He hated the darn thing, but with kids all over the place, he needed to be accessible, and it was the safest way to go when he was driving.

"Hi, Mr. Corallis. This is Mrs. Chaperson."

"I'm almost at the school. Did you need to reschedule?" The principal had set up the meeting via email, wanting to discuss Maddie's progress. No doubt, Ms. Serval had gone to her, feeling like she wasn't getting anywhere with "the dad." He couldn't help but imagine Serval telling Chaperson that "her

dad just doesn't get it." Same attitude he got
from Nina. Maybe it was a women versus men
thing. Or maybe he really was missing something and failing at parenthood. Failing at protecting his little girl and helping her heal.

The rain let up, causing the wipers to
squeak. He turned them off so he could hear
better.

"No. Our meeting is still on, but I wanted
to give you a heads-up, just in case you need
to make arrangements, that Maddie won't be
able to finish the day at school today. She'll
need to go home with you due to an incident.
I'll explain when you get here, since you're
on your way."

Great. Just great.

"Have her pack her stuff," he said, discon-
necting.

Ben's face heated. An incident? Now what?
When were things going to run smoothly?
Even the darned streetlight wasn't cooper-
ating. He tightened his grip on the steering
wheel and looked back at Bentley's.

The bike was gone.

"No, ma'am. I don't understand. Not this
time." Ben's jaw ached. Maddie sat, with her

backpack already on, just outside the glass wall panel separating the principal's office from the main office area. She stared at her feet as she ground the toe of her sneaker into the linoleum. He lowered his voice just in case she could hear through the glass.

"Was the kid hurt?"

"Well, no, there was no deep skin break or blood, but still, he was grazed. Throwing a pencil is dangerous. It could have been worse." Mrs. Chaperson put her hands flat on the desk. "You have to understand, Mr. Corallis, we have to stick to the safety rules. No exceptions."

No exceptions was her way of telling him that Maddie, who'd lost her mother and wouldn't speak, didn't deserve any special consideration. Unless they classified her as special ed. Not happening. Maddie's mutism was temporary. It had to be.

"I don't expect anyone to make exceptions, ma'am. But I do expect some insight and understanding to be used in the situation. Clearly she was upset about something and reacted, for lack of being able to 'use her words.' I agree fully on the zero-tolerance policy regarding safety, but I also have zero tolerance for my child being picked on, and I'd like to know if Ms. Serval noticed anyone provoking her. And I'd also like to know if that child was also given in-school suspension for the next two days for bullying."

He'd had no clue what in-school suspension was when she first mentioned it and had to ask. Suspension was something he'd experienced after a sixth-grade brawl when some dude wouldn't stop chanting "fatty, bratty, no daddy" behind his back on the playground. The situation had been different. He'd never known his dad and his mom was around, just not much because she was working double shifts. But blood had been drawn. This in-school thing was a new twist. A stepping-stone to student Alcatraz. The mental image of Maddie being forced to sit in the office all day to do her work while classmates walking by gawked made his skin crawl. Why were kids so mean? Even the little bags of fun dollar-store items Nina had put together for Maddie's classmates when she'd turned ten last month hadn't helped. He'd really hoped that her birthday would be a positive trigger. It wasn't.

She'd been provoked. Picked on. She'd

only thrown a pencil, for heaven's sake. Why was the victim being punished here?

"I can't discuss the other child," she continued, "but they've been spoken to for touching another student's property. *Bullying* is a strong word, and of course I'll continue to investigate and keep a closer eye on things, I assure you. We take that seriously. But you have to understand, she's not on in-school suspension for just the pencil incident. It's because this was her third incident that was significant enough to be brought to my attention. I have here that back in October, she shoved another student in line and they fell down and scraped their knee. According to others in line, Maddie had been called a name. And, on a separate occasion, she wrote a very...unacceptable swear word on a piece of paper and threw it at a student. Three major offenses is the limit. But what's important here is that these behaviors aren't overlooked, so that she can get help now before things get worse. She's acting out, Mr. Corallis. Kids do say mean things at times, but she needs to learn how to cope without violence in the real world. You won't always be there to defend her."

Ben hated the truth in her words. He gnawed at the inside of his cheek. His Maddie was swearing? He tried to remember if he'd ever cussed in the children's presence. He consciously tried not to, but a guy didn't spend years in the marines and not pick up some colorful lingo. Just one more way he was being a bad parent.

"From what I've been told," she continued, "today Maddie brought a trinket or piece of jewelry from home and it was causing a distraction. Her teacher noticed it hidden in her desk, but she didn't say anything because Maddie seemed to be having a decent day. But later she became preoccupied with fiddling with the thing in her desk and not paying attention. Then when the students were lining up to go to art class, the other student involved saw it and grabbed it from her."

Ben pressed his lips together, processing what she'd said. Her mother's necklace. The one with three child-shaped trinkets adorned with the kids' respective birthstones. He'd ordered the one for Ryan online and had it sent to her since he couldn't be there for his birth. He'd given the necklace to Maddie months ago, thinking it would help. That necklace was a special keepsake. What if she'd lost it at school? Or it had gotten stolen?

"I've since returned it to her—she seemed overly stressed by it being confiscated and I knew you were on your way—but, please, have her keep it at home."

I do have common sense, thank you.

"Why not just have her speak to the school counselor about this whole thing?" The counselor was an extremely patient, intelligent person who seemed to truly understand Maddie. He could see the difference in his daughter's mood on the days she came home with a note letting him know she'd done an activity with Mrs. Eggers.

"She's scheduled to meet with her on Monday. This week is short because of Thanksgiving." She pressed on when he shook his head. "I understand this is difficult for you as a parent, and I truly wish the county budgeted for a full-time counselor at each school, but with the cutbacks…" She raised her hands and dropped them. "It's the best we can do."

Ben stood and nodded, not so much in agreement as in acceptance that he wasn't getting anywhere. An emotionally fragile fourth grader being handled as if she'd committed aggravated assault. The fear of liability in this day and age. As far as he was concerned, a kid didn't need to beat another one up to be called a bully. Maddie was being picked on and harassed in other ways. And she couldn't—wouldn't—speak up to tell anyone. So she was lashing out in frustration. Could anyone blame her?

"Also, before you leave, Ms. Serval wanted me to mention that Maddie has also seemed extra tired. Dozing off during independent reading. Is she sleeping well at night? Getting to bed on time?" Mrs. Chaperson asked, standing and coming around the side of her desk.

Ben's back and shoulders itched.

"Of course she is."

Except maybe last night, because while Hope had been reading a bedtime story to the boys, Maddie had brought him a deck of cards. He'd given in, despite the hour. If she actually approached him to play something, which wasn't often, he wasn't about to say no. What if that game of Fish had turned out to be the key that unlocked her silence?

Mental note—look up just how many hours of sleep a kid her age is supposed to get.

Mrs. Chaperson smiled sympathetically.

"Good. We just like to cover everything."

Ben looked out at his daughter. A part of him had to wonder if she'd caught on to the fact that if she acted up she'd get to go home. Yet another part of him, the part that had seen fear and desperation firsthand in the faces of children trapped in an assault zone, or the hardened faces of those in war-torn areas who'd seen too much, that part of him believed that in all her silence, Maddie was crying out for help. Feeling cornered, he pinched the bridge of his nose, then braced his hands on his hips.

"I'd rather she stayed at home the next few days," he said, "instead of here for the suspension. Especially given the short week. She'll understand it's a punishment and that throwing anything is unacceptable. You have my word. But I don't think humiliating her in front of her peers is going to help her situation. In-school suspension is only going to give them something new to tease her about. It'll make things worse on all levels. I'm sure school policy isn't intended to cause harm, and I don't want this to cause potentially irreversible damage, making it take even longer to get her to speak again." *Liability.*

Mrs. Chaperson took a deep breath and watched Maddie for a few seconds. Her voice softened.

"Okay. We'll handle it this way this time. But I have to warn you, if there's a violent incident again, she could be expelled, unless you agree to have her placed in special classes where we're better equipped to handle her emotional needs. I have to answer to higher authorities and handle complaints from other parents. Special-ed classes would put her with staff who give more individualized attention and work with needs…so that she can get better. Consider it, because suspensions go on a child's permanent school record."

"Noted." Ben walked out of the office. Maddie immediately stood up and started to follow him out.

"Mr. Corallis, if you don't mind signing her out here," the school secretary called. She held a pen for him. He took a step back and signed. The only thing he was grateful for today was that they were being careful about who walked off with his kid.

He left with Maddie at his heels and held the main door open for her, seeing her chin quiver as she hurried past him. She hadn't shown any such sign of weakness inside. Not a tear. His little girl was stoic. A minimarine. Unwilling to concede that she was the only one at fault. Maybe a little stubborn there, too.

He caught up to her, wrapping his hand on her arm to slow her down. "Hang on a sec, squirt."

She yanked her arm away and marched toward his SUV. Ben rubbed his palm against his forehead, then let his hand fall to his side.

Please. Help me get through to her, Zoe. Help me.

CHAPTER SIX

Dear Diary,
Sometimes I wish I could just die and go be with Mommy. No one bothered me when she was here.

"IS THERE ANYTHING I can do to help?" Hope asked, stepping into the Harpers' kitchen after changing into the dry sweats Nina had lent her while they ran her things in the dryer. The sweats were baggy on her, but definitely warmer than wet clothes. The rain had started up again before she'd reached the house, and Nina had insisted that Hope would catch pneumonia if she didn't get dry. Eric had been banished from the house for not insisting on driving Hope earlier instead of lending her a bike. He was serving out his sentence unclogging the leaves that had piled up at the drain by the basement door so that rainwater wouldn't back into the house.

"You can get the kids to finish their food so I can finish cooking," Nina said, waving Hope toward a set of stools at the kitchen island while she continued to clean vegetables at the sink. Chad sat on one of the stools making mounds with his broccoli and shoving dinosaur-shaped nuggets around them with a toddler fork. He was leaning to one side, propping his cheek on his other hand, and had looked up with big eyes when Hope walked in. At a right angle to the last stool, Ryan sat strapped in a high chair, playing with a red, white and black mirrored toy-and-gadget center suctioned to his tray. An unopened jar of baby food and a tiny rubber-coated spoon sat on the counter just out of his reach.

"My two favorite men," Hope said, sitting on the stool in between the boys. An oven alarm buzzed. Nina dried her hands and pulled a tray out of the oven, then set it on the kitchen island. The aroma had Hope forgetting that she'd already stuffed herself with a burger and fries. She was going to return to Kenya a good twenty pounds heavier if she wasn't careful.

"I'm not a man," Chad said. He straightened up but continued to poke at his food. Ryan squealed and kicked the side of the island from under his high chair tray.

"You could have fooled me," Hope said. "You're not eating baby food and formula like Ryan, for one thing." Chad stuck his tongue out at Ryan.

"Hey, that's not nice," Hope said, patting his leg. "My grandma used to tell me that if I stuck my tongue out, a bird flying by would think it was a worm and snatch it."

His tongue disappeared, but then he narrowed his eyes.

"There aren't any birds in here."

He had her there.

"But," Nina said as she set goodies on a napkin, "it's hard to chew without having all the parts of your mouth where they're supposed to be. Don't stick your tongue out unless you don't have teeth to hold it in, like a baby." She tipped her head at Ryan.

Nina set a napkin in front of Hope. It was decorated with a little boy in a black hat with a buckle on it and girl in a white bonnet. Hope frowned.

"Pilgrims," Nina said. "If it's your first

time in America, then you've never experienced our Thanksgiving holiday."

Hope shook her head. "No. But I've heard of it," she said.

Hope knew that the holidays were going to be tough on the entire family. Nina looked exhausted. Hope bit her lip. She should never have agreed to leave the kids with their grandparents today, or to come over at all. Having the children around… Five plates of various cookies and pies crowding the countertops… Clearly Nina was distracting herself to soften the pain of never being able to spend the holidays with her daughter again. Hope didn't want to say anything in front of the boys, though.

Nina placed a square piece of chocolate cake on the pilgrim boy's face.

"Try one of these, Hope. Tell me what you think. Ah!" she added with an admonishing shake of her finger at Chad, who was going in for a stealthy grab. "You don't get any if you don't eat your food."

Hope made bug eyes at Chad, then took a bite.

"Oh, my gosh. I think you just ruined me

for any other food on earth. What is this? It's heavenly."

"Peanut-butter-fudge brownie. Jack's favorite. Great bribe power, too. It's like truth serum. It always got him to talk." The corners of Nina's mouth turned down. Obviously her brownies weren't enough to get Maddie to talk.

Nina straightened her shoulders and quickly recovered. "But somehow it hasn't worked to make someone eat their broccoli and chicken nuggets," she said, looking right at Chad.

Chad abandoned his fork, stared at the dessert and then looked at Hope as if he'd fallen in love. This one could kill with cuteness. She set the rest of her brownie down, only because shoving the entire thing in her mouth wouldn't have set a good example. She gave Chad an exaggerated look of surprise.

"Oh, but that's not broccoli."

"It's not?" Chad scrunched one cheek up and wrinkled his nose. "It smells like it to me."

"I don't know how you can smell anything but those brownies, but I assure you—" she reached over and picked up a piece of broccoli, propping it on its end "—this is a dino-saur tree."

Chad's lips spread into the most adorable smile, and he opened his eyes wide, sucking in a noisy breath of fake surprise.

"A dinosaur tree?"

"Yes, and this mean dinosaur—" she picked up a chicken nugget and pretended the dinosaur was eating the broccoli "—is going to eat the tree. Yum! 'Save me, save me!'" She made the tree run toward Chad, who opened his mouth and snatched a big bite of it. "Ouch!"

Chad started giggling. The game went on until he'd stuffed the last bite of triceratops in his mouth and uncovered the purple dino picture on his plate.

He growled ferociously, followed by a fit of laughter that had Hope joining in. The air in the room shifted even before she heard Ben's voice.

"Chad. Don't laugh like that when you're eating. You could choke."

Ben stood in the doorway to the kitchen, hands on his hips and jaw clenched like a T. rex. Nina sighed, whipped off her apron and scooted around him to hang it on a hook in the pantry. Chad's laughter fizzled out, and he solemnly took a sip of milk from his plastic cup. He eyed the rest of Hope's brownie and glanced at her, but didn't dare take it. Not in front of his father anyway. Ryan cooed and babbled, slapping his tray, happy to see his dad.

"That's okay. I know the Heimlich," Hope said, flashing her best smile and trying to salvage Chad's fun. She split the brownie on her napkin, popping half in her mouth and giving half to a thrilled Chad. Ben's face was motionless.

"I'm kidding," Hope said, covering her lips with her fingertips to make sure every crumb stayed in. His eyes followed the motion.

"He's fine, Ben," Nina admonished. "She got him to eat his entire plate. Down to the dancing purple dinosaur. When has that happened?"

Ben's shoulders sank a few millimeters.

"That dancing purple dinosaur is enough to give grown men nightmares," he muttered, walking past the counter and picking Chad off the stool. So the man did have a sense of humor lurking somewhere in there. She watched as he took his son over to the sink and washed his mouth and hands, then set him down. Chad ran off.

Hope waited for him to step away from the sink area, then carried the dino plate and matching cup over and washed her hands.

"Have a brownie," Nina said, placing a hand on his shoulder. "Come on, sit down."

"I need to get the kids home. Maddie's curled up in a ball in your armchair," he said, motioning with his thumb through the kitchen doorway.

"Oh, let me see if I can at least get her to eat a snack," Nina said. "Besides, I was about to feed Ryan his jar. I just needed to finish with the oven. And if you want I can help her get her homework done before you go home. Take a break while you have reinforcements around."

"I don't mind feeding Ryan," Hope said, drying her hands and heading for the stool next to the high chair. "I was just getting Chad to eat first," she said, then looked pointedly at Ben. "I'll be careful. I won't make Ryan laugh."

He dropped his gaze and said nothing, then gave a curt nod and left the kitchen. Nina pressed her lips together and followed. Hope wanted to check on Maddie, too, but forced herself to stay put.

She opened the baby-food jar and scooped up a bite of mashed sweet potato and brought it near Ryan's mouth. Half of what went in oozed back out. She caught it with the spoon and brought it to Ryan's mouth again, trying not to listen to the conversation in the living room. If there was anything she'd learned in medicine, the one thing that tore her up, was that no matter how smart she was or how educated, she could still be powerless to help…or heal. The will to get better had to come from the person suffering and, sometimes, all they needed was a safe, open door to walk through.

Ben Corallis was anything but an open door.

"IF YOU DON'T want to go with Grandma to get a snack, then you need to pull out your homework and get it done. Not going to school tomorrow doesn't mean you're on vacation yet."

Ben sat on the edge of the sofa next to Maddie. Her backpack leaned against the coffee table because she'd refused to leave it in the car, even though he'd told her they weren't staying long. The entire drive over from school, she'd stared out her window, giving no indication that she was listening to his lecture on why neither throwing pencils—aka grenades, from the way it'd been put to him—nor hand-to-hand combat at school was acceptable. He kept his opinions of the situation at school otherwise to himself.

"Come on, honey," Nina coaxed, crouching next to her. "I made your favorite brownies."

Maddie slowly lifted her head from where she'd had it buried in a pillow and sat up, bringing her knees to her chest. She blinked her eyes to adjust from dark pillow to light room. She looked tired. Maybe he should just let her do her homework tomorrow.

"I'll get her pad in case she wants to write down what she wants, or draw a picture." Nina got up and went to fetch the pad from the coat closet that she'd cleared of coats and used exclusively for grandkid supplies. Ben had lined it with shelves. The writing or drawing pad had been something recommended in her first therapy sessions. Maddie actually made use of it, depending on her mood. But whenever she shut down after something happened at school, it would take forever for her to open up about it.

"How about getting your math done here, while we wait for Ryan to finish eating, so that you can watch that show you like when you get home?" Ben asked. He took the backpack and started to unzip it. Her face turned red, and she tried to yank it from him.

He pulled it away from her. "Hey, what's the problem?"

Her pooling tears and quivering chin made him feel like scum. Why didn't she want him looking in her backpack? Was there more going on here? Maybe the other kid hadn't been the only one to touch something that wasn't theirs. Had she stolen something from school? What had her principal said about strike three? Still holding the pack, he met Maddie's eyes directly.

"Is there something in here that doesn't belong to you? And I don't mean your mother's necklace."

She frowned, and the tears in her eyes spilled onto her cheeks. She didn't respond with either a shake or a nod.

"*Did* you steal?"

This time her nostrils flared, and she gave him an evil glare.

He pulled her notebook, agenda and math text out of the main pocket. The second zipped pocket hid nothing but an empty lunch box. He unzipped a small side pouch, hoping the necklace was there, safe and sound. He reached in…and pulled out a bracelet. *The* bracelet. The one Hope had given her right off her own wrist. He closed his eyes, then opened them and held the bracelet out to his daughter.

"Why'd you take this to school?" *Why are you clinging to something that a practical stranger gave you? Why was this important enough to fight for and cry over and destroy my day? Your day?*

Was thinking she'd risked losing her mother's necklace easier to take than her attachment to Hope's bracelet? He exhaled. "Did you think I'd take this away from you?"

Maddie nodded, wiping her cheek with her hand.

She didn't trust him. From her point of view, he'd shown up, and then her mother was gone. Cause and effect. That was what she was clinging to. He couldn't blame her for not trusting him.

He handed her the bracelet. She hesitated, then slipped it on her too-small wrist. Ben stood up and saw Nina watching from the end of the room, hugging the pad and pencil to her chest, her face damp. She nodded her head as if to say it would be all right and she'd finish calming Maddie down.

Nothing was all right.

He walked silently to the kitchen, stopping momentarily to look back and watch how Nina set the pad in Maddie's lap. He was a terrible father. He didn't have a maternal or parental bone in him. He wasn't doing them any good. This wasn't his territory.

He stepped into the kitchen and in a fleeting second of fatigue, he thought he saw Zoe feeding Ryan. He pinched the bridge of his nose, knowing full well that the curls and dark, slender neck were Hope's. She faced away from him, making airplane noises as she brought a spoonful of food in for landing. Whether Ryan understood the game or not, he seemed to be enjoying himself. The playfulness in Hope's voice tempted him to leave her be. Wasn't he the one who had told her, during her first diaper change, that there were worse things in life...? But a clawing ache quickly reminded him that life wasn't about playing. Life was about survival and doing your duty. Doing what you were meant to do, what you'd vested your life in. Without that direction, a person would be lost. And being lost was dangerous.

Ryan gave him away by looking in his direction. Hope turned her head, and her smile faltered.

"I don't think Ryan will finish this jar, if you're wanting to play with him," she said.

Play? Ben took a deep breath. "You didn't by any chance borrow my wife's bike today, did you?"

The baby spoon stopped in midair. Her face paled.

"Purp—"

"Yes. That one."

She set the spoon in the jar.

"I'm so sorry. I didn't know. Eric told me I should use it. I assumed it was Nina's."

Eric? Nina, he might have believed. She had it in for him lately. But Eric? He couldn't have at least warned him? Checked with him?

The porch door cracked open and Eric peered in.

"Nina's not coming right back, is she?" he whispered.

Ben folded his arms and leaned against the fridge. "I wouldn't know," he said.

Eric stepped in and closed the door behind him.

"When that woman gets in a mood, it's hard to believe she's the queen of sweets." Eric stole a sugar cookie off the nearest plate and sat at the breakfast table just as Nina bustled in, grabbing a plate and piling brownies and cookies on it, presumably for Maddie, given the way she started back for the living room. She spotted Eric and stopped in her tracks.

"I thought I told you to go do something outside," she said, fuming.

Eric stopped chewing and rubbed at his knee.

"My injury started acting up again. Must be the weather."

"That's not going to work this time," she said, walking over and taking the cookie out of his hand. She went to the sink, opened the cabinet underneath and tossed it in the trash.

Ben stared at Nina. "So you knew Eric had given Hope Zoe's bike?

"Only after the fact," Nina said.

Hope turned away. She cleaned Ryan's face with a baby wipe and gave his tray the same swift treatment, then gathered the empty jar and got up.

"You should have said something to me, Eric. You've made me feel very uncomfortable."

One look at Ben and Eric stood military straight, though Ben caught him wincing.

"You listen to me, all of you," Eric said, lowering his voice to keep it from carrying into the living room. He pointed at Ben and Nina. "You think you're the only ones who miss her? I didn't plan it. I was just there, and then suddenly I wanted—needed—to see her bike going down our street again." His last words were hoarse and strained. He rubbed his fingertips hard across his forehead. He looked at Hope. "She and I... We used to ride together. Ever since she was a kid. It was our thing. Some dads shoot hoops with their daughters. We rode." He looked at all of them. "We rode," he repeated, only this time his voice cracked. He pushed past them and left the kitchen.

A massive sob escaped Nina. Then another. She dropped the plate of treats onto the counter and rushed after him.

Ben couldn't move.

Chad came zipping through the kitchen doorway with a plastic reptile.

"Chad," Ben said. "Stop running."

Chad kept circling Hope, every third turn plopping to the floor and rotating his eyes in silly circles, oblivious to the tension in the house.

"Chad, I said stop." How much sugar was in those brownies? Not to mention the caffeine in the chocolate. Bedtime was going to be a blast.

"I really need to get home," he said.

"Should we be leaving Nina and Eric like this?" Hope asked. She unbuckled Ryan and lifted him snuggly against her chest. She swayed gently. Chad got up and made the reptile eat his brother's feet. Hope reached down and brushed the top of his head with her hand without missing her rhythm or taking her eyes off Ben. She stood there with his boys as if it was second nature to her and she'd been a part of their lives all along.

We.

"I think they need some time alone," Ben said.

She nodded. "Should I put Ryan in the playpen I saw in the living room until we get Maddie and Chad ready?"

"I'll put him straight into his car seat," Ben said.

He went to take Ryan from her. For all the weapons he'd assembled blindfolded and bombs he'd dismantled, Ben paused awkwardly, his hands inches from the baby, trying to figure out how to remove him without making contact with the live wire.

"Ben."

His eyes met Hope's. Her skin looked as smooth as a baby's, and her cheeks glowed the way Ryan's did after waking from sleep.

"I'll carry him out," she said with a hushed calm. "You can gather up Chad and Maddie."

Something unspoken passed between them. An understanding. An unwelcome awareness.

"Right." He took a step back, then strode out of the kitchen.

HOPE TUCKED HER face against Ryan's tiny head and breathed in his soothing—grounding— baby scent.

It was nothing. She repeated the words in her mind. *It's just the excitement and adrenaline of being on your own, in another country. You're letting your imagination run wild.*

The Harpers' living room was empty. The coffee table was littered with paper and crayons, but Ben already had the others at the car, and she had no time to help clean up. Hope pulled Ryan's hat and jacket out from his baby bag, opting to wait on checking his diaper till they got home, and harnessed him in his infant carrier. She took him out to the car and clicked the seat onto its base. Ben leaned into the back from the opposite side and was busy securing Chad in his navy blue safety seat. Only Maddie, clinging to whatever she'd been coloring earlier, bridged the gap between them.

Hope gently bit her bottom lip and set the baby bag under Ryan's feet, pulled out toy keys to occupy him and closed the door. Through the window, she saw Ben reach across Maddie to double-check the slack on

Ryan's straps. To say he was careful didn't do the man justice.

It didn't matter how handsome, capable or protective Ben was or how her heart broke for him and his family—he was off-limits.

He climbed into the driver's seat just as the battle in the back broke out.

First, Maddie grabbed the toy cars that Chad kept crashing into each other in repeated midair collisions. She threw them onto the floor of the car where he couldn't reach them, so he went for the paper she was holding instead.

"Let me see!" Chad kept grabbing for Maddie's paper, and she kept pushing his hand away.

"Chad, come on. Leave your sister alone," Hope said, twisting in her seat.

"No," Chad said, still grabbing. Maddie pushed harder. Then pinched. Chad shrieked.

"Stop!" Ben reached back and snatched the paper. He looked at it. Hope couldn't decipher his expression. "It's really nice, Mads," he said quietly.

He handed the drawing to Hope.

At ten, Maddie could draw a million times better than Hope could at twenty-five. The drawing showed Hope with her hair held back by the orange scarf she had on when she arrived. The colorful peasant-style skirt. The bangles on her wrist. She was holding the hand of a girl wearing a single bangle. Maddie. Hope's throat tightened.

"Maddie, you're a beautiful artist," she said. "I'm so impressed."

Maddie cracked a sheepish smile. Hope started to hand the drawing back to her, but Maddie shook her head.

"You want me to keep it?" Hope asked. Maddie nodded and waited, as if Hope would decline. "Thank you," Hope said. "It's an honor to have an early original from someone who could be a famous artist someday. This is so special."

She reached back and wrapped her hand around Maddie's. The smile she got in return was warm and full of promise. Which scared her, because if Maddie grew any more attached, Hope would end up shattering that promise to pieces when she left. This was supposed to have been nothing but a few months away while helping a family friend. A working vacation. But this was different. This was becoming personal on so many levels.

She looked at Ben. He swallowed visibly and started the engine. *Time to go home.* She was sure he was thinking the same thing. The line, even in medicine, between helping and hurting could be so gray, so thin and fragile. She'd broken it before. She couldn't risk that with Maddie. Drawing her out of her shell only to have her retreat even deeper.

She needed to end her trip early.

She needed to return to Kenya, for everyone's sake.

CHAPTER SEVEN

Dear Diary,
I like Hope. She's really nice and pretty.
And I heard Daddy humming while he
boiled pasta yesterday. I've never heard
him do that before. I think we all like
her. I think Mommy would have liked
her, too.

BEN CLOSED THE door to Ryan's room. Chad's
door was cracked open with nothing but the
glow of his night-light coming through,
which meant Hope had been successful in
winding him down. He approached Maddie's door, noting the light coming through
the crack at the bottom. She needed to get to
sleep already. He raised his knuckle to tap on
the door and stopped at the murmur of what
sounded like whispers.

Girl talk.

His nose tingled, and he rubbed it with the

back of his hand. Zoe used to do that. Sit with Maddie, alone in her room, and talk about whatever it was that mothers and daughters talked about. He couldn't fill those shoes no matter how hard he tried.

Maddie was bonding with Hope after just a few days. He'd been trying for seven months now. He'd be back at square one when she left. This wasn't working for the long haul.

He opened the door and caught Maddie stuffing a notebook under the covers. A pink pen fell to the floor. She was alone.

Hope isn't in here?

Maddie stared at him, scrunching the covers up to her neck, then grabbing her monkey and scrunching him, too. The bracelet sat on the nightstand next to her. He remembered how she'd acted over the backpack. *She needs to trust you.* He made as though he hadn't noticed her hiding anything. The first therapist they'd seen had suggested she keep a diary, but she'd shaken her head at him. Ben hadn't seen one. At least not under her pillow, in her nightstand or anywhere he went when it came to putting away laundry and tidying up.

"Hey, Mads. You need to get to sleep,

okay?" He took two strides over and kissed the top of her head, pausing. Hoping. "Sleep," he said. He turned off the bedside lamp, then went to the closet and turned the light on in there, the way she liked. She slipped down onto her pillow.

He left the room and leaned against the hallway wall as soon as he closed her door. His pulse raced and his lungs pumped as if he'd rounded his tenth mile. Hope wasn't in there, and he'd heard whispers. He covered his face.

It was Maddie.

HOPE TUCKED HER fingers between her knees for warmth as she sat on Ben's back porch steps. She wore the pink jacket Maddie had chosen, but had misplaced her gloves. It seemed that even on milder days, temperatures really plummeted after dark. But after today, she needed to be alone. She needed the blank slate of darkness to think. The air was quiet and crisp. Even the rustling of dried leaves she'd grown accustomed to hearing had been muted by the earlier rains. She untucked her fingers and drew her knees in, wrapping her arms around and resting her chin on them.

She was going to miss them.

The door behind her creaked open, and a band of kitchen light ran across the porch and down the steps at her side. Her skin thrummed, and goose bumps waved down her arms. *It's just the cold.* The door closed.

"Hi," Ben said.

"Hi," Hope said, looking up.

He lowered himself onto the step next to her, leaving a safe couple of feet between them, and handed her a steaming mug.

"Thank you." She took the mug and cradled it. The heat seeped through her palms and to her core. And it smelled so good.

"Hot chocolate," he said, raising his own mug to his lips. A moment of silence passed. "Is it all right if I sit here?" he asked.

She chuckled.

"Yeah, I suppose that came out a little late," he said. The corner of his mouth quirked, and he ran his thumb along his mug. Embarrassment looked rather cute on him.

"I don't mind you joining me. It's your porch after all. And you came bearing hot drinks," she said, taking a sip. She moaned.

Any form of chocolate was pure ambrosia. "Delicious. Thank you again."

"I didn't see you inside and I noticed this door was unlocked. I see you worked magic with Chad," he said, smiling. She nodded.

"Did you think he made me run away?"

"He very well could have. He's a handful."

"He just needs less sugar and more *structured* physical activity," Hope teased. "He's an attention getter, for sure. And I adore him, somersaults and all. You have incredible children, Ben Corallis."

"I know," he said, staring into his hot chocolate.

"I've decided to leave, soon. I'll really miss them."

"Leave? You just got here," he said, setting his mug on the landing between them and turning to face her. "You can't leave yet."

"Ben, you know I have to. You saw Maddie's drawing. You've seen what's going on. I'm already in love with that little girl, and it'll break my heart to leave her, but I don't want to see hers broken. Not more than it already is. You know I'm right," she said, putting her now-half-empty mug next to his.

"I did worry about that, but I heard her to-

night. I walked by her room, and I thought
it was you talking, but she was alone and
she clammed up when I walked in. I know
I heard her, Hope. It's a big step. It's a step
she's taken because of you. I don't know why
or how, but I know it has something to do
with you being here. You can't go. Not now."
He put his hand on her forearm, and Hope
felt her chill melt like chocolate. "Please," he
said, then let go. "Give her a chance."

Maddie had spoken? Hope's lips parted,
but she wasn't sure what to say. He thought
she was healing his daughter, but he didn't
know that she wasn't good at healing children. Give Maddie a chance? Guilt. She
hated it. She'd come to help out in general,
and now Maddie's recovery lay specifically
on her shoulders?

She put her forehead against her knees.
She'd never forgotten the day she'd volun-
teered with a group to go vaccinate children at a rural village. They hadn't planned
to do more than that, but there was one
boy. He'd looked to be no more than three
or four years old. Flies had landed on his
lashes and sunken cheeks, drinking the fe-

verish sweat that beaded on his face, but he'd never blinked. Hope had reached out to take him from the Masai woman—his mother—who'd brought him and was pleading with Hope in a dialect she recognized but didn't speak. Hope had rushed him to the medical tent, ready to help. Ready to save. But he'd died. Of all the children they'd been there to help, it was too late for him.

It had been too late for the man in the emergency room, too.

And now Ben wanted to put Maddie's recovery in her hands?

Ben didn't understand that his daughter would speak when she wanted to. Not because Hope was special or had the power to help children.

She looked up and took a deep breath. The cold air made her chest ache. *Stay until she speaks, then I don't care if you go.* That was what she heard between the lines.

"Okay," she whispered. "I'll stay. Because you're asking me to."

She didn't have the courage to tell him that, deep down, she didn't want to leave. And not just because of the kids.

BEN CLICKED ON SAVE, then logged in to his email and attached the file. He'd finalized a detailed plan for the security business, including his and Cooper's different responsibilities and how much of an investment it would take, down to the penny. He hit Send. Sooner or later Coop would agree. He could look the plan over at his own pace, without Ben pressuring—at least not in person—and see that this would be worth it for both of them.

He'd give him a week. If he still refused to work with Ben, then that was it, he'd move on. If Maddie regained her voice, then he knew what he'd have to do. Go back on duty and let Nina and Eric have their way. They'd get to raise his kids the way they saw fit. He'd take on the financially supportive role. Just like before.

A rap at the front door had him closing his laptop. He answered, guessing it had to be Nina because she was the only one who knew he hated the sound of the doorbell.

Nina and Eric stood there. Eric dutifully held at least three plastic containers of cookies, and Nina carried a plastic bag.

"Peace offering," Eric said. "Though I

can't take credit for making them. Sorry about yesterday."

"Come in," Ben said, standing aside.

"These are Hope's," Nina said, holding up the plastic bag. "She forgot them in the dryer when you all left." Nina followed Eric inside.

"You can set them here," Ben said, waving at the console. "She's playing in the yard with the kids." It was turning out to be a sweat-shirt kind of day. Not too cold.

"How's Maddie doing today? Any better?" Nina asked.

"Not really, but she seems okay." Ben and Hope had agreed to keep Maddie's tiny bit of progress to themselves, for fear that if every-one got wind of it and made a big deal about it, she might withdraw. Worse yet, she'd hate him for eavesdropping.

"We won't stay but a few minutes. Would you mind if we went out back? I'd like to apologize to Hope, too," Eric said.

Ben nodded. He and Eric. Military men. They were expected to be tough. He knew the man was hurting. He was Zoe's dad. How could he not? Imagine if something worse had happened to Maddie, his own little girl.

But he'd never realized just how deep Eric's pain went and how poorly he'd been coping all these months—until yesterday.

"I don't see why not," Ben said. "Stay as long as you like." And he meant it. He, as a parent, needed to step back and let them be grandparents. This wasn't just about him raising his kids his way or trying to prove he could do it. This was about them clinging to all they had left of their daughter. The same three kids who were all he had left, too.

They went out back, and Ben cleared his work off the breakfast table before joining them. Nina was at their wooden play yard, pushing Ryan in an infant swing while talking to Hope, who was spotting the end of the slide for Chad. Maddie swung independently next to Ryan. And Eric stood inspecting the state of Ben's woodpile. Over a year ago, they'd had a tree fall from a storm. Luckily, Ben had been on leave at the time. He'd done a lot of sawing and chopping those few days. The wood had lasted them a long time.

"If you're not planning to use all that wood, we'll take some," Eric said.

"Sure."

That was it. They were good. Both looked off at the women. Yeah. They were going to be here awhile.

"You shouldn't be riding a bike that far in this weather. It's unpredictable, and it's not safe on wet roads. Wet leaves are as bad as ice," Ben said, sticking a store-bought chicken casserole in the oven. He reached past the plastic guard that kept curious little hands out of danger, turned on one of the stove's back burners and set a small pot of eggs to boil. Chad wanted "dino eggs." He glanced out into the living room. Maddie, reading a story about a girl and her dog, lay on her belly next to Ryan, who lay on his back underneath a baby gym. Chad, who'd been watching TV, jumped up and ran to the bathroom, announcing his intentions. That summed up parenthood. In one end and out the other.

"Why doesn't Nina's stovetop have one of those?" Hope asked, referring to the plastic safety guard.

She didn't? How'd he miss that?

"Uh, she will have one soon," he said. They'd had this one up ever since Chad could reach. Pretty soon Ryan would be learning to walk and then grabbing everything in sight. "Back on subject. If you want to borrow a spare car, I know of one."

Eric had offered her use of his bike, saying that maybe if she lowered the seat, it would work for her. She was fairly tall. But Ben didn't like the idea of her being on a bike near a main road. Helmet or not. A bike that didn't fit her well would be even riskier if she lost control. The truth was, he also didn't want her at Bentley's or anywhere near there. It wasn't his place to put restrictions on her, though. She was a grown woman. Bringing up Bentley's would lead to "why nots," and that would mean talking about Zoe's death. Which he didn't want to do.

"Actually, I don't drive, so a car won't do me any good, but you're right. Today looks a bit dreary. I might wait and go out tomorrow," she said, folding a pair of little-boy jeans and adding them to the many stacks of folded laundry on the table as he cooked.

"You don't drive? As in, not even in Nairobi? 'Cause you know you can use a foreign license here."

"Not even back home. There's never been

a need. I have a driver. And trust me, it's safer that he deals with the insane driving there, not me."

Ben stared at her.

"You have a driver? As in, a private chauffeur?"

It was amazing the things he didn't know about her.

"Yes," she said, shrugging. "He and his wife have lived with us my entire life. She's our cook and was my nanny. They're really like family."

Did that mean Hope was like family here? More than just a temporary nanny for his kids?

"Man. Sounds like a perfect life. And you came halfway around the world to ride a bike, change diapers and fold laundry?"

Her lips spread into that gorgeous smile, which creased the corners of her big brown eyes. A man could get lost in that face...that smile. Forget wars existed. Forget pain.

"When you put it like that, it does sound crazy," she said, reaching into the basket. Her smile faltered, and she licked her lips, but instead of saying more, she pulled out a pair of boxers, then smiled again, holding them up by the waist.

"These look rather large for Chad."

Ben went over and snatched them from her. "I'll take those," he said.

She laughed, bringing her hand to her chest. Her fingers brushed her neck where her fitted green sweater dipped just under three rows of polished tiger's-eye beads that matched the highlights she had in her otherwise black hair. He stuffed his boxers into his pocket and retreated back to the stove to lower the flame on the eggs.

"You're good at changing subjects, aren't you?" he said.

"Ben." She sighed. "You don't have to worry about me. I can take care of myself. As long as I don't have to cook."

What did he want her to do? Stay trapped in his house if she wasn't watching the kids? They'd agreed she needed time off to herself to enjoy her time in the States, and he'd agreed that, even with her here, sometimes Nina and Eric needed time with the kids.

"Fine. But go ahead and use Zoe's bike. I'll bring it over here," he said, staring at the bubbles boiling over the eggs.

"Ben—"

"No, I mean it. It's a bike. It's your size. You'll have better control, so it'll be safer. I won't have you getting hurt. And I'd like Maddie to have it here anyway…for her. So just use it. And if it's too cold, there's a bus stop a few blocks away that heads to the campus area and mall. I can also drop you off wherever you want to be."

"Okay."

He turned off the flame and swung around.

"The kids have appointments at our pediatrician's office tomorrow," he said, "so they'll be with me." Their doctor was used to handling all three in one room. There wouldn't be room for another person even if she came. It would be a good time for her to go do whatever she wanted. What did she do in her free time back home?

"Got it," she said.

He left it at that and went to make sure Chad hadn't flushed himself down the toilet. And then he took the boxers from his pocket and stuffed them in a drawer, along with everything he wanted but didn't need to know about Hope Alwanga.

CHAPTER EIGHT

Dear Diary,
I found the box of Christmas stuff that
Grandma brought over. I heard Daddy
fighting with her about not decorating
this year. I'm afraid to ask. But that's
okay. I don't want him sad. I can watch
the lights across the street from Chad's
bedroom window instead.

HOPE WAITED FOR the truck in front of her to
make a right turn, then she followed. Ben
had brought Zoe's purple bike over last night
and had left for the appointments a while
ago. Hope could have taken the bus, but why
would she on such a gorgeous day? She'd be
back at the house before Ben had anything
to worry about.

She recognized a man walking down the
sidewalk as the one that restaurant owner,
Brie, had seemed interested in. Bentley's

wasn't far ahead. He had his hands tucked into the front pockets of his jeans. He approached the next intersection, clearly favoring one leg. He stopped to make sure it was clear, then stepped off the curb just as the truck in front of her made a right. A horn blared, and for a second, Hope was sure he'd been hit. Adrenaline coursed through her, and she automatically switched to emergency mode, stepping hard on her pedals to get to him quickly. The man jumped back onto the curb, and she gasped in relief. Had he not seen that truck coming?

And here she was with not much more protection. Just the helmet. Ben would freak out if he knew. So would Simba. She passed the man and pulled into Bentley's parking lot, leaving her bike at the same spot as before.

It took a few seconds for her eyes to adjust to the change in lighting. It was a really bright day, and despite the windows, the wood throughout Bentley's soaked it in and gave the place a more tavern-like ambiance. At this hour, she expected a buzzing lunch crowd, but the parking lot said otherwise, and only a handful of the tables were filled.

"Hey there," Brie said. "I'm surprised you're

back. I was sure Wolf had scared you off for good. Grab a seat and I'll leave him by the bar." Brie led Wolf away on his leash before Hope could reply.

She went ahead and took the same first booth as before.

The man walked in, blinking several times to adjust. He focused on the bottles lined behind the bar and a hook rack next to them that said, "Enjoy another beer, but first your key goes here." He didn't seem to notice Brie approaching—or the way she scratched her cheek and tucked her red hair behind her ear as she walked up to him. Hope wished it was her place to warn her. Clearly the man wasn't interested.

"Same table, Cooper?" Brie asked.

She knew him? He sure didn't act like it.

He startled when she greeted him, then answered with nothing but a "yeah." He followed her, limping, hands still tucked into his front pockets, shoulders slightly hunched. "The usual," he said without taking the proffered menu or looking up. Wolf whimpered from his spot by the counter.

Brie immediately corrected him with a verbal cue, then turned back to the man. "I think I can remember that." She tucked her notepad back in her apron and walked to the kitchen. She came out seconds later and headed for Hope's table.

"So how are you enjoying our little town? It must seem boring to you. Not much sight-seeing around here." She forced a smile, but couldn't hide her annoyance with the guy she called Cooper.

"Actually, I think it's lovely. I—"

"I suppose you're right. This is home for me, though. Grew up here with my uncle's family. Went to the university here, too. My family has owned this pub for as long as I can remember. It took a lot of talking to convince my uncle to let me take over, rather than sell out."

Must have been easy for her. Her uncle probably gave in just to shut her up.

"Someone out there always wants to tear down and build something new, you know? Sure, this block is all older shops, but the way I see it, shiny new things only stay that way for so long. This place has character. I love every crack, including the initials college students have carved in so-called secret spots on the sides of these tables over the years. I used to do my homework at this very table, long before I was old enough to serve."

Hope tilted her head and ran a hand along the table's edge. Sure enough, there were carvings. Initials joined with plus signs or hearts.

"Listen," Hope said, thinking that perhaps that word would help her get a few more in. "I came by thinking that maybe you could help me with something."

Brie glanced back at Wolf and seemed satisfied that he was doing okay. She sat across from Hope.

"Sure." She shrugged. "If I can."

Hope looked at Wolf. He was wearing his blue vest today. This was a stupid idea. What was she getting herself into? She rubbed her hands against her jeans.

"Wolf really doesn't bite? Ever?"

"Never. Oh! You want me to help you get over your fear? Like exposure therapy and all that? I'm no psychologist, but sure, let me bring him over here and—"

"Wait," Hope said, pulling her hands out from under the table and reaching across. "Please, wait just a second. Hear me out."

Brie settled back down.

"I'm here visiting a family friend and help-ing out with his kids. To make a long story short, his daughter hasn't really spoken since she lost her mother." Brie's eyes narrowed. Good. She was finally listening. "She loves animals and I know that you're raising Wolf as a service dog, but I've also heard that pup-pies are raised to be therapy dogs. I was won-dering if maybe you'd be willing to bring Wolf to meet her. Just to see if it makes any difference. If you're sure he doesn't bite."

Hope took a deep breath and waited for Brie's answer. She'd studied enough to know that phobias weren't logical. The logical side of her brain told her not all dogs bit and that many people connected with animals better than with other humans. The emotional side of her brain wanted her to put Maddie's feel-ings ahead of her own. If this helped her...

Brie looked as though Hope had slapped her across the face. She wasn't speaking.

"Okay, a bad idea," Hope said. "Don't worry, it was just a thought." She began to get up to leave the booth.

"No, no." Brie covered her mouth, then set her hand down. "I'm sorry. I happen to know a lot of folks around here... Hometown, this restaurant… Who did you say you're staying with on Lancaster Street?"

Hope hadn't, but she'd mentioned the street when she'd asked about delivery last time.

"Ben Corallis. You know him?"

Brie's nose turned red, and her cheeks tinged with the same shade. She scratched her ear and tucked her hair back.

"Yes, I know him," she said, clearing her voice. "But mostly I knew his wife, Zoe. She was my best friend. The person I called if I needed to talk, and she did the same when the kids were in bed and Ben was overseas."

"Oh, my God. I'm sorry. I had no idea," Hope said.

Brie got up. She sniffed. "Let me go get his order, and I'll be back."

Hope nodded, knowing she needed a minute alone. She should never have come here. It was a crazy idea, but watching a million different expressions flit across Maddie's face, especially smiles, as she was reading that book, made her think…

Brie took payment from the last couple in the place, then disappeared and returned with their change before running back to check on Cooper's order.

A staccato beat emanated from the corner of
the room. Cooper pulled out a cell phone and
agreed to go in for some sort of appointment
a little earlier than planned. He got up and
headed for the bar. Wolf wagged and licked at
his leg again. The man stooped down.

"Hey, boy. Wolf. It's a good name." Wolf
put his paw on the man's knee. "Yeah, I know
you can tell. Just keep it to yourself. Deal?"
He scratched Wolf behind his ears and stood
up so fast when the kitchen door swung open
and Brie stepped out that his shoulder hit the
bar stool next to him. He straightened it, and
his face turned almost as red as Brie's hair.

"Uh, I'm sorry. I know dogs in training
shouldn't be distracted."

"It's okay," she said, looking between Wolf
and Cooper. "He likes you for some reason."

As if she didn't.

"Did you know Ben had someone staying at his house?" she asked, nodding over
at Hope. Cooper frowned and looked. Hope
got out of the booth and walked over to them,
keeping a safe distance from the dog. She
didn't like being talked about like some intruder. She stuck her hand out to Cooper. He
shook it.

"I'm Hope. It's nice to meet you."

"Hope, Cooper is a friend of Ben's. Hope here is a friend of his, too."

Now, that didn't sound right.

"I'm helping his family as a nanny," Hope clarified.

"He might have mentioned something," Cooper said. "Uh, I need to go, so if you don't mind canceling the order, Brie. Sorry." He turned to leave.

"I can have it packed to go for you. It's almost done," Brie said, stepping after him and clinging to the fact that he'd managed to say a complete sentence to her. The guy shook his head apologetically.

"I can't take it where I'm headed."

"Cooper, wait," she called after him again. "Don't forget we're serving a turkey special tomorrow. And of course the band will be here Friday. I noticed you always come for the bands, so…" She shrugged, trying to make it all sound matter-of-fact. He nodded, but turned and left without another word. Brie seemed to deflate.

"I need to leave, too," Hope said. "Never mind about my idea. I didn't know."

"Hope, don't go. Grab a stool. Please."

Hope hopped onto a bar stool several seats away from the dog, her illogical side reminding her that she liked her ankles. Brie sat next to her.

"How are the kids?"

She didn't know? She wasn't seeing them? But she'd been Zoe's friend.

"I'm a little lost here," Hope said. Something was off. Maybe talking about the kids to a "friend," who apparently wasn't in touch, wasn't a good idea. "Everyone here seems to know each other. How could you not know how Ben's children are doing?"

"I haven't seen them in a long time. I don't really know Cooper well. I met him briefly at Zoe's funeral. He dropped some stuff off from Ben shortly after. He used to come in here to drink at the bar, but not anymore. No alcohol. He comes to eat, listen to music and then he leaves. I think he likes the food, just not me. Probably because Ben ordered him not to."

"What?"

"Ben Corallis is the reason this place isn't doing well. He blamed me for Zoe's death, and he made sure everyone knew it."

CHAPTER NINE

Dear Diary,
It's Thanksgiving. I don't want to go to
Grandma and Grandpa's, but I know
they're going to make me. I want to stay
in my room. Mommy loved to cook and
she won't be there to help.

HOPE COULDN'T BELIEVE the size of the bird
Nina had managed to fit in her oven. Chickens were much easier to come by than tur-
keys in Kenya, and her expat patients, or
friends like Jack and Anna, had told her they
cooked chickens during their American holidays abroad.

The sound of cheers carried from the living room, where Eric was watching American football with his leg propped up on an
ottoman. She could hear him trying to coax
Chad to pay attention to the game. Ben was
feeding Ryan a bottle in front of the televi-

sion and Maddie was out there, too. She'd made it quite clear she didn't want to help in the kitchen. Hope couldn't blame her. She wanted to go find out what all the game excitement was about, but Nina needed help and she was the only person free.

Hope carefully cut the tomatoes she was supposed to add to the salad. The cucumbers still waited their turn. Nina smiled and motioned toward Hope's cutting board.

"With pieces that perfectly sized, we may be having that salad at Christmas. It's salad, not surgery."

"But it'll look good," Hope said. She rubbed her cheek on her shoulder to soothe an itch while keeping her hands clean. Sure, she had cutting skills—with a scalpel. In the kitchen, not so much. In fact, her precision with a scalpel had her professors once urging her to go into surgery. She hated surgery, almost as much as she hated seeing children sick or suffering. She was hating salad making, too.

"Right before it gets chewed up," Nina said. "Honestly, you don't have to be quite that careful. The salad needs to make it to the table before the pumpkin pie."

Hope stretched her back. *Don't let it bother you. It's a tough day for them. You can deal with being compared to Zoe for today. You'll live.*

"I've never tasted pumpkin pie," Hope said.

"Never had pumpkin pie? You're in for a treat," Nina said, mashing boiled potatoes in a large bowl. "Does pumpkin even grow in Kenya?"

"Yes. We call it *malenge* and use it mostly in savory dishes." Hope scraped the chopped tomato into the bowl and started on the next one. "We have a dish for special occasions, *mukimo*. It's made with pumpkin leaves, potatoes, corn and beans. The same ingredients you have here, but a very different dish."

"You eat pumpkin *leaves*?" Nina asked, stopping midmash.

"You don't?" Hope really wanted to ask Nina exactly what had happened when Zoe was killed, but she didn't dare. Not today. She reached for the cucumber and rolled her shoulders. "The dish I'm powerless against is a sweeter one made with pumpkin, coconut milk, cardamom and sugar. I'll do anything for it."

"Good to know," Ben said. He filled the doorway to the kitchen. He was holding Ryan with his hand pressed protectively against the baby's back. Ryan's ruby-red cheek was nestled against Ben's shoulder, and his eyes were closed. The juxtaposition of tiny, innocent, helpless child against towering, jaded, protective man was almost poetic.

"Food's not ready yet. No loitering. Anyone in the kitchen has to work," Nina warned.

"But my hands are full, and it looks as though you've got a sous chef." Ben raised a brow at Hope. "You should come over here every day for lessons," he added. Hope opened her eyes wide and shook her head at him while Nina's back was turned.

"Grandma, I made a touchdown!" Chad yelled, squeezing between Ben and the door frame. He circled the breakfast table while punching a fist into the air, then headed back for the living room. "Hoorah!"

"He needs to stay out of the kitchen," Nina said. She set some butter in the microwave to melt and wiped her hands on her apron. "I need to hold this little munchkin for a minute before I finish cooking." She reached up and peeled Ryan off Ben's shoulder.

Ryan's face contorted and turned even redder...then relaxed. He patted Nina's cheek and gurgled with his eyes closed.

"Whew!" Nina said, waving the air.

"Your timing, not mine." Ben grinned, raising his palms. Nina rolled her eyes.

"Then you get to baste the turkey."

She left, and Ben opened the oven to beat the turkey. Hope had no idea what that would accomplish. He started squirting it with an oversize dropper.

You're alone. Ask him why he blames Brie for his wife's death. Why he'd ruin a person's livelihood. She was living under his roof. She had a right to know what kind of man he really was, didn't she?

"Ben—" She cut herself off when Maddie appeared at the kitchen door, carrying an armful of stuffed animals. She stood there studying Hope from over their heads.

"Please, tell me that you and your friends are going to take over my job here," Hope said to Maddie.

Maddie shook her head just as Ben looked up from giving the turkey a bath. "Are you hungry?" he asked.

Again a head shake. Ben and Hope exchanged glances.

"Well, there happens to be an empty stool here," Hope said. "You're welcome to keep me company—or not." She resumed her chopping as if salad making was fascinating business.

"You're right, Hope," Ben said, taking the hint. "Half the fun of Thanksgiving is hanging out before the food's ready. Building that appetite." He shut the oven door, went to the pies on the counter, bent down and inhaled. A colander of red berries sat dripping dry next to a food processor by the sink. He grabbed one and looked over at Hope as he tossed it in his mouth.

Hope put the last of the salad ingredients into the bowl.

"Did your uncle Jack and auntie Anna send you those animals? They look African."

Maddie nodded. Ben ate another berry.

"Which one is your favorite?"

Maddie held up the monkey.

"We have lots of them where I'm from. Especially at Busara, where Jack lives. I've heard crazy stories about one that follows

Anna around throwing things to get her attention. You should come and visit someday."

Maddie's eyes opened wide, and she nodded.

Hope moved to the sink to rinse the cutting board and knife.

Ben grabbed a few more berries and moved out of her way. She glanced at the berries as she washed and set the board to dry in the dish rack.

"What are these?" she asked as she went back to the island to toss the salad. Maddie's face wrinkled. Ben made a guttural sound of appreciation as he popped another in his mouth.

"Cranberries. Very sweet. Taste a bit like honey. Go ahead and try one. There's more than enough for the relish Nina makes."

"Okay."

Hope went back to the sink, popped a few cranberries in her mouth and chewed.

She screeched like a monkey, slapping her hand to her mouth and scrunching her face. She swallowed as fast as she could. She shuddered and her eyes watered.

"You said sweet! How in the world do you keep a straight face eating those things?"

"Skills," he said, with the corner of his mouth turned up.

A muffled giggle came from Maddie. They both heard it but kept their eyes on each other, afraid of reacting the wrong way. Maddie ran back to the living room, and Ben turned to where she'd been.

Hope put a hand on Ben's arm, and he covered it with his.

"It'll happen, Ben. She needs time, but it will happen."

IF BEN HADN'T bought into Nina's reasons for giving thanks, he certainly had one now. Maddie had laughed. It wasn't words, like he'd heard the other night, but she'd let it out in front of him and Hope.

And that morning, he'd found Maddie with her face pressed against the window in the family room, as if she wanted to break through. He wished he could break through to her. It was Hope, however, who'd finally gotten her ready to leave the house to go to her grandparents'.

She'd taken Maddie to the bathroom, and then Mads had reappeared with braids. Ben never bothered much with her hair, other than to tell her to brush it—he didn't do girl hair. Occasionally, if tangles got too out of hand for even that magic spray from the drugstore, he enlisted Nina's help. But this morning, Maddie had her hair in two long braids, the fancy kind that looked woven against the head—the way Zoe used to fix it.

Maddie had looked at him expectantly, her eyes bigger and brighter with her hair pulled away from her face, as though curtains had been opened. And when he'd told her that her hair looked nice, he was rewarded with the tiniest of smiles, which meant he'd said the right thing. And then, instead of walking past him to head out the door, she'd grabbed his hand and pulled him outside.

Ben had followed, feeling as if he'd scaled a mountain, yet also feeling awkward. A father holding his daughter's hand shouldn't have felt awkward.

And then, here at her grandparents', she'd giggled. He'd been teasing Hope, had lost himself for a moment. He'd let go. Let himself have fun. And it had made his daughter happy. Made *him* happy.

Don't let your guard down. Don't relax. You lost Zoe that way.

He released Hope's hand, and she pulled hers away.

"I'm going to toss," she said, pointing toward the salad.

"I'm gonna go catch some more of the game," he said, and left the kitchen.

NINA WAS BUCKLING Ryan into his bouncy seat near the sofa where Eric was sitting. Chad had abandoned the football game and was playing with a train that circled the base of the Christmas tree his grandparents had already set up in front of the bay window.

"Where's Maddie?" Ben asked.

"Upstairs watching cartoons on the TV in our room," Nina said. "We still have an hour or so before the turkey will be done."

Ben had worried for nothing. Again. His kids would be fine—happy—living here. He'd send his paycheck and take leave to visit. Maybe he'd even sell his house and put the money in savings for them. Maybe if he did that, every wall, every nook, every cranny, wouldn't remind them of their mother being gone. And maybe Mads would be able to move on.

Cooper hadn't responded to his email

about the start-up company. It was looking more and more as though returning to duty, plan B, was going to happen. His only other option would be to land a job in Washington, DC. Some of those high-clearance jobs paid well. But since he'd been cautioned about uprooting his daughter so soon, he'd still have to consider leaving her and her brothers with their grandparents. Maddie and Chad were used to them, seemed comfortable around them. Ryan was still young and adaptable. Ryan was the only one of the four of them who wouldn't have any real memories of his mother. Only photos and stories. His eyes burned. If he returned to duty, there'd be a chance that Ryan would never have memories of his dad, either.

Ben fought the urge to go home to hide and think…away from everyone. Isolate himself, like Maddie was doing with her silence.

He fidgeted with the keys in his pocket. He was here because deep down he knew the kids needed to be here. He knew Eric and Nina needed them around. And he'd invited Coop, because it was better for him to be with friends than a bottle. If Coop didn't show up, Ben would take turkey and stuffing to him and shove it down his throat.

HOPE COULDN'T BELIEVE she'd eaten so much, but that pie. Had she known how sinfully good it would be, she'd have saved more room. She couldn't help but watch in awe as the men inhaled their third helpings. Ben had looked more than a little irritated when she and Cooper had told him they'd met at Bentley's. Brie would undoubtedly be disappointed when Cooper never showed for turkey at the pub.

They had not gone around the table giving thanks, the way Nina wanted. But Ben had come into the kitchen while they were getting ready to set the table and convinced her to spare them, stating first, that he didn't want to regret coming, second, that Cooper and Hope would feel uncomfortable with all the emotional vomit and third, that Maddie would be put on the spot.

Hope had thought he was being a bit harsh, but the part about Maddie was true. It was why Nina had agreed and let Eric say a group thanks instead. A speech that had included thanks for the two fine men at the table returning home from war safe and sound. She didn't miss the way both Ben and Cooper had flinched at the words. Safe and sound... but not unbroken.

"I MUST STILL be jet-lagged," Hope said as she started on her second cup of coffee. The table was still loaded with dessert but no one had room. "I'm embarrassed to say I'm so sleepy."

"It's the turkey. You either have to sleep it off, or caffeinate, then sleep it off," Cooper said with a wry smile. He reached for his mug of coffee.

His arm bumped against Chad's unfinished cup of milk. It toppled on its side and rolled into Hope's lap. Everyone's hands flew up reflexively to stop it, and the kids, watching a cartoon on TV, craned their necks to see what the commotion was about.

Cooper apologized profusely, turning his head to assess the mess while pushing his chair back to get up and help.

"It's no problem," Hope said. She lifted the bottom-weighted cup back onto the table. "Don't worry. Not much spilled."

Everyone passed napkins down the table. Hope had a surplus.

"Eric, do you want to tell them or should I?" Nina said, changing the subject.

"What?" Ben sat forward.

"Surgery on my knee," Eric said. "An outpatient procedure. They said that they'd go in with tiny incisions and see what's wrong, and if it's something they can fix, they'll do it right then. It's called an ortho something."

"Arthroscopic surgery," Hope said.

"Yes, that's it," Nina said. "I plan on being at the hospital, of course, and driving him home. We wanted you to know, Ben and Hope, in case something comes up with the kids."

Ben put his elbows on the table and leaned forward. "I'll come to the surgery. We can take my car."

"You don't have to do that. It's an out—"

"But Eric has at least fifty pounds on you, Nina," Ben pointed out. "If they give him painkillers that make him dizzy, or it rains and he slips with the crutches on the driveway, how are you gonna pick him up?" Ben insisted. "Plus, you said once they're in, they may have to do more. Hope's home with the kids. There's no reason for me not to come."

The least I can do for Zoe is be there for her parents for things like this.

"I agree with him, Nina," Eric said. "I'm sure it'll all go smoothly, but just in case, for your sake."

"Fine," Nina said.

"Is that what you're getting into, Hope? Bone doctoring?" Eric asked.

"My parents own an orthopedic practice, yes. I'll eventually join them."

"Why ortho?" Ben asked.

Hope couldn't answer, because for the first time in her life, the only answer she had sounded too pathetic to say out loud.

Because my parents expect me to be just like them.

CHAPTER TEN

Dear Diary,
Some kids at school were saying that
being good means you'll go to heaven
or get presents from your parents—
not from Santa, since we're too old to
believe in him. I know Mommy's in
heaven. Everyone says so. But if I go
to hell for making her die, I'll never see
her again.

HOPE PICKED UP the pewter frame from the
fireplace mantel in Ben's house and held it
closer for a better look. Zoe was so pretty.
Judging by all the other photos Hope had
seen on the inset shelves, she'd been great
with the camera, too. Ben said she'd taken
them all. That she'd been a photography
major before quitting college. She certainly
knew how to capture moments…and emotion. Hope picked up another photo of the

three kids together, surrounded by flowers. She recognized the front steps to the house, where the picture was set up. In it, Maddie cradled a newborn Ryan. She was beaming. Hope's chest ached. They'd lost more than just a beautiful person. They'd lost their glue, the one person who had held them all together despite Ben being so far away all the time.

I'm sorry for what happened to you, Zoe.

She heard Ryan gurgling through the baby monitor and waited a second to be sure he wasn't waking up. Silence. Chad was also taking a nap. That little guy could harness energy like a wind turbine. She looked around the room to be sure she'd tidied up all the toys he'd been playing with. Here on out, she was setting rules for Chad picking up his own toys. If he had that much energy, he could direct it, use it for the greater good of mankind, like cleaning so she wouldn't have to.

This nanny thing was giving her some perspective on parenting. No wonder her parents had set so many rules for her and given her so much structure. Kids were exhausting. And her mom always said that a parent never stops worrying, even when their children become parents themselves. She thought about the pain Nina and Eric were in over Zoe and how much they, and Ben, worried about Maddie, Chad and Ryan. She worried, too.

She wasn't expecting Ben back from the hospital for some time, and with the boys in bed for naps, Maddie at school and everything tidied, she needed to do something other than take a nap herself. She didn't feel comfortable doing that while on kid watch.

She tiptoed into Chad's room, her room, and brought out one of the medical texts her dad had insisted she take along. So far, bringing them was proving to have been a big waste of luggage-weight fees. But if she dug into a few pages, then she wouldn't have to lie if he asked if she'd done any reading.

She started to settle onto the couch, but then jumped up, remembering to set the kitchen timer. She didn't want to miss Maddie's bus, and it wouldn't be too long now. Ben had reminded her at least five times that little kids by themselves at a bus corner were an invitation to kidnappers. For crying out loud. She didn't need to be reminded of that, but he was Maddie's father and had every right to say whatever he wanted. To set all the rules like hers had. She opened her book.

Orthopedic Surgery and Treatments for Athletes. It was bound to make time fly.

HOPE JOLTED WHEN the timer rang. She took a groggy few seconds to get her bearings. She'd fallen asleep before finishing a single page. Thank heavens she'd set the alarm.

She put away the book and hurried out onto the front porch, leaving the door cracked so that she could hear the boys if they got up. In several long minutes, the bus pulled up at the corner, only two houses down and close enough to watch her get off the bus. Maddie ran home, ducking her head to hide a shy smile behind her loose hair.

Hope waved with two hands as the bus's gears shifted and it drove off with a high-pitched puff. "Hello, beautiful girl!"

Maddie lifted her head as she climbed the porch steps and smiled outright. Hope took her inside and locked the door behind them.

"How was school?"

Maddie shrugged and nodded simultaneously, slipping her backpack off her shoulders. Hope squatted in front of her and pushed a strand of hair off her face.

"How would you like it if I put a snack on the table while you do your homework, and then we can have some fun afterward?" She emphasized *fun* and was rewarded with an enthusiastic nod.

Babbling came through the baby monitor.

"Sounds as though somebody woke up happy. Would you like to help me change his diaper before starting homework?"

Maddie gave Hope a thumbs-up. Hope smiled.

Deal with what's dealt, help the helpless and give laughter to the living.

A happy Maddie was a good sign and a relief.

"I bet you're the greatest big sis and helper ever."

Maddie stilled and her eyes widened, almost as if she'd seen a ghost, then another smile spread slowly across her face.

BEN'S BACK ACHED. He did his best to stretch it while waiting for the light to change. It didn't help. Between sitting in the car and the hospital chairs, he was done. What he needed was sleeping kids, a quiet house, a hot shower and a firm mattress.

He'd called the house three times over the course of the afternoon and evening, each time letting Hope know that he'd be running later than expected. It turned out there was a lot to clean out of Eric's knee. Then there was a pharmacy run, so that Nina wouldn't have to leave Eric alone. For a military guy, the dude had no pain tolerance. That or Nina had spoiled it out of him over the years.

The entire day had brought back memories of Cooper's surgery. The docs had managed to save his leg, but the therapy had been grueling. Coop had been the definition of *stoic*…until he'd reached his limit and turned to drinking. Everyone had their limits.

Ben was glad the kids were with Hope. Having someone around whom you trusted was an incredible stress reducer. Someone to lean on. Cooper had no one. It was why he'd joined the marines to begin with. It had given him a chance to be part of a group. A family.

Ben had people around who cared. And for now, at least, he had Hope, too.

He drove down his street, slowing before turning into his driveway. For a second, he thought he was seeing stage four of the Joneses' electrical holiday fiasco reflecting in his windows. His gut tightened and his lower back twinged with the threat of a spasm. *What the...?*

"No way."

He pulled up his driveway, slammed the car door behind him and stormed up to the house. He unlocked the front door.

It was a war zone. With music. So much for decompressing.

His pulse ratcheted up, and his throat constricted.

The cardboard box full of decorations that Nina had brought over had made its way out of the coat closet where he'd stashed it out of sight. The lack of a Christmas tree hadn't slowed them down. Lights were strung all over the ficus tree in the far corner of the living room by the front window. Snow globes and figurines were on every surface. The kitchen counters were covered in artwork, most likely left there to dry, and the breakfast table held jars of finger paints set on protective sheets of foil.

Ben zeroed in on his target. The source of music. The off-key thrum of the last string played still buzzed through him. His chest heaved.

Hope and his kids sat in a circle on the floor, Maddie and Chad on either side of Ryan's bouncy seat. She held a guitar. *Zoe's guitar.*

From the way Hope's lips opened and closed as he stood there, she knew bad stuff was about to hit the fan.

"What are you doing with that guitar?" he said, his voice deep and slow in an effort to control himself.

Hope hesitated, looking at the children, then back at him. She leaned the guitar carefully against the sofa and got up. Maddie saddled up to Ryan and Chad. Her chin quivered, and she stared at Ben as if he'd grown horns.

"Don't worry," Hope said. "We were just about to start cleaning up. We were having fun, as promised, since everyone did what they were supposed to do. Maddie finished all her homework. Chad helped me—"

"Kids," Ben snapped. "To your rooms. Maddie, take Ryan with you. Now."

Maddie burst into tears and ran to her room, leaving her brothers behind. Hope fisted her hands at her sides. She glared at Ben before taking Ryan to his room.

"Why you mad, Daddy?" Chad asked, looking up.

Ben closed his eyes.

"I'm not mad at you. Just go to your room."

"Chad, come here," Hope said from the hall. He went to her. She whispered something in his ear, and he hurried off. She marched up to Ben, coming toe-to-toe with him and pointing after the kids.

"What has gotten into you? You upset them for no reason!"

"This is my house. I never gave anyone permission to do this," he said, "and I never gave you permission to play my wife's guitar. The bike was one thing. That was Eric's fault. This?" His hands cut through the air. His lungs felt as though they were shrinking.

Zoe was everywhere.

And he'd let Hope into her home. He'd let a woman he was starting to have confusing feelings for into Zoe's house. He'd let her control Zoe's things. He was betraying Zoe. Betraying everyone, including himself.

Hope's eyes darkened.

"If you don't want me here, all you have

to do is say so. But don't you dare raise your voice at me." She went to the end table, whipped Maddie's pad off it and slapped it against his chest. He held it. Maddie's handwriting was scrawled in the cursive she was learning at school.

"We want a tree like Grandma has at her house."

"Can you play Mommy's guitar for us please? Like she used to."

The list went on. Maddie's wants. Her *needs*. The look on her face when he'd walked in. How could he not see that? His jaw tightened and his eyes stung. And the look of disgust and disappointment on Hope's face mutilated him. He'd screwed up. He'd failed his kids. He'd failed Zoe.

Hope pointed to the painted sheets drying on the table. Handprints and the thumbprint flowers.

"They made get well cards for their grandfather. Do you want to fault me for that?"

"The decorations… This was her thing… That was crossing the line."

"And did you draw that line for yourself or for the kids?"

Ben curled his lips in. He wanted to fight.

He wanted to explode. He was angry because Hope was right. Angry because he was so blind. And angry because it was so much easier to cope with anger than facing his failure as a husband and a parent.

But he had to keep everything and everyone in control, because how else could he keep them safe? He couldn't risk letting his guard down again. The last time he did, the cost had been too high.

"They want to remember their mother and enjoy that memory," Hope went on. "But they want permission from you. Permission to lift the weight and just be kids again. They're looking to you to make sure that it's okay to be happy again. That it won't mean they don't love or miss her." Hope's eyes welled with tears. "Maddie's falling apart in her room. She's going to think she made you mad because this was all her idea."

He covered his face, digging his fingers into his scalp. He understood what Hope was saying. Maddie was going to regress because of him. Just when she was starting to get better, he'd gone and made her worse. He'd hurt her.

He turned away, confused and disoriented in his own home.

He braced his hands against the entry console and hung his head. It throbbed with the jabbing rhythm of artillery fire. Ryan's crying could be heard without the monitor being on.

"I can't," he said, shaking his head. His voice came out rough. "I can't. I need to walk."

"Go," Hope said in a voice tinged with disappointment. "Just go."

BEN HAD DONE more than walk. He'd run, pushing harder and harder. Not for the high, but because he wanted to feel drained. Purged. Punished.

It was late by the time he was back in the house. The street was still, and his neighbor's lights had been turned off for the night. His house was quiet, but for the steady sound of Ryan breathing through the monitor and the whir of the heater kicking in. And although the decorations and lights were still in place, the ornaments that hadn't been unpacked had been closed up and put away. A neat pile of their artwork on the end of the counter was the only evidence left of their painting mess.

Instead of relief, he was plagued with a feeling of abandonment. Hope lay sleeping, curled up in the corner of the couch with a pillow tucked under her head and her knees pulled up tight. Her arms were tucked behind them for warmth.

He took the throw off the armchair and covered her. He peeked in on the kids. Each one lay sleeping and probably having bad dreams about their dad, angry and yelling… or their mom dying. Or maybe Hope was right. They needed to remember, but because of him, they were enjoying time with their mom the only way they could.

In their dreams.

CHAPTER ELEVEN

Dear Diary,
I'm evil. I'm bad. Everyone hates me.
Even Hope. Daddy got mad at her all
because of me. I'm stupid and I ruin everything.

HOPE WOKE UP with a start. Why was she on
the couch? She looked down at the afghan
that had fallen off her shoulder and into her
lap and knew she hadn't taken it off the chair.
She'd wanted everything in its place when
Ben got back.

She put her hands to her cheeks and closed
her eyes, remembering the night before. He'd
been gone so long. She'd soothed Ryan and
waited, tucked Chad in and sat at the edge
of Maddie's bed as she cried herself to sleep.
She'd tried rubbing her back. She'd even tried
to explain that everything would be okay.
That her father was just tired. But Maddie

hadn't wanted to listen. She'd piled stuffed animals on top of herself and kept sobbing.

Hope got up, folded the afghan and laid it over the back of the armchair. Ben's sneakers were by the door. When *had* he gotten in last night?

It didn't matter, other than the fact that she was certain Maddie wouldn't be up to going to school today. Hope didn't have the authority to call her in sick. Ben would have to. She looked at her watch—6:00 a.m. She remembered from the planning for yesterday morning that the bus came around 7:30.

She tiptoed to the hall bathroom and eased the door shut as quietly as she could, then leaned her back against it. She wasn't going to wake Maddie up. If Ben wanted to blame her for that, too, well, so be it.

But she knew one thing for sure. She wasn't leaving. She couldn't, even if all it would take was a phone call and a ticket, or just staying over at Nina's. She wouldn't, because of the children.

BEN ROLLED OVER to get the streak of morning sun out of his eyes, then bolted upright, cursing to himself as he looked at the digital clock by his bed. How in the world…? Maddie would have missed the bus. Who knew what trouble Chad had gotten into if he was already up, let alone how drenched Ryan would be.

Hope's out there. He remembered the hell of last night and dropped his head back against the pillow, missing by an inch and hitting the headboard. He cursed again and got up, not sure if he was prepared to leave his room and face what had happened.

He grabbed a clean T-shirt from the drawer. The monitor he kept in his room was on. Unlike the alarm he'd apparently forgotten to set before crashing. Yet no noise had woken him. Was it because he subconsciously knew Hope was there? Had he let his guard down, let himself sleep in, because he trusted her with the kids?

Just like the day he'd returned from duty and let Zoe convince him that she'd take care of things because he was tired?

Voices carried from the kitchen. Happy voices reminiscent of mornings when he was on leave. Hope's face, with those mesmerizing eyes full of knowing, understanding and rebellion, came to his mind. He tried forcing

Zoe's face to take its place. It didn't work. What was happening to him?

The window shades had already been opened, and morning light gave a glow to everything in the room, including Hope's hair as she bounced up and down to soothe a whimpering Ryan against her shoulder. Chad's favorite superhero cereal bowl sat half empty on the table. The pediatrician had told Ben to get rid of the sugar in the house and revamp his shopping list. He still needed to do that. Chad was sitting in front of the TV watching a cartoon.

Maddie wasn't there.

Hope, still soothing Ryan, set his bottle by the sink and turned just in time to catch Ben watching. Her face looked freshly washed, making her appear even younger than her knew her to be. Ten years younger than he was, he reminded himself.

"She's in her room," Hope said, reading his mind. "She refused to come out for breakfast. I didn't think school—"

"You're right."

Hope swung sideways, making her skirt swish back and forth. Ryan did not seem happy. He gnawed on Hope's pinkie finger with slobbery desperation.

"Ben, I think Ryan is cutting his first tooth," Hope said. "Do you have any infant acetaminophen or ibuprofen? Or gel?"

Something shifted in Ben. Ryan was getting his first tooth. He hadn't been around when Maddie and Chad cut theirs in, though he'd heard about the pain and sleepless nights from Zoe. He hadn't been around for a lot of firsts, and it suddenly hit him. If he managed to start a new career, build a company so that he could support his family without reenlisting, he'd be around for all of Ryan's firsts. This tooth was just the beginning.

But that would mean he could screw up again, like last night. Emotionally scar them. He frowned and ran his hand back over his head. Coffee. He needed coffee.

"I, uh, don't know what you mean by gel, but I have the other stuff for pain and fever."

Of course he did. He wasn't the best at fatherhood, but he did have the basics covered.

He took a chair from the table and put it in front of the fridge. He figured if, at six feet, even he needed help reaching the undersize cabinet over the fridge, it had to be the safest place to store medicine. Sure, there were child locks strategically placed on cabinet doors, like the one under the sink where the dishwashing liquid and disinfecting wipes were kept, but Maddie was old enough to open those. She was a smart cookie, but when it came to medication, he felt better having it out of reach.

He undid the lock on the top cabinet. Despite the height, he wasn't skimping on safety. If any child could figure out how to scale the smooth surface of a fridge, it would be Chad. That kid would excel at the trials of the junior ROTC high challenge or rappelling and high tower courses. Someday.

"Here you go." He handed down a plastic bin full of pharmacy items and got down.

"Here it is," Hope said, pulling out a small dropper-capped bottle filled with pink fluid. She measured out the dosage and got Ryan to take it with minimal spitting. The last time Ryan had had a fever from some bug going around, Ben had carefully measured out the dose his doctor had prescribed and had a mini panic attack when half of it had come right back out and he'd had no way of knowing just how much. *Corner of the mouth, side of the cheek*, he noted to himself as he watched.

"There you go, baby," she cooed. "You'll feel better soon."

Ben took the box of meds, locked it back up and returned the chair. Neither of them brought up last night.

"It really would help if you get a tube of gel—teething gel that numbs the gums—and perhaps a teething ring. The kind you put in the fridge is great. You may actually have a few teething rings from when Chad went through this."

"I thought you had no baby experience," Ben said.

Hope raised a brow. "Zoe has a lot of how-to books in the nursery. I trust it's okay that I read them for Ryan's sake?"

Direct hit.

"I'm going to check on Maddie," he said, "and then I'll see if he has teething stuff in his room." Zoe had a few boxes stashed on the upper shelf of his closet, each labeled with an age and size range. Those he'd figured were hand-me-down clothes. One box said Toys, Etc... Maybe he'd find teething

rings in there. If not, he'd head to the drugstore.

Ben knew it was Chad when he felt his leg
tackled. He looked down. Chad had all fours
wrapped around him as though he was pole
climbing, only he hung his head back as far
as he could. Almost upside down.

"Are you feeling better, Daddy?"

Ben rubbed the back of his neck. How was
it that little kids, not a fraction of your size,
had the ability to knock the wind out of you
with words?

"Yeah, bud. You're gonna break your
neck." He held Chad's upper arm.

Chad laughed and let go with the other
hand to salute him. If Ben hadn't been holding on… The little daredevil.

"I wanna do some-ping," Chad said, releasing Ben's leg. He climbed onto a chair,
then sat on the edge of the table.

Ben needed coffee. Would having some
before looking in on Maddie make him a bad
parent or a better one?

He grabbed a mug of coffee to take back
with him.

"Let me check on your sister first. Then
we can go in the yard."

"Yes! Get your gear and get outside!" Chad said. He spoke in the tone of a four-year-old drill sergeant.

Ben froze with the mug halfway to his mouth. He glanced at Hope to see if she'd caught what Chad said. From the look on her face, she had.

That boy worships you, watches your every move and listens to every word you say. All of them do.

Ben took another gulp instead of acknowledging Chad's marine lingo. He started down the hall, but doubled back.

"Last night... I'm sorry—"

"Don't be. I'm in your home, not the other way around," Hope said.

Except that it feels as though you belong here, and that's what's messing with me.

"It doesn't matter. You're here to help, and I... There are still some things I'm figuring out. I didn't need to come down on you like that."

"Thank you."

Ben stared at his son, now sound asleep, drooling onto Hope's shoulder. She ran her fingers lightly up and down Ryan's back, seemingly not bothered by his leaky mouth.

Ben pressed his lips together. He couldn't figure out Hope Alwanga. She should have been dying to get out of his house after the way he'd lost it last night. He hooked his thumb toward the hallway and retreated without another word.

BEN MADE QUICK time of his shower that morning. He hadn't wanted to waste anymore of the day, and he really wanted to check in on the Harpers and let the kids deliver their handmade cards to Eric by the evening. But first, he called and made an appointment with the last therapist he'd checked out—they'd had a cancelation for the late morning, and he'd taken it, which worked perfectly. Now with December underway, appointment schedules seemed harder to snag.

He'd made a promise to Maddie. The ultimate epiphany. The only way he could get her to leave her room. He'd promised to take her to get a pet. Just the two of them. A father-daughter thing. So the plan was, first the therapist, then the pet, then home to gather everyone else.

And now that the plan was completed, for the past fifteen minutes, all of them—Hope and the boys included—sat around the table staring at the fishbowl and single male beta fish.

"What are we supposed to do with it?" Hope asked.

"You watch it," Ben said. "It looks nice. Fish are supposed to be relaxing. And Mads gets to feed it once a day."

Maddie and Chad had their noses to the bowl.

"I think there's poop coming out of its belly," Chad observed. They all took a closer look. Yep, poop.

"Maybe you could draw pictures of it, Maddie," Hope said. Maddie shrugged.

They all watched for another few seconds.

"Okay. Why don't we carry it to your room, Mads? Find a good spot for him."

Ben picked up the bowl just as Maddie scribbled on her notepad and held it up. The therapist today, a woman who seemed to know her stuff, had told Maddie not to hold back. That whatever she felt like writing was okay. No one would get mad. The message had been for him, too. He read what she'd written.

"That's what you're naming him?"

Maddie nodded.

Ben.

She'd named him after her dad. No doubt her way of letting him know that he was as boring as a fish.

BEN WALKED IN on Hope scrounging around in the drawer underneath the microwave. The drawer where he tended to stash his laptop and work.

"Looking for something?"

She leaped up with her hand on her chest. "Oh. You startled me. Yes, Chad asked for some bathroom stationery. I have a crayon he can use, but I can't find any more paper. We used the stack that was in the craft supply box yesterday for the finger painting." She faltered slightly when she brought that up. "I think he must be constipated again and needs some entertainment while he's in there," she added, getting to the point.

"Bathroom stationery," Ben repeated, deadpan.

"Yes." She splayed her hands and dropped them. She'd given up on finding bathroom stationery. Ben started laughing. Uncontrollable, let-it-all-out laughter. Stress release.

"What's so funny?

He shook his head and couldn't get the words out.

"What?" Hope asked again, hands on her hips now, and clearly a little annoyed.

Ben walked over to a closet at the very end of the bedroom hallway. She followed, obviously curious as to why he was laughing. Man, he was going to have to tell Eric and Cooper about this. He pulled a roll of toilet paper out of the closet and put it in Hope's hand, looked at her, then spewed laughter again.

Hope looked at the roll, then back at Ben and began to laugh, too.

Good thing Chad hadn't asked her for "moon floss." Ben had taken for granted that, over the years, Zoe had gotten used to the terms he'd used when he was on duty and then brought home.

The doorbell rang, and Ben went to answer it, still chuckling. It wasn't until the second ring that he realized he wasn't reacting to the doorbell the way he used to. No prickles, no nerves. He opened, still curious and not expecting anyone.

The nerves came back at first sight.

"What in hell are you doing here?"

Brie stood at the door with a golden dog in a service vest. He knew full well which dog. The one Zoe had signed them up for. The one he'd refused. And Brie. She had some nerve showing up here. His ears filled with pressure.

"Ben—"

"Go back to your pub," he said. "We have nothing more to say to each other."

"We don't. But I'm here to see the kids," Brie said.

"You're not welcome to see the kids."

Brie blinked and looked away, but didn't move. She met his gaze again. "We need to talk, Ben. It's been months. It wasn't my fault. I cared about her, too."

"Cared about her? I *loved* her."

The dog looked at him, and Ben felt his chest cramp. Tears spilled from the corners of Brie's eyes.

"Okay. If you need a scapegoat, someone to blame out of nothing but anger, you can keep blaming me, even if you know the facts and you know I wasn't working that afternoon. I'm careful, Ben. Even more so now, but I've always been." She wiped her face on her sleeve. "I haven't seen Maddie, Chad or Ryan. I can share stories with them about their mom. Go ahead and hate me all you want, but let me try to help them. Especially Maddie."

"I invited her," Hope said from behind him. Ben knew they'd met. She'd been to Bentley's. But Hope had invited the woman to his home, the woman whose bar had just happened to be the last place the drunk had been before he'd climbed into his car, pulled out and killed Zoe. Eating at Bentley's was one thing, but becoming friends with the woman who used to caution Zoe about married military men who didn't wear their rings?

He'd explained to Zoe that he didn't because he if he was ever captured, he didn't want anyone knowing he had a wife...or kids. Brie wasn't privy to the details of what he did and where he went while on duty. She had no clue about the covert operations and level of clearance he really had. Yet she'd taken that peace of mind from Zoe. What kind of friend was that? What kind of friend kept running a business that served alcohol after a drunk killed her friend?

Ben looked at Hope.

"Do you know what she's done?"

Hope shook her head. "I know what I went back and read from her copies of the police report and investigation. I know that the few words you said to a local newspaper reporter kept a lot of people from returning to Bentley's. I know that Wolf there might be able to help Maddie, and that's all I care about right now. Blame and anger can be destructive, Ben. Just stop and look at the kids. Look at yourself."

Ben swallowed. He didn't know how to let go of the blame or anger. It was the only way he had of avenging Zoe's death. A death he could have prevented had he been the one to go to Bentley's that day.

He looked at the dog Brie called Wolf. If he hadn't refused the puppy, would Maddie have coped differently after the funeral? Was he indirectly responsible for her mutism? Was he as guilty as Brie in all this? Or was the point that *neither* of them were? He'd been blaming Brie for existing, for her pub existing, when Zoe's death had been an accident. A tragedy. The kind of moment that led to the expression "live as if there's no tomorrow…"

Only he hadn't been living or letting anyone around him really live. He'd been pretending. Surviving. There was a difference.

He covered his forehead with his palm and let go of the doorknob.

"Maddie and Chad can see the dog. I'll be in my room."

And he walked away.

HOPE PUSHED RYAN in his kiddie swing and watched as Brie introduced Maddie and Chad to Wolf. They remembered her. In fact, Maddie got excited when she saw Brie and ran to give her a hug. Hope wished that Ben had seen that. She wished he was out in the yard witnessing the change in his daughter's face as she interacted with Wolf. And Chad... Wow... Chad was absorbing everything Brie was telling him about dog handling and how he needed to be calm and in control. Like the leader of a pack. Chad was acting as if he'd matured several years in a single hour. Wolf was an amazing dog.

She slowed Ryan's swing, noticing his head drooping. Falling asleep while someone rocked you in a swing—what a life! She picked him up and cradled him as she continued to watch. A curtain opened on the second floor. The nursery. Ben was watching, too.

Hope hugged Ryan close and pressed her lips to his head.

Ben might never forgive her for asking Brie to come over, but Hope had no doubt she'd done the right thing. She'd thought Simba was nuts when he'd suggested she travel across the world to help with three children, and here she was, in love with them as though they were her own. At least when the time came to return home, she'd know that she'd made a difference.

That she *could* make a difference.

CHAPTER TWELVE

Dear Diary,
I love all animals, but a fish is no puppy.
Daddy's just plain weird.

HOPE SET THREE BAGS filled with Christmas presents for the Harpers and Ben's children in the cargo area of Brie's compact SUV. Brie added her bags and shut the door before letting Wolf into the backseat.

"Thank you for taking me shopping," Hope said. "There is no way I could have taken all of this home on a bike."

"No need for thanks. I enjoyed this. I'm always so stressed out this time of year. That takes the fun out of Christmas, you know? Especially this year, with Zoe gone. I appreciated the company," Brie said.

They both climbed in, and Brie got the heater going right away. Hope buckled her seat belt before sticking her gloved hands under her thighs. The temperature had really dropped, even below what the weatherman said were December averages. Brie's uncle was holding down the fort at Bentley's so that Brie could get her shopping done. After that, they'd decided, since it was a Sunday, to close early so that he could head home and Brie would have a chance to put the tree up in the pub. Hope was looking forward to helping Brie, especially since the only decor her parents ever put up at Christmas was a very small artificial tree. The entire atmosphere surrounding the holidays here in the States was so different from back home.

Hope hadn't had the chance to swing by Bentley's in the past week since Eric's surgery. For one thing, it was getting too cold for her to ride the bike. She'd tried the bus once, and it was okay, but Brie had brought Wolf over to the house one other time. Ben had actually stepped out onto the back porch that time and watched Maddie and Chad interact with Wolf for a few minutes, then when it began raining and they'd moved into the kitchen, he'd actually stayed there with them. It was a step forward.

Eric was getting better daily and wore a

knee support to help, but he was still off his feet a lot, except for physical therapy exercises. He and Nina had been through a lot of changes this year—their son moving across the ocean, their daughter losing her life and their granddaughter suffering in silence, and now coping with Eric's old knee injury. Which was why Hope really wanted to get them gifts.

And she'd gotten Brie one, too, although Brie didn't know it.

"One of these days, you have to promise that you'll come and visit Kenya and stay with me and my family," Hope said.

"*That* would be the trip of a lifetime. One of these days," Brie said. "Are you still up for hot chocolate and tree decorating? I'd totally understand if you're too tired. I can just drop you off at the house."

"No. No. I'm good. The day wouldn't be complete without getting that tree up. It's so strange that everyone here gets them up so early. We only put ours up for a day or so before Christmas, then it comes down. I love how everything here sparkles for weeks on end. It's so fantastical."

"It really is. It can be crazy when you have

a business, though. I can't seem to keep up. Most restaurants and stores had theirs up before Thanksgiving." Brie sighed as she turned into the parking lot for Bentley's. "Sometimes I wonder if I'll ever be able to compete with all the new places popping up." She paused, looking straight ahead. "Or recover after what happened."

Wolf let out a yelp.

"What's up, boy?" Brie asked, turning toward the backseat.

Hope nodded toward Bentley's entrance. Cooper was reading the closing-early notice Brie had made for her uncle to hang on the window near the door. Cooper began walking away with his hands tucked into the pockets of his winter jacket.

"He's leaving. My uncle must've already put up the closing-early notice," Brie said.

"Why don't you get out and invite him in?" Hope said. "Hurry up."

"I can't do that." Brie craned her neck to get a good look at him. Wolf whimpered. "I know you said it's not me and he's just reserved, but I don't know."

"Brie, you'll never know if you sit until you freeze in place." Hope jumped out of the car and waved. "Hi, Cooper!" He looked up, but didn't seem to recognize her. "Hope. Ben's friend. Thanksgiving."

"Oh, yeah. Hey." He waved back and started to walk on. Until Brie stepped out.

"Hey there," she called out as she opened the back door for Wolf. "If there's a closed sign on the door, it only applies to strangers. I'm not sure I can conjure up the usual, but I'm sure I can manage something."

Wolf sat obediently waiting, but his tail was like a windshield wiper on high speed. Cooper ducked his head, then crossed the parking lot to them.

"Does some hot chocolate sound good?" Brie added. Hope was positive that the cold air alone wasn't responsible for her red cheeks and matching nose. Or his.

"Yes, ma'am. Hi again." Cooper stuck his hand out and shook hands with Hope. He hesitated, then held his hand out to Brie. She shook it. Finally. First contact. Hope was honored to witness the event.

"May I point out that this poor soul isn't used to temperatures in the thirties," Hope said. "For me, midfifties is cold." She slapped her hands against her jeans. Her coat and knit cap were warm, but her face felt numb.

"You're just trying to make us jealous." Brie grinned. "Let's get inside."

Cooper followed them until they approached the door. He waited for Brie to unlock it but hurried to hold it open for them. Mr. Quiet was quite the gentleman.

"Ooh, this is so much better," Hope said. "I was freezing."

"Let me check to see if Uncle Ralph or Arnie are in the back. Either way I'll get those hot drinks started to help us melt down," Brie said.

Cooper unzipped his jacket but left it on. He glanced at his usual table, but didn't move. Hope made sure he couldn't catch her making big eyes at Brie behind her back. Technically, the place was closed, so obviously he wasn't sure if he was supposed to go sit like a customer or what. Brie's eyebrows lifted when she caught Hope's signal.

"Um, so, Cooper," Brie said as she pulled on the green beanie cap rimmed with dogs in Santa hats. "How handy are you with lifting big boxes?"

"Very handy, ma'am. Just point to it and tell me where you'd like it."

"Great!" Brie said. "If you hang out and help us put up the tree, anything you want to eat or drink is on the house. And, Cooper, please. Call me Brie."

"Yes, ma'am. Brie."

Hope quickly excused herself to use the restroom. She didn't need to go, but she couldn't keep a straight face out there, and she didn't want to embarrass them. No question now that Cooper liked Brie.

Hope looked in the mirror and straightened her malachite-and-unpolished-ruby beaded earrings. They weren't holiday earrings, per se, but they had the right colors, and they went well with her solid green fitted sweater. She had to admit, her looks had never mattered much to her, but lately she was more conscious of them. She went ahead and washed her hands, since they'd been in every store imaginable, and left the bathroom.

She slowed her steps as she reentered the main seating area. It was like looking into one of those snow globes before it was shaken. The evening sun sparkled through the stained-glass window on the upper half of the door and along the tops of the windows near the bench seats. Shiny ball ornaments shone along green garlands that trimmed the bar area and the edge of the stage. Brie had really done some magic to the place. And she didn't miss Brie's placement of three hearty brown mugs of hot chocolate on the round table near the corner of the stage: Cooper's table.

Hope slipped onto one of the chairs at the table and wrapped her hands around the closest mug. She watched as Cooper stood abruptly when stout, ruddy-cheeked Uncle Ralph, whom Hope had met the last time she'd come by, walked in with Brie and Wolf at his heels. Cooper shook her uncle's hand. Hope loved the way Cooper said, "Yes, sir." Respect and honor. That was how everyone was supposed to treat their elders. That was what she'd always lived by. The way Brie's shoulders relaxed said she appreciated it, too. Her uncle's approval, whether for the pub or the man, meant the world to her. Hope understood that need.

Uncle Ralph said something about a strain and placed his hand on his lower back, and another "Yes, sir. No problem, sir" came from Cooper. Brie couldn't take her eyes off him, and the way she said, "Follow me, I'll show you the way" sent a flutter through Hope.

Life seemed so perfect, so pristine and picturesque, when you looked at it from the outside in. Any dream, any desire could be brought to life in that glass bubble. Grass certainly did look greener from the other side. Hope had been feeling defeated and burned out back home. Depressed by the suffering she saw. She'd seen and felt the suffering here, too. With Ben's family. And now, even with how perfectly the scene before her was unfolding, she knew nothing was perfect, but if love was present, it didn't have to be.

Hope looked at the stage next to her. What would life be like right now if she didn't try to make it perfect? If she stopped trying so hard to do what everyone expected of her and to prove herself?

Not only are you an Alwanga, you're a woman. You have to work harder to prove yourself and be successful. Her mother's words filled her ears. She set her mug down and played her finger around the rim. A person didn't build a successful career without some sort of desire driving it. Her parents had always been driven. Sometimes it took blocking out everything else in her life, surrounding herself in silence, so that she could find peace from their pressures. A moment to just stop and gain perspective. Like now, looking into the bubble… A snow globe, like the ones they'd set out at Ben's. She smiled at Brie's glowing face and Cooper's humble reserve. Something fluttered and floated past the corner of her eye. She got up and hurried to the windows just to be sure.

"Hey, everyone! It's snowing!"

The snow dome had just been shaken.

BEN OPENED ANOTHER one of Cooper's kitchen cabinets and looked inside. More mugs from different states and countries than one guy would ever use, and a random box of toothpicks in the corner.

"I'm not taking no for an answer unless you've read through that file I sent you. I'm telling you, Coop, just read it. This could work." He needed to know once and for all at this point. He was also using it as an excuse to come over and find out if a major intervention was needed.

"You're not going to find anything in those cabinets," Cooper said, putting his feet up on his old couch.

"Who says I'm looking for anything?" Ben asked.

"Really? Man, subtlety is *not* your thing. I told you I'm not drinking."

"Then why is it you won't return my calls? And why is it I was told you've been making almost daily visits to Bentley's? Of all places."

"Who told you that? Ah, Hope," he said, figuring out the obvious.

"She mentioned that she sees you from time to time, and I took it from there. Don't hold it against her. You know I can get people to talk." Ben regretted the words as soon as they left his mouth. Anyone but his own daughter.

"It's a free country," Cooper said. "Can't a man get some grub? I didn't get the memo that said I needed to check with you first."

"It's not what you eat that I worry about," Ben said.

"For crying out loud, I was asked for some help with a box, we all ended up helping get a tree up for the place, then Brie insisted on giving me and Hope a ride home because of the weather. If you don't believe me, go interrogate that girlfriend of yours some more."

Ben felt sucker punched. Coop had *not* just called Hope his girlfriend, had he?

"Cooper—"

"Don't Cooper me. You waltz in here pretending to be a friend. Saying I'm the only guy you'd trust as a business partner. But you don't trust a thing. What kind of man do you think I am?"

"Coop, we've known each other forever. Been through things no one could understand. I have your back and you have mine. Like always. I want to be sure you're okay."

"Worried?" Cooper leaped off the couch and slammed his fist against the wall, then paced. "You think I'm messed up. Maybe I am, but not for the reason you think. I haven't had a drink since I attended your wife's funeral. I made a promise to you and I've kept it, and all you've done is look for any reason to suspect me. I was in a bad way. The painkillers after surgery. The alcohol. But I put that behind me so I could be someone. So I wouldn't hurt anyone. And look where it got me."

Ben was out of the galley kitchen in two strides.

"I don't get it. Look where it got you? What? No job? Man, you're the one sitting here letting your bank account bleed to death. I've been begging you to snap out of it and work with me. I'm handing you a job on a damn platter. You want to do something else? You don't want to work with me? Fine."

"I can't. I can't do anything."

"Of course you can. You're a marine! You don't let an injury stop you. If you can get yourself to a pub, you can get yourself anywhere. Don't you see what you're doing here?"

"No! I don't see!" Cooper glared at him, his nostrils flaring and fists clenched, looking as if he was about to tear the place apart. Instead, his chest deflated, and he turned his back on Ben.

"I don't see," he repeated. "I'm going blind."

There was a frozen pause, like that moment bullet meets vest and knocks the wind out of you.

Cooper sniggered. "Yeah, see?" He faced Ben again. "A blind man would look real good for a security company. Give those clients a little extra confidence." He laughed, but there was an eerie ring to it. He swung his arm and knocked several frames and a stack of mail off the table. "See that? That's what it's going to be like. Pathetic. Useless."

Ben couldn't move. He stood in his buddy's tiny apartment and felt the walls closing in. Blind? He'd recovered from his leg injury, and they'd cleared him of any brain trauma. He clearly recalled Cooper telling him that the doctors who treated him had said that other than a permanent limp and twisted red scars running down his leg, he was fine. That his MRI was negative. That if he'd suffered any trauma to his brain from the blast, it was mild. No visible head or eye injury, no loss of peripheral vision when they checked by holding fingers up and making sure he could see them. He'd been cleared.

"I don't understand," Ben said. Shell-shocked didn't come close to how he felt. Cooper walked over to his sliding patio doors and looked outside.

"Apparently, I got close to one too many blasts. According to the new doc I saw, my hearing came back fairly quick after each incident, blurred vision and headaches cleared up, too, because the impact was mild. I was far enough away. Nothing actually hit my head. All normal combat stuff. But add up all the times and you have luck like mine. He called it repetitive mild traumatic brain injury. Too mild for visible signs, but now I have nerve damage.

"Oh, and here's the kicker," he said, turning around. "Back when they first screened me for mental issues, they blamed my tired eyes on sleep trouble, and lack of sleep on stress. Who'd believe a drunk anyhow, right? Blame the bottle. Treat the PTSD. It was all psychosomatic. And I believed them. I ignored the symptoms because I believed it was all in my head until they got bad enough for me to go back. And now they'll try to stop it from progressing, but it's likely too late. And the damage that's already done? My peripheral vision loss? It's permanent."

Ben tried processing what he'd heard. Tried to think of signs he'd missed. Something he might have noticed and pointed out sooner to help his friend.

Ben stood legs akimbo, wanting some sort of direction. Some way to fix this.

"Coop. Man, I'm so sorry. Tell me what to do. Whatever you need. I got your back."

"No, you don't, Ben," Cooper scoffed. "Everything lately has revolved around you getting your life back. Well, I can't help you there. I don't have a life. You wanna know why I go to Bentley's and sit there? So I can see what it'll be like when all I can do is hear. Listen to music. Listen to people talking about their normal lives. I listen because, even before I realized I was bumping into stuff too often, looking at a computer screen or trying to read anything killed me. That's why I sit around. Not because I'm some lazy ass wallowing in pity. I also go to Bentley's because I can walk there. Yes, I *walk*. I walk because I won't risk suddenly not being able to see while I'm behind the wheel. I won't risk hurting someone. You want my car keys? Take them. You've been worried about me turning into one more drunk driver. Well, no worries, man, 'cause I won't be driving at all. Your wish came true. Punish the drinkers. Now get out."

Ben palmed his face, then dropped his hands to his sides. Coop was right. He, Ben, was either a person's best friend and protector or their worst enemy. It depended on which side of the battle they were on. It came with the job. And here he'd been failing to protect his friends and family. That made him a traitor, didn't it?

Ben's blood rushed through his veins, making his ears throb. He'd failed again. Zoe was dead. Maddie couldn't speak. And now his friend was going blind. And he was the common denominator. Who else's life was he going to ruin?

Blame. Looking for excuses. Was this what he'd been doing with Brie and Bentley's, too? He took a deep breath. Coop was angry. Cooper *needed* to be angry.

"Coop, I didn't know. You should have told me."

"Why? You blamed the short time I drank, just like they did. All you've done is stick to the fact that I'd turned to alcohol. Besides, you've had enough going on yourself. Go look in the mirror. You need someone to be angry at. Someone to be your vent victim. Believe it or not, I get that. You didn't need to know about my problems. And get this... I don't need your sympathy. Not when I've seen what you really think of me," Cooper said, jabbing a finger at him.

Ben walked to the kitchen, scanned the floor blindly, then went back to Cooper. There was one last thing he could do. Coop had been dealing with all this on his own. Holding it all in. Ben knew the torture. The loneliness. Cooper needed to lose some cargo before it sank him.

"You don't know what I think. You're drowning in self-pity, and that's what brought you down after your leg injury. You need to snap out of this and talk to me," Ben said.

"Get out."

"Coop."

"Get out, Ben. Now."

"I'm not leaving." If Cooper needed a punching bag, Ben could take it. Ben deserved it. No way was he walking out of here now.

"You must have a death wish. I said to leave."

Ben stared him down. Oh, he had a death wish, all right. He'd lost count of the number of times he'd wished he was dead instead of Zoe. Cooper blinked. His friend needed to let go of everything he'd been holding in before his life really did detonate.

"You know what else I think?" Ben said. "All those reasons you gave me for going to Bentley's were bull. I think a certain redhead is the real reason. But you're not man enough, so you just go sit in a corner and wallow. Kind of creepy, don't you think?"

Telltale color crept up the back of Cooper's neck. Good. He'd pushed a button.

"It's not like that. I'm not wasting my time picking up girls who'll either feel sorry for me or not want anything to do with me when they figure it out. I can't burden anyone with this. Make them feel obligated to help the blind man."

"Hope told me about how that dog, Wolf, acts around you," he pressed on. "She mentioned it because she thought it was interesting how he seems to respond to you. Not because she knows."

The color drained from Coop's face, and he raked his fingers across his head. He limped over to a secondhand recliner angled in front of his TV and slumped into it.

The explosion that had ripped through Cooper's leg had also killed his K-9 dog, a Belgian Malinois. His dog had rotated through other handlers, but the incredible bond he'd shared with Coop was almost legend around the base. Ben knew that losing his dog in the line of duty had been a massive setback in Coop's physical and emotional recovery. Cooper shook his head, but couldn't look Ben in the eye.

"Wolf is a golden retriever. I'm not crazy, but clearly you are if you think some dog would get to me."

No doubt it had. "The way I see it, you can't stay away from that place because of the woman and the dog."

"Says the man who refuses to set foot in the place because he can't handle the memory of his wife."

"This isn't about me. This is about you living out your life stuck in this apartment. Is that how it's going to be? No purpose? No life? Afraid to talk to a woman? Afraid to work? What happened to 'once a marine, always a marine'? Even if you're dead. So losing your vision? Suck it up, because you're right—some of us *have* lost a lot more."

Cooper pushed against his good leg, stood, then lunged at Ben.

Mission accomplished.

HOPE HURRIED ALONG the shoveled sidewalk that led from the post-office entry to the rack where she'd chained her bike. Ben had left the house to take care of something work related, and Nina had come to get the boys earlier so that Hope could get some errands done while Maddie was still at school. Hope had spoken to her family twice since she'd arrived in the US, but the time difference was a challenge. In any case, she wanted to send postcards to Chuki, Simba, her parents and Jack and Anna. Postcards were more fun, in her opinion. She also let all of them know that she planned to give them their Christmas gifts in person.

The air had warmed up slightly in the past few days, enough to melt what hadn't been plowed, but still cold. Even so, after her near-breakneck slip this morning—which Ben was never going to hear about—on a patch that had refrozen overnight, she was trying to stick to the more salted areas.

She rubbed her nose with the back of her

glove and sniffed from the cold. She turned the corner, ready to unlock her bike. *Zoe's bike*.

It was gone.

She stopped in her tracks, every panicked breath swirling like smoke in the air. She looked down the walk she'd just come from and back again. It was purple. It would stand out. How could she have lost it or let it get stolen? She was sure she'd turned the combination on the lock. It took a few miserable seconds for her to recognize Ben's vehicle a few spots down. He held a hand up to signal her. *Oh, dear heaven, thank God.* The bike was safe. But what in the world was he doing here?

Hope stepped carefully over a pile of snow that separated the sidewalk from the asphalt, opened the door and jumped into the front passenger seat.

"Ben? What are you— Oh, my gosh, what happened?"

She pulled off her gloves and reached out to examine his left upper cheek. Ben flinched at her touch, but then held still. He'd taken a beating and had a split lip and a good-size laceration and contusion on his cheek to show for it. She pressed gently to see if the cut on his cheek was deep enough to warrant stitches, all the time hyperaware that he was watching her.

"What in the world happened?"

"Just helping a friend."

"Helping a— Are you crazy? You should know better than to get in a physical fight. If this is how you handle friends, please tell me I'm not one of them."

The corner of his mouth curved up, but he winced and touched the cut on his lip, then held her hand, the warmth of his hand penetrating her skin, and gently pushed it toward her.

"For the record, I did not beat anyone up. I let Cooper have at it and then put him in an arm hold until he calmed down."

"Cooper did this? Cooper, who has been sticking around to help Brie close up every night at Bentley's? Ben, we have to warn her."

"No, it's not like that. He'd never hurt her. But there is something I think she should know about him. I'll tell you on the way. First, I need your help."

CHAPTER THIRTEEN

Dear Diary,
We had a substitute at school this week.
Matthew Butthead raised his hand and
told the class that I had a substitute
mommy. I almost got mad, but then I
didn't, because Miss Hope is the best
substitute mommy in the world. I want
her to like me enough to stay.

HOPE DROPPED THE gauze she'd used to clean
Ben's wounds into the trash bin he'd pulled
near the table. He was keeping his eyes
closed, which she was thankful for. She was
in medical mode, but Ben Corallis was not
like any patient she'd ever treated, and standing so near to his chair, out of necessity, was
distracting to no end.

She studied the lines of his face. Lines that
told of grim battles and painful loss. Of fatherhood and frustration. Of yearning. The

furrows between his brows relaxed as she ran her fingertips along his cheek…inspecting…caressing. She placed one hand against the soft prickle of his hair, the other gently along his jawline and turned his head slightly so she could dress his wound.

"Hold still, just like that," she whispered, a habit she'd been teased about before. Anytime she was focused, her voice would become barely audible.

"Mmm-hmm," he responded with the same hushed, intimate tone that drew her attention to his lips. His eyes remained closed as she cradled his face.

"I've seen movies where guys like you cut their own limbs off or stitch their own wounds. This is just a bandage."

"I could cut off my arm if I had to," he murmured. She smiled as she opened the tube of triple antibiotic and applied it to his cuts.

"Is that so? Then, why am I doing this?"

His lips curved, but he stayed still, eyes closed, and she had an unbearable urge to kiss each lid and make everything better.

"I'm pretty sure you insisted," he said.

"Besides, why would I treat myself if I have you?"

Hope held her lower lip between her teeth. *If I have you.*

"Of course I insisted. You came to me wounded." She took a slow, deep breath, his clean scent washing through her, playing with her mind. He'd come to her wounded, but he had deeper wounds. Wounds she could never heal.

She needed to focus and not read into anything. She tugged the straps of a butterfly bandage across his cut, drawing it as closed as possible without stitches. Lucky for him, the wound wasn't too deep. Not like the ones that didn't show. He already had several old scars, from what she could see, and it appeared those wounds had never been sutured. As tough as he was, she had a hunch he hated needles. It was always the toughest-looking male patients who hated them.

"How did you know where I was?" she asked.

"I'd called to talk to you about Cooper and you didn't pick up, so I called and checked Nina's. She told me I might catch you at the post office. The bike gave you away. You promised you wouldn't ride it on bad roads."

"Mmm, I did. But I was careful and it wasn't far. You're a worrier."

"Just protective."

"Ah. Protective men, I know well. My big brother is quite protective."

"I can't blame him."

They both stilled. Hope licked her lips and diverted her attention from his eyes that begged her to see through them, to the bandage she was smoothing much longer than necessary.

"What I mean is, that's a big brother's job. To chase off interested men and boyfriends," Ben said. "Isn't it?"

She picked up the tube of antibiotic ointment she'd used and began cleaning up the first-aid supplies.

Was he fishing? Or implying that he was an interested man?

"Yes, he chases off interested men he doesn't approve of. Boyfriends, I wouldn't know about." She patted his shoulder. "I'm finished."

He opened his eyes and she handed him the bin of supplies. He got up to return it to the cabinet over the fridge. Hope went to wash her hands and get a disinfecting wipe to clean off the table.

"You mean to tell me, you've never in your twen—"

"Twenty-five," she filled in. He had to be fishing.

"—twenty-five years had a boyfriend?"

Hope pressed her lips together and splayed her hands.

"None. There is one friend my brother doesn't bother chasing off. We grew up with him, and he thinks someday I'll come around. Honestly, I've never had time. I live with my parents, which, yes, I know, might seem strange, especially for someone my age with my work, but it's not that unusual over there. They've always been protective and wanted what's best for me. My life has always been about education and career. Not socializing. My coming here was a huge step for them. If my brother didn't know and trust Jack and his family, I wouldn't be here."

Ben pushed the chair back in its place at the table, but kept his hands on its back.

"Wow," he said, apparently absorbing the

full meaning of what she was saying. He frowned and angled his head to look at her.

Hope's cheeks burned. She'd just given him way too much information. Whatever boundary had existed between them, she couldn't find it anymore. Friendship… Caring… Had they erased the line? Were they friends? She went to the freezer, opened the door and found what she expected on the bottom shelf. She wrapped it in a paper towel and handed it to him, no explanation needed.

"In fact, you came up."

"I came up?" he said, letting go of the chair and holding onto the ice pack.

Hope nodded and followed him to the living room. He eased into his recliner.

"As I recall, Jack assured my brother that if you found out that anyone was bothering me, you'd make them wish they never existed," she said, curling up on the end of the couch nearest the chair.

"Is that so? Has anyone bothered you?"

"No one has bothered me, Ben. I'm just emphasizing how much my family worries. I may not be a parent, but I worry about those I care about, too. And I also know there's never a guarantee that they'll always be okay or that I could have made a difference."

"Is that why you want to be a doctor?" Ben asked. Either he wanted to ignore what she was trying to get through to him, or he missed it altogether.

"Why not? I come from a family of them. It was a given. Does it surprise you because I'm a woman?"

"Absolutely not. I've answered to women who outranked me…and who were arguably scarier," he said, cocking the corner of his mouth, then cringing. He reached up reflexively and touched his bruised lip. "Just wondering."

Hope scratched at her knee and realized she was sitting in the same spot she had the very first night she'd been brought here. The first night she'd met Ben. She looked down at her hands. Hands that had been doing more diaper changes than signing prescriptions. Why did she want to be a doctor? If her internship had eaten her up so severely that it drove her across the world to escape it and heal physically, mentally and emotionally, then perhaps it wasn't what she was really meant to do with her life. Being proud of her accomplishments and having others take pride in her felt good. It made her feel valued. But for some reason, it wasn't bringing her complete and utter joy. She lowered her face, thinking of all the people she couldn't help. The impossible system and rural poverty. The children who suffered or lost their lives because of it.

"That tough a question, huh?" Ben asked, startling her. Had she been contemplating it that long?

"No, it's not. It's just…" She propped her elbow on the arm of the couch and pressed her knuckles against her lips, staring at the stone coasters on the coffee table. "It's just that my being a doctor was always the plan." She lifted her face and rubbed the smooth lapis teardrop that dangled from her ear.

"Ben, I was born with a ventricular septal defect. A hole in my heart."

He frowned and put his cold compress onto the table and leaned forward. "Catheter procedures were barely cutting-edge back then, but my hole was too big. It required open heart surgery. My parents, being doctors, knew the risks going in…all the possible complications. But it doesn't matter

who you are. When your child is suffering
or in danger, when your infant ends up with
complications after surgery like I did, you're
just a parent worrying desperately for your
child. I was their priority back then. Not
their careers. Simba probably felt quite ne-
glected." Hope smiled, knowing that whether
her brother did or didn't back then, he cared
about her now.

"They put everything on hold for me. All
their colleagues went out of their way to give
their baby, me, the best care and chance at
life. If my parents hadn't been who they are, I
might have not gotten the treatment I needed.
I'm in medicine because it's how I can give
back to all of them. Repay their sacrifices.
They gave me life, so I listened when they
gave me a direction for it. Helping them grow
their orthopedic practice is the least I can
do."

"Are you okay now? The surgery. Are you
still at risk?"

"I'm fine, Ben. I've always taken antibiotics when having things like dental work
done, just as a precaution, but I'm okay. I'm
fixed."

"So you're doing this for your parents. Not for you."

Hope uncurled her legs and hugged her waist.

"Why would you say that?"

"You just did. It's what I heard." He leaned an inch closer. "If I asked you if you were so madly in love with and fascinated by bones that looking at an X-ray made your pulse race and palms sweat, would your answer be an exquisitely over-the-top, passionate yes?"

Were they still talking medicine? Hope glanced at his mouth, and her pulse raced and palms got damp. The thought of X-rays had no part in it.

"What's your point?"

"Does there need to be one? Sometimes it's just about what you're feeling. Why not study the heart? Or work with children? Try to give other kids like you were a better chance?"

She needed to stop trying to decipher every word he said, every double meaning. She was reading into things again. She nibbled at her lower lip and saw his eyes track the movement. She stopped and pushed her hair back.

"I didn't know how much I loved children

until I came here. But loving them doesn't mean I want to witness their suffering day in and day out. I've seen children die from lack of access to care. I've also seen them die from tragedies. Horrific accidents. Adults, too. I don't know how much of that I can take seeing.

"I was at the hospital when the Westgate Mall attack in Nairobi happened. I'm sure you recall the attack from the news. Thirty minutes and I would have been done with patients and at that very mall with my friend. We'd planned to meet there. Instead, I never left the hospital because they needed everyone, whether we were still medical students or not."

"Westgate Mall? Oh, man." Ben ran his hand back over his head and shifted in his seat. "I've seen the footage from that shooting. Unspeakable. I'm so sorry you had to witness any of that firsthand."

She pressed her lips together and gave a small shrug. "Deal with what's dealt, help the helpless and give laughter to the living. That's what I always tell myself. It's also why I want to finish my internship and keep on track for ortho and working with my parents. More fixing and less death."

"Have you ever thought of practicing elsewhere? Like here in America?"

"Honestly? It never crossed my mind. I suppose I could do it if I wanted to, but it would take a lot of time. Kenya's medical education is different. We start medical school right out of high school and go six years before beginning internships, and still more years to get our masters or doctorates if we pursue them. I'd have to pass boards here before applying for residency. It's not easy to get in, but with enough persistence and motivation…"

Would she want to do that? As it was, she was struggling to motivate herself to get through her internship in Kenya.

"You came here to get away," Ben said. "That tells me something was wrong, Hope. What do you really want to be doing?"

Hope covered her face and shook her head. "I don't know." She sighed and leaned back. "I'm not sure. I understand and appreciate all I've been given, including the structure and direction. A kid needs that. That sense of security and knowing boundaries and having guidance. But I think, as a parent, it's tough to know how much of it to give and when to pull back. I don't blame them. It's partly me. I've never had the courage or confidence to speak up and tell them how I feel, but maybe I've held back because I don't know what I want. I've been *told* for so long, I'm not sure anymore how much of what I'm doing and putting into a medical career is me, or how much is them."

Hope pressed her fingertips against her eyelids. She'd said it. She'd finally admitted it to someone. To Ben. He put his hand on her knee and she uncovered her face.

"Technically," he said, "you could do anything you want to. You know that, don't you? You're your own person, Hope."

She reached out and let her hand touch his. "I know that, but I'm still not sure what I want."

"Like I said, ask yourself what is it you love, and be honest with yourself about it."

Was it a question of *what* or *who*? Ben looked straight at her, sincere and concerned, and she could not take her eyes off his for the life of her. What if she was falling in love with him? Was this what she was feeling? Falling for a widower and father of three who lived as far away from her life as possible? Was she ready to even consider uprooting herself, leaving the only country she'd ever called home, deserting the career she'd invested years in already? Was she ready to leave her family and become an instant mother?

She was insane to even think about it. And she had no idea if Ben even thought of her that way. An attraction and flirting was a far cry from the scenarios she was imagining. The man had lost the woman he loved and would probably never love anyone that way again. She needed to be practical and stick to reality. Like the fact that she'd be returning home.

"You have choices, Hope," he went on, "whether you realize it or not. I have no choice except being here. I'm trying to make it work, but I have to be able to support my kids. My career, my life, has always been out there, serving. If things don't work out here workwise, then I'll return to duty and leave the kids with their grandparents. So choose while you can...before things in life take away those options."

His watch timer beeped. The bus.

"I'll go outside to meet her," Hope said, standing abruptly. "You don't want her to see your face like that before you can come up with an appropriate explanation."

Hope hurried to the door, shocked at what he'd just said. He'd leave his children and return to duty? He'd let them suffer more loss? She put her hat on and wrapped her scarf around her neck. Ben held his side as he unfolded his legs to get up.

"If your body is starting to hurt, you should go ahead and take something for it."

"I can handle it. High tolerance and all that."

Stubbornness and all that. Hope put her hand on the knob.

"You know, Ben, if you're willing to leave Maddie and the boys and go back to duty, if given a choice, then maybe high tolerance for pain is your problem."

Ben drove in silence.

Maddie kept looking at him through the rearview mirror. They'd left the house as soon as her bus arrived because he wanted to pick up the boys. He'd simply told her that he'd had an accident but was all right. He'd been told by the recent therapist that using the word *accident* was okay, especially if it was done in a way that would desensitize them to the word and show the kids that not all accidents caused death.

Hope hadn't looked at him at all since they'd gotten in the car. He wasn't sure what had happened. It felt good having her around. She changed the energy in his house. And something about her, the touch of her hands on his face, had changed the energy in him, too. She calmed him, drew him out of his head and into the present. He hadn't wanted it or expected it. He wasn't sure if it was right. All he knew was that everything and everyone—him, his kids, even Nina and Eric—did better when she was around.

And then one comment about returning to duty, and she flipped. Just like Zoe would have, if he'd had the chance to tell her that he intended to…because three kids meant he needed an income and benefits he could count on.

He glanced over and saw Hope reach into her tote and pull out one of those silver bracelets she'd taken off before mending his face.

She reached back and handed it to Maddie. He looked in the mirror at his daughter's reaction. You'd have thought she'd been handed a block of gold, or a quadruple-scoop ice cream cone...or a litter of kittens.

He could figure out just about anything but women. How'd she do it? How'd she know when and what? Total silence and she pulls out a ring of metal from her bag of tricks and everything brightens up. Except he now knew that under her smile, Hope hid her share of pain and conflict. The stuff she'd shared? She'd shrugged it off, but Ben knew a person couldn't brush away painful experiences that easily. His little girl was proof of that.

Hope was wrong about him and pain and his tolerance for it. He'd felt it plenty. Which was exactly why he knew he did best out there as a marine, providing for his kids from far away. This hands-on parenting thing? Obviously he'd missed that gene.

Maddie unzipped the smallest pocket on her backpack and pulled out the first bangle Hope had given her. Ben almost reacted. He wanted to react. She wasn't supposed to take it to school anymore. Not after what had happened. But with one look from Hope and an almost imperceptible shake of her head, he swallowed his words.

Maddie slipped both of the bracelets on. The bulk of her pink sweatshirt held them in place better than when she was bare armed. Hope twisted to face her in the backseat.

"You know what that one is for?

Maddie shook her head.

"Do you remember what I told you about the bracelets being magical?"

Ben saw Maddie nodding an emphatic yes. It was no wonder he didn't get any of this. It involved magic.

"Well," Hope continued, "there's a rhyme that goes with them. 'When you wear one, good things come your way. When you wear two, happy memories won't fade away.'"

Maddie ran her fingers along the thin metal.

"I know the perfect place you can keep them so that they don't get lost. Your father can put a hook on the wall and you can hang them right over your bed."

Kind of like an American Indian dream catcher, Ben thought.

Ben pulled into the Harpers' driveway.

Maddie unbuckled and ran inside. Ben put
his hand on Hope's when she opened her
door. He expected disappointment. He was
ready for it. But instead there was sadness in
her eyes, and it beat him up worse than any
gash or bruise could. He tightened his hand
on hers, then let go. "Thanks. For being there
for her…and for everything."

"WHAT HAPPENED TO your face, Daddy?"

Chad came running as Ben followed Hope
inside. She was right about the kid copying
his every move. What had happened to his
face wouldn't set a good example.

"Yeah, what happened to you?" Eric asked,
walking in from the kitchen with a cane for
support and a cookie, the aroma of caramel-
ized sugar and cinnamon following him. At
least he wasn't on crutches. Nina had told
Ben that if it weren't for Hope insisting he do
his therapy exercises, Eric would have been
giving everyone a hard time about it. Something about a young, pretty face.

"Well…you see…" Ben stooped down and
picked Chad up, positioning him in the crook
of his arm. He carried him over to the Harpers' Christmas tree. Maddie sat cross-legged,

fingering the ornaments. One had a music box inside. She pulled on a looped string and let go. He didn't recognize the tune. He looked at the lights, twinkling hypnotically. Zoe used to stare at *their* tree. Even with the ficus still lit up at his place, it wasn't the same. It couldn't hold all the ornaments.

If Zoe were here, she would have given him that same look Hope did in the car. Sadness. So how was not putting up their Christmas things honoring Zoe? What was the point in depriving the kids? Hope had been right in questioning why he set rules and boundaries.

"I had a tree accident," he answered at last.

"A twee accident?" Chad asked.

"Yep. I was hit by a tree trained to attack anyone who didn't plan on putting one up. There I was, minding my own business, when I passed a place selling Christmas trees. I said no, thanks, and the next thing you know a tree came at me, followed by an army of them, green branches flying everywhere. I ducked, but couldn't escape."

"Uh-uh," Chad said in disbelief, but his look of awe said he believed every word. Maddie knew it was made up, of course, but sat listening intently. Ben leaned over so he was level with Maddie. Chad stayed perched on his knee.

"What did you do?" Chad asked.

"I told those botanical beasts that if they set me free, I'd promise to take my kids to get a tree right away."

Maddie scrambled to her feet, and Chad pierced the air with a battle cry.

"We're getting a real one!"

"Chad, go use the bathroom before we go anywhere," Ben said.

Eric chuckled from his spot on the couch. Hope smiled and peered at Ben from under her lashes. He never wanted the memory of that smile to fade.

"What do you say?" he asked her. "Have you ever gone tree hunting? I'm having a hard time picturing Christmas trees growing in Kenya."

Hope stepped away from the corner where she'd been leaning against the wall, watching them.

"You're correct. Other than hunting down our plastic one from the storage area, I have not had a real tree-hunting experience, but

I think you and the kids should go by your-selves."

What? She was still upset with him?

"But it makes sense for you to come. I kind of assumed you would, since we'd head straight back to the house afterward." What had he gotten himself into?

"I can wait here. Just swing by when you're done," Hope said.

Maddie took Hope's hand and tugged her even closer to Ben. She wanted her to come, too. For an entirely different reason, he was sure. Ben started to reach out to take Hope's hand himself. He wanted to pull her out the door. Make her come, because he needed her to be there. He was taking the kids to get a tree because a crazy voice in his head was telling him it was the right thing to do. Whether it was going to be a good thing, he didn't know. What if he messed up? What if being in that tree lot proved too hard to take, and he ruined the entire night for his kids? He wanted her home when he helped the kids hang all the ornaments Zoe had collected over the years. How could he get through that without Hope there to pick up the pieces if he broke down?

Maybe she didn't want to.

"I heard something about going to get a tree," Nina said, coming out of the kitchen wearing a red sweater with poinsettia prints. Ben pulled his hand back, but from the way Nina paused and looked at both of them, she'd seen the action.

Nina cleared her throat. "I'm so glad. This will be a good thing, Ben. Tree shopping. Just you and the kids. You've been needing to spend some family-bonding time with them." She turned to Hope. "You can help me in the kitchen. I have a few recipes I can teach you so that you can make them once you return home. Something to remember us by," she said with deliberate, practiced sweetness.

Irritation pricked at Ben, but he couldn't do more than nod. Hope flinched at Nina's words, but she maintained her composure.

"That's just what I was telling him. He should go spend time alone with his family. Have fun with them," Hope said, tipping her chin. She and Nina stared at him.

Women, Ben thought. Each with a different agenda for messing with his plans.

"Is Ryan up?" he asked.

"He's still napping. But he's due to wake

up. I don't think you can handle all three on your own in the tree lot, unless you plan on keeping Chad on a leash, can you?" Nina said.

Actually, he did have one of those toddler leashes. It was one of the first things he'd bought when he'd been thrown into full-time fatherhood. He didn't think Nina had ever seen him use it, but how else was he supposed to make it through a grocery store with a loaded cart? Strapping Ryan to his chest in an infant carrier and clipping Chad's toddler leash onto his belt had given him tremendous peace of mind on many occasions. He was pretty sure it was in the glove compartment.

Maddie clung to Hope's hand and narrowed her eyes at him. He narrowed his back at her.

"I can handle all three. But I can't help you there, Mads," he said, referring to Hope. "If she doesn't want to come, I can't force her. I guess it'll just have to be one memory of her time here that she'll have to live without."

"You don't play fair," Hope said, stroking her fingers through Maddie's loose hair.

"Who's playing anything? I'm just saying."

Ryan started crying from his crib. Apparently the kid had already developed a sixth sense for being left out.

"Why don't you go get Ryan ready, Hope?" Nina said. "That'll speed things up. He thinks he can handle all three. Let's get him out the door before he chickens out."

Before he changed his mind? Or before he stood up to her and insisted that Hope come along? Nina was working hard to keep Hope at home. Hope had a right to, being there to help with the kids and visit America, but one tiny action—barely a fingertip touch— and Nina was out to make it clear that she wasn't okay with anything more developing between them.

Out of respect for Zoe, he had to think that Nina was right, and he was out of line. He just didn't like the way she'd insinuated herself into the situation. He'd been telling Hope earlier to stand up for herself and not let anyone dictate her path. And look at him now. Chicken sh…droppings. He was trying to get in the habit of cursing less for the kids' sakes. Nina went to get Chad bundled up.

"Maddie," Hope said, tilting her chin up so she faced her. "I have something you can take with you. Don't let me forget when I get back with Ryan."

Hope didn't take long changing Ryan and getting him into warm gear. She'd really become a pro at multitasking with the children. She clipped Ryan in his car seat, then searched her bag.

"Here it is," she said, handing Maddie a pocket camera she must have picked up at the drugstore when she ran errands. Nothing fancy like the ones Zoe had used, the ones she could have built a name from but had given up for motherhood—for him—but the way Maddie lit up was priceless. Hope hunkered down to Maddie's level.

"It's digital, so your father can help you transfer pictures whenever you want, or show you how to do it," she said, glancing at Ben. Sure. After he had the chance to set up every child-safety protocol possible on the computer at home. And then some. "Take it, Maddie, so that when you come back, you can show me—not just tell me—about your tree hunt."

Maddie wrapped her arms tight around Hope's neck, and Hope gave her a kiss on the cheek. Ben swallowed hard. He scratched the side of his neck. He needed control. He needed out of this. Maddie ran to the couch to show her grandpa the camera, and Chad did frog jumps through the room.

"Actually, I can't, I just remembered that I have to—"

"Ben," Hope said, stopping him. She stepped closer, grounding him without contact. His breathing slowed. "Listen to me, Ben," she whispered. "You'll survive this, too."

CHAPTER FOURTEEN

Dear Diary,
I had a dream that Daddy liked Miss
Hope. I mean the way grown-ups like
each other. I asked Mommy if she was
okay with it and she said yes. I'd be okay
with it, too. I think he likes her in real
life.

BEN WASN'T A FOOL.

He was a marine, and marines did not go
on a mission without combat gear.

He stood at the entrance to the crowded
tree lot. He hadn't taken all his kids, on his
own, through a crowd at night. Grocery
stores were well lit, and he'd always managed between putting the kids in the shopping cart and the grocery items in their laps,
and Chad's leash.

A well-bundled Ryan was strapped to his
chest. Chad was secured in a harness that

pressed against his down jacket, making him look like that tire-commercial balloon man. Ben tugged the carabiner that latched Chad's politically incorrect leash to Ben's belt loop. Harness secure. Check. Maddie stood no more than three feet from him, as instructed. He pulled a receiver out of his pocket and hit the test button. The gadget he'd secured to her flashed and beeped. Tracking device operational. Check. If she wandered and someone kidnapped her, and she couldn't scream... He wasn't taking that chance. It had been one of the items on his list of security gadgets his company could offer—the company that wasn't happening. He'd gotten one at the beginning of the school year in case of field trips.

He hooked his thumbs behind the straps of his camo backpack and ran a mental checklist. Bottle, baby wipes, diapers, plastic trash bag for diapers, teething gel, Mad's writing pad, ziplock bag of cheese crackers, one emergency baby food jar of sweet potatoes and a couple of extra bottles of disinfecting hand gel. Was he forgetting something? His watch read 1700 hours. They needed to get on with it, because he was going to have to get the tree set up with water before it was time for all three kids to hit the racks.

Santa stood a couple of yards from the entrance ringing a bell and calling out, "Come here, children. Ho, ho, ho."

Was Ben the only one who found that a little creepy?

"Santa!" Chad yelled. He started off, and Ben reeled him in.

"Don't even think about it, kids," he warned. He gave Santa "the look."

"Okay. Stay close. Let's do this."

The place had just about every type of evergreen he could identify, some in heights that would scrape the paint off his ceiling.

"I like this one," Chad said, scooping up trampled-on snow and showering it on any branch he could reach. The kid had a good eye. A dark, lush spruce with even branching. He'd probably have to temporarily move the ficus to a different spot in order to fit this tree in the living room.

Maddie patted his arm and shook her head.

"You don't like it?"

She pointed, instead, to a rather lanky tree at the end of the yard. The blue-green tinge of the needles was nice, but its branches were

few and far between. He could see where
some had been cut off near the trunk. That
explained the red sticker sale tag.

Maddie took out her camera and took a
picture of the tree, then pointed at it again.
She dragged him closer by the hem of his
jacket.

"I don't know, Mads." Her chosen tree
looked as if it was waiting for Charlie Brown
to show up. He looked at his daughter and
back at the tree. Then she did something she
hadn't done in the almost eight months since
losing her mom. She blew him a dramatic
kiss with both hands, then cupped them
under her chin in a begging attitude. People
funneled past them, music played and Chad
was about to rip his belt loop from the seams,
but Ben couldn't move. Couldn't stop looking at his little girl's face. The coy look in her
eyes. The spark that had been missing. The
life-loving energy—that she'd gotten every
bit of from her mother—glowing from her
cheeks. He reached down and held her chin
in his hand.

"Mads. You're right. This tree is perfect."
Broken, but holding together.

He waved down one of the sellers and was

told it would be a few minutes. Chad examined Maddie's tree and scrunched his face.

"Daddy? Have you lost your mind?"

Ben raised his eyebrows at the little rebel.

"Yes, Chad. I think I have. Because we're not just getting one tree. We'll get Charlie here, but tomorrow we're going to a tree farm. Don't tell anyone, though. It'll be a surprise."

Because we're taking Hope, and nobody's stopping us. Not even her.

HOPE ROLLED ONTO her back on her mattress and gripped fistfuls of her hair. About an hour ago, Ben had called Nina on his cell, asking if she wouldn't mind dropping Hope off at the house because he was running late. Hope had already asked her the same favor, claiming that she had a migraine coming on. Nina had indeed kept her busy with a baking lesson, but all Hope could think of the entire time was what Nina had implied earlier. She hadn't said anything afterward. She hadn't cornered Hope over flour mixes. But the tension was there. And yet Nina was right. Hope was a fifth wheel. Nothing but a spare tire, not meant to roll with the other four.

She was becoming too comfortable with Ben. Too close.

She could change her ticket and be in Nairobi within the next few days. Everything would be back to normal.

Except that Ben and his children wouldn't be there.

Her eyes burned, and she sniffed back tears. She wasn't a part of their family. She was an intruder at best. Someone who was crossing the line. Drawn to a man and his children when they'd suffered such loss, not even a year ago.

She wasn't sure what it was, what she was feeling for Ben, but she did know it was too soon for him. Too soon for her to figure out if whatever seemed to be passing between them was just curiosity, or friendship, or sympathy, or something more. In the end, it didn't matter. If she returned home, he'd have the space he needed to bond with his kids and see that he needed them as much as they needed him. If she left, he'd have the time to figure things out—if he didn't return to duty first.

If he didn't run away.

She was trying to run away.

The sound of laughter drew her to the window. It was dark, and with her room lights on, she couldn't see anything but the neighbor's wonderland of lights. But she knew. Only one boy could squeal like that. She ran to turn off the room light and peered through the curtains. She watched as Ben hoisted, then tossed Chad into the air a few inches from his hands, let go and caught him. He ruffled his hair and sent him to knock on the door as he bent into the car to get Ryan. Maddie was skipping—skipping!—after Chad. Hope put her head against the ice-cold windowpane. There she was, once again, gazing into a snow globe with no way in.

You're the key, Hope.

Her mama's voice sounded in her head, telling her that her future was in her hands.

The problem was that this time, the key didn't fit.

Now, THIS FELT like a family outing.

Ben glanced sideways as he drove carefully down the winding country roads that led to a tree farm that offered balled and burlapped evergreens. Mounds of mud-spackled plowed snow lining the road gave way to an unmarred, glistening blanket of white that stretched endlessly to their left. To the right, the blanket wove its way through a splintered forest and a herd of deer on high alert.

Hope's excitement had the kids craning their necks as she pointed out the herd. Here she was, someone who lived where many only dreamed of going just to see exotic wildlife, bubbling with the thrill of being surrounded three hundred and sixty degrees by snow and spotting deer. Things most took for granted around here. The way she probably took giraffes and wildebeests for granted.

He smiled and concentrated on the road and her voice as she began humming to the holiday music on the radio.

"Do you two know this song?" she asked Maddie and Chad. Ben looked in his rearview mirror and saw Maddie nod and Chad shake his head. Chad didn't know "All I Want for Christmas is My Two Front Teeth"? He should have recognized it.

He would have, if Ben had taken Nina's advice and put him in preschool this year. Even half a day to get him used to structured learning. But he'd been too stubborn and defensive. He had wanted his kids as close by as possible, just so he could feel in control and falsely secure. He'd been so involved with Maddie's school issues, he'd put his son's early education on hold.

The coal from all the mining towns in America wouldn't be enough for his stocking this year. Maybe the chances of building a company with Coop going under was a blessing in disguise for the kids. Now, whether he found a position in DC or returned to duty, he knew the best thing for the kids was to live with their grandparents.

Eric and Nina had raised two before. They knew what they were doing, whether he wanted to admit it or not. He'd let his pride and need to prove himself and make things right for his family get in the way of what was best for them. He looked at Hope again. Hope, who didn't have kids of her own, was a more natural parent than he was. She caught him looking and blushed.

"What?"

"Nothing. Just remembering what an awful guitar player you are. You sure can carry a tune, though."

"I wasn't that bad, was I?" She looked back at the kids. Maddie scribbled on her pad and held it up. Hope read it out loud. "'You were terrible but I liked it anyway.' Okay, I admit it. I've never played an instrument. I can't even get the right rhythm on a drum. We have traditional handheld drums. My brother is great at it. Me, not so much."

"But you can sing, apparently," Ben said.

She smirked and shrugged.

Ben turned down a long bumpy drive. Three small farm buildings formed a half circle. A backdrop of evergreens at different stages of growth framed the setting. Stands of handmade wreaths and garlands welcomed visitors. He parked in front of what looked like the office.

"You all ready?" he asked. The clicking of belts unlatching gave him the answer. "Remember, only one that's burlapped and small enough to keep alive so it sets roots."

"You know they'll have no idea," Hope said. "You'll have to veer them toward the right one."

"Yeah, I know. No Charlie trees for this project," he said, winking at Maddie and reaching behind to give her cheek a gentle pinch.

The plan was to pick a tree that they could eventually plant in a spot just to the right of their house, not too far from the outdoor water outlet. A live tree that would grow in remembrance of Zoe. One they'd make a tradition of stringing with lights every year.

"Everyone have their gloves and hats on?" he asked, trying to keep himself in the moment.

"Let's go!" Chad said, grabbing an armful of snow and throwing it in the air. Then he did it again, though it didn't make it too high.

"We may need to skip the hot chocolate or cider with him," Ben said.

"Definitely," Hope agreed. "Kitchen pantry overhaul when we get home, too."

"Long overdue."

Maddie and Chad ran ahead of them to check out a carved wood bear wearing a Santa hat. Hope helped Ben hoist and secure Ryan into the harness on his back so his hands would be free. He put his hand on Hope's back as they followed the trail and signs with instructions on what to do. It was simply a gesture. Guiding her. That was all. But it felt…so right.

Maddie and Chad disappeared behind one tree that hadn't been dug up yet. The farm had plenty of trees ready to go, and Ben figured they'd pick one of those, but the day was about more than grabbing and going. He wanted to get away. Share this with Hope.

A snow missile came flying at him, obliterating itself against his thigh. Maddie's red coat made for useless camouflage behind that green tree. Another flew but missed.

"My turn!" Chad's snowball barely cleared two feet.

"This is war!" Ben called out. He reached down, grabbed a handful of snow and made a ball, then threw it, aiming for the tree. "Aw, I can't believe I missed."

Laughter emanated from behind the tree. He and Hope looked at each other because they'd heard two distinctly different laughs. More snowballs came flying.

"Come on, Hope. I can't fight the enemy alone."

Hope tried her hand at snow combat. She made a beautiful, formidable warrior. Ben stepped behind her and grabbed her around the waist.

"Human shield!" he yelled as she laughed and tried to get away. She shrieked when a snowball hit her jacket.

"No fair, Ben. Let me go!"

He didn't let go, instead turned her to face him. And in that second, nothing else existed. Everything disappeared into the puffs of breath that danced between them.

He kissed her. Brushed her lips with his in one quick, private, stolen kiss because the moment was so perfect. With two kids behind a tree and one behind his back, it was a second in time captured for him and Hope. She stared at him wide-eyed, then touched her lips with a gloved hand.

Ben tugged her hat down around her mesmerizing face.

"Let's go get a tree," he said.

"Yes. Let's."

THEY ENDED UP getting two, with double of everything needed for setting them up. And after dropping one off at the house and eating a very late lunch, they headed to Nina and Eric's. Nina didn't even bother to mask her stiff reaction to the fact that they'd gone to a tree farm. *All* of them. Her only consolation was Ben telling her that the kids asked to come over and play with their grandparents. They hadn't really, but he figured catching flies with honey might work with her. He and

Hope only needed an hour or two for their second mission. It was already getting dark.

He passed this street almost daily and always sat at the intersection holding his breath for a green light, but never, since Zoe's accident, had he turned into the parking lot of Bentley's. The closest he'd come to that was when he'd spotted Zoe's purple bike parked out front shortly after Hope had arrived in the States. Ben really wanted to park and wait in the farthest spot from the door, but making Hope run across the parking lot with the bitter wind now coming through in gusts would have classified him as pond scum.

He pulled up close to the main entrance, but kept his eyes straight ahead. He could do this. This wasn't about him anymore. Hope unbuckled.

"I know what you're trying to do, but I really feel bad about pulling her from work," Hope said. "Can't it wait?"

"She owns the place. Don't you think she has servers or a bartender who could keep things going for an hour or two?" he said, propping his elbow on his side door and rubbing his jaw as an excuse to look away.

"You haven't been in there lately, have you?"

"No." Ben rubbed his palms along his jeans. "No. I don't go in there. But I never assume I'll have another chance. Things happen. I want to do this now."

He wouldn't even be here if he didn't think Brie was the one person who could help his friend. When he'd left Cooper after their brawl, the guy had calmed down. He'd even apologized for Ben's face by telling him he deserved it. Ben knew that was code for "We're still brothers, but no way I'm getting mushy." But what if he *wasn't* okay? Worse yet, what if he decided he didn't have anything to live for?

"Trust me," Hope said, "she hasn't needed much help, so she saves money by doing it all herself, other than her cook and occasionally her uncle."

Ben frowned. He'd had that serious an impact on Bentley's?

"I'll let her know we're here." Hope got out. Wind blew into the car as she shut the door firmly against it, trapping him inside with the aroma of Bentley's famous burgers and potato skins. His temples pounded, and he held his breath in spurts, trying not to re-member. He and Zoe on their first date. Sen-timental Zoe getting him those burgers every time he came home. Sometimes he hated the way tastes and smells entwined themselves in memories like viruses. At least the bad ones.

The sound of Hope opening the SUV door saved him. She climbed in, and seconds later, Brie and Wolf came rushing out of Bentley's. Both woman and canine climbed into the back. The smell of grilled food intensified. He was going to be sick.

He stepped on the gas without saying hello until he was near the parking lot exit. There, he rolled down his window and took a deep breath of icy air, then turned to look at Hope and Brie as if everything was normal. Hope looked at him wide-eyed, as if he'd rolled down the window because he'd passed gas in front of her friend.

"I'm just anxious to get to Coop's," he ex-plained. "Thanks for doing this, Brie."

"Of course. Uncle Ralph was here any-way, looking at my accounting. I want to help Cooper, I just don't know that he'll let me. He didn't answer my phone call or come by today. I'm not sure he'll want me showing up at his door."

"Brie, Hope told me how he has been around you, and I happen to know he loves dogs and seems to have a connection to Wolf. Something tells me he won't turn you away."

Ben drove down the street and turned into the apartment complex where Cooper was staying. The light was on at his place. Ben was thankful it was on the ground floor, and he wouldn't have to haul the tree upstairs. He parked where Cooper wouldn't readily see his car, but Ben and Hope could keep watch.

"Brie, wait in here till I untie it. No use in freezing."

He grabbed the stand he'd bought, not knowing if Coop had one, and set it and a box of lights on the hood, then made quick work of the tree. He carried it over and leaned it against the wall near Cooper's door, then signaled for Brie and Wolf through the windshield. She grabbed the stand and box and ran over.

"Okay," he said. "Knock and see if he'll let you two in."

Ben joined Hope in the car. They waited. After her third knock, Brie looked over at them and shook her head…just as the door opened and cast a light on her. They watched her lips move, her motion to the tree, and finally they saw him step out and carry it inside. Brie and Wolf joined him.

Ben and Hope exhaled at the same time.

"Now we wait."

"Do you know how long it took us to decorate the tree at Bentley's? We may be here awhile," Hope said.

"He can handle the tree on his own. Everyone in our division knows about Cooper and Christmas trees. It didn't matter where we were, even if it was desert for miles, he always managed to make one if the holidays rolled around and he wasn't going home. I think his best was out of empty ration packets." Ben chuckled. "When I mentioned Brie to him, there was something in his face that I've never, ever seen at the mention of a girl. And then there's Wolf. If anyone can pull him out of his funk and get him to realize his life isn't over, it's the two of them."

"It breaks my heart that he's going through this. She really cares about him, Ben. I believe in fate and things happening for a reason. Things we can't understand. Maybe they were meant for each other. Maybe her connections and work will help him get a service dog faster, if need be."

"Maybe. Not sure how it all works, but this goes way beyond that." Ben turned and faced Hope. "Cooper had a different type of service dog once. A K-9 who was killed during the blast that injured his leg. His K-9's name was Wolf."

HOPE WIPED HER tears as Ben told her about Wolf. She connected the dots. She'd witnessed the dog's behavior around Cooper firsthand. Incredible. Was it possible? Or a mere coincidence? Was there really such a thing as holiday magic and miracles? Goosebumps trailed down her arms.

Ben scrubbed his hand across his stubble. "I'm worried about him. I'm worried about Maddie. Even Chad and Ryan. I'm not sure what I'm supposed to be doing anymore," he said.

Hope took his hand and held it. She rubbed the pad of her thumb across the rough skin of his knuckles. He didn't pull away.

"All you can do is be a friend. Be a father. You're doing what you can," she said. "Only a true friend would be sitting in a dark car on a cold night, just so a woman and a dog could deliver a tree."

The corner of his mouth quirked, and he squeezed her hand. Hope was certain he would have kissed her again, but for the sound of a door slamming and the sight of Brie running out with Wolf. Her hand was over her mouth, and she was crying.

"Oh, no." Hope unbuckled.

Ben was halfway out his door, but Brie was already climbing in after Wolf.

"Honey," Hope said, turning backward with her knees on her seat and rubbing Brie's knee. "What happened?"

Fleeting images of the damage to Ben's face Cooper had done spun through Hope's head, but Brie didn't look anything but wind-blown, and Ben had assured her Cooper would never hurt a woman. That he'd only hit Ben because Ben had wanted him to.

"Brie, talk to me," Ben said, leaning back with one hand on Wolf, who kept nudging Brie's cheek.

Brie struggled to still her sobs. "H-he told me he was sorry if he'd given me the w-w-wrong impression, but that he's not interested in me that way. A-a-and that I shouldn't call him. Then he thanked me for the treeeeee." The word trailed off on a wail.

Hope got out and climbed into the backseat. Ben's face looked pale and drawn. His jaw clenched and unclenched.

"Just drive us back," Hope said, knowing the sight of a girl crying was enough to make most men panic. She put her arm around Brie and let her sob into her shoulder. If she ever had any doubts about how much her friend had fallen for Ben's, they'd just been blown away.

BEN SCANNED HIS laptop screen for one last read-through. He opened his email, attached the file and pasted the brief cover letter he'd written into the body of the email. He hit Send. One down, five more to go. He systematically went through each one, pasting in the matching letter and greeting and hitting Send.

He sat back and listened to the house breathe. Ryan's monitor sputtered with static, then stopped. Nothing moved but his blinking cursor. He'd done it. He'd made his move.

He'd been so sure that he'd eventually convince Coop to go in with him. Now he knew why his buddy had so vehemently resisted. And without his expertise, Ben wouldn't be able to pull together a company. Not the way he'd envisioned.

He never thought he'd have to fall back on plan B. Reenlisting had always been his first choice before Zoe died. But with Maddie's problem, he'd done his best to stay around. That wasn't going to be possible anymore. And at this point, if he didn't start putting money into his account on a regular basis, his savings were going to be depleted. Even the insurance money from Zoe's death would be gone. He was responsible for his family, and if that meant he needed to be away in order to provide, then that was what he'd do.

But he couldn't bring himself to reenlist. After the past few days with his kids—and with Hope—he couldn't bear the thought of only seeing them once in a blue moon. And if Maddie ever regained her voice, hearing her through technology, no matter how amazing it was for those stationed far from their loved ones, wouldn't be enough for him.

Semper Fi. He loved his country. He served because it was who he was. Yes, he was a husband and father, but for the sake of survival and coping with the things he'd seen and had to do in order to protect his family and country, he'd distanced himself. He realized that now. Hope had made him see it. He was a father first. He would always be a marine, but he was a single father, and his kids were counting on him. And given the future Cooper was going to have to adjust to, Ben felt better being closer to all of them.

Just not as close as home.

But a job in DC would at least give him the flexibility to fly up as needed.

He shut down his system and went and lay down on the couch, tucking a pillow under his neck. He faced the tree they were calling "Zoe's tree" in all its glory, right in front of the large window overlooking the street. Its lights were set to twinkle, and every branch carried an ornament…a memory. Maddie had loved the idea of planting it permanently in their yard after Christmas, and had drawn a picture of their house with it out front.

Maddie's little "Charlie Brown" tree took up a narrower area between the bedroom hall and the entryway. She'd chosen the spot. Ben figured she wanted it to be the first thing she saw when she came home from school. Other than white lights, the only things she'd hung on it were the two bracelets Hope had given her. Ben left it at that. He didn't know what was going through that little girl's head, but she seemed happier. The school had sent a note from her last counseling session, and she appeared to be doing better there, too. The note said she was lucky to have such a caring and involved father. Yeah, right.

They had no idea how very little her "positive behavioral changes" had to do with him. He had a feeling that once Chad started preschool, something Ben was looking into for the second half of the year, he'd be getting office calls on a daily basis. Only, he wouldn't be the one taking those calls. Not if he landed one of the contract jobs in DC. With the potential to earn six figures with a company that contracted with the government, he had to give it a shot.

The only reason he'd survived as a single parent was Nina and Eric. And Hope had made all the difference in the world, too, but she'd be back in Kenya, focused on her career. He had a support system here. Everyone down to school staff and grocery clerks knew his family. He wouldn't have that if he moved them. With Maddie showing small improvements, he wasn't about to uproot her.

He'd have to talk to the Harpers. Eric would soon be back to doing all the things he used to. Would he and Nina be able to act as guardians for three grandkids? Was that asking too much? With a solid salary, though, he could hire someone to help them out, full-time if they wanted. He'd do that. And he'd rent his house to Coop if he wanted. He could have it arranged and rigged for whatever his needs were. He'd have him stay there for free, only Coop wouldn't go for that, and he wasn't going to cut the man's pride any lower than it was right now. He'd keep it cheap, though. And if he did get a dog, he'd have the room he needed. He didn't in that tiny apartment.

He'd taken Cooper to a few of his appointments last week. The VA was a stickler for making sure they distinguished between an ailment caused by an injury or exposure during service and a disease that was unrelated. The optometrist who'd originally picked up on Coop's nerve damage during a routine exam Coop had gone in for because of frustration with his vision had been right. And between those records, and the extensive test results and the opinion of a neuro-ophthalmologist that came highly recommended, no one could argue the cause. But things weren't looking good for his left eye. The doctor hoped they could slow down progression in the right and save some of his central vision. There were no guarantees.

Ben pulled his phone out of his front pocket and scrolled down to the Harpers' number. It was late. Late enough for Eric and Nina to have gone to bed. It had been past the kids' bedtime by the time he and Hope had returned from dropping Brie back off at Bentley's. Hope had wanted to go inside with her, but Brie had insisted she'd be okay. Ben felt rotten to the core. Yet another plan of his had failed. He knew strategy and tactics... just not here in civilian life.

The kids and Hope were in bed. He wanted to wake her up. Just to talk. He wanted to hear her voice.

He cursed himself. It was wrong. It was wrong of him to want that. Or to have kissed her. It didn't matter that Zoe wasn't alive and that the last time he'd seen her in person had lasted less than thirty minutes eight months ago and had been ten months after his prior leave. Other than a few short Skype visits, they hadn't been together in almost a year and a half. But she was still his Zoe.

He walked over to the tree teasing him with ornaments. He hadn't really taken a close look at them. He'd let Maddie and Chad do most of the hanging because more than that would have been asking too much. Hope had helped them reach a few higher branches. The kids' three first-Christmas ones were clustered near each other. Another stood out. A small silver frame engraved with *First Anniversary*. He removed it from the branch. Inside the frame was a copy of an ultrasound. Maddie's. Shrunk to fit. His eyes burned, and the muscles on the sides of his neck became corded and tight. Zoe had put that black-and-white copy in there because he had been gone. They couldn't take a celebratory picture together, and she'd wanted something from that moment in time. He hadn't even been here for that.

He put the ornament back and swallowed the tears that threatened. Zoe had deserved so much more. He'd taken away her life from the start. She'd given up college and pursuing a degree in the arts just a few months after they'd gotten married and he was scheduled to deploy. She'd gotten pregnant, and the morning sickness had had her floored the first three months. He did remember that, because guilt was a hard thing to let go of. She'd spent their marriage living like a single mother of three. And each year their focus had turned more and more to the kids. Her raising them and him providing. It had been hard not to become strangers to some extent.

And now he couldn't even keep everything she'd devoted herself to building—a home and family of three fantastic kids—from falling apart. He'd wasted her life. She'd left him with the ultimate gift, and he was breaking it.

He bent his knees and crouched in the middle of the room. He rocked on his heels and held his head in his hands.

Forgive me, Zoe. Please, forgive me. I wasn't here for you, but I did love you.

With that, months and months of holding it all in came to an end.

CHAPTER FIFTEEN

Dear Diary,
I saw Daddy kissing Miss Hope. Chad saw it, too. I put my finger to his lips, but he's such a blabbermouth. I don't want anyone talking about it. I don't want it ruined. I don't want to say something that will make Hope or Daddy go away.

HOPE HAD WOKEN UP the morning after they'd put up the tree and found Maddie curled next to her, sound asleep. Less than a week till Christmas. She was glad school vacation had started because Maddie looked so at peace. She didn't want to wake her anymore than she'd wanted to crawl out of bed herself. There was something indefinable about the comfort that came from holding a child. It put the world in perspective. It brought everything down to a fundamental, basic need. Love.

Several days had passed since they'd gone tree hunting, and it seemed that Ben was hardly home anymore.

According to Nina, he was helping Cooper get to the appointments he had with some specialists. Hope didn't understand the way Ben had handled Cooper at first, letting Cooper use him as a punching bag, but clearly he understood what his friend needed. Maybe it was a guy thing. Or a marine thing.

She missed him. She wasn't about to admit it to anyone, but she did.

She put Ryan on the floor of the living room where she could keep an eye on him yet give him a bit of freedom, and hurried to wrap the presents she'd bought the day Brie had taken her shopping. She had locked them in her suitcase for safekeeping, but with the tree up, she couldn't wait to set them under any longer. Nina and Eric had picked up Maddie and Chad, wanting to take them to get something special for their dad.

The door opened, making her jump. She quickly scanned the gifts to make sure Ben's had been wrapped already. *Yes. Okay.*

"Hey, you," he said. "Channeling elves, are we?"

He set his keys down on the console and kicked off his slushy boots.

"Hi. You left early," Hope said, not liking how unintentionally suspicious she sounded.

He pressed his lips together, keeping his smile from spreading, reached into his pocket and pulled out a small, narrow, wrapped box.

"I did leave early," he said, coming over and slipping it under the tree. Her name was written on it.

"You didn't have to get me anything," she said, taping her last box and glancing over at Ryan, who was rolling sideways.

"I know."

She bit her lip and looked at the box.

"You're the kid who opens gifts and re-tapes them. Aren't you?" Ben asked, sitting cross-legged near her. She wrinkled her nose.

"Kind of."

He belted out a laugh.

"I thought so. Go ahead. But don't tell the kids. They may follow in your footsteps."

I'd need to be around them much longer than I will be for that to happen.

She grabbed the box and ripped open the wrapping, scrunching it into a ball and dropping it on the floor next to her. She opened the box.

"Oh, Ben."

She lifted out a simple necklace. A silver teardrop pendant. Was it a message, a symbol of how sad he'd be when she returned to Kenya, or a symbol of possibility? The promise of rain—one drop that has the power to spring new life from nothingness. From death. She closed her eyes to hide the tears that threatened.

"Thank you. It's perfect," she said.

He took it from her and clasped it around her neck. The brush of his fingers at the back of her neck sent shocks of awareness through her. She could feel the warmth of his face near hers. She opened her eyes, and he pulled back slightly.

"Looks as though you know how to tempt a guy," he said, nodding toward Ryan.

Ryan was crawling for the first time— straight for the crumpled ball of wrapping she'd tossed. And Ben was witnessing a first with his son.

"Come on, baby," she said, slapping her jeans. Ben cheered like Ryan's greatest fan.

Then Hope trusted her instincts. She turned to Ben and kissed him.

"Congratulations on a first," she said.

Then she kissed him again.

BRIE HAD BEEN HEARTBROKEN, which was why Hope wanted to stop by and see her before she closed early today for Christmas Eve.

She pulled up to Bentley's, locked the bike in place and took off the helmet. It was cold but not too bad. She went inside and sat down at the bar to wait for Brie to finish taking a payment.

"Hey, girl," Brie said, moving around the counter to process the credit card. She sounded down. "A visit from you is the best thing that's happened today."

"It can't be that bad," Hope said.

"Look at this place. I'm closing in thirty minutes, and I've had a total of five customers the entire day. Uncle Ralph couldn't even find anything wrong with my bookkeeping or where I've put advertising dollars. I'm telling you, it can't just be all the bad publicity we got. All the new shopping centers popping up are killing me and every other 'old' business, too. It's not fair. We were here first, you know? Give me a sec."

She went back to finish up with the last customers. From the way she spoke to them all, full of energy, no one would have known how she was hurting. She came back and handed Wolf a reward, then started polishing glasses as she spoke.

"It's just frustrating."

"Are you sure it's not just the holidays? People traveling out of town and such?" Hope asked as she leaned her arms on the roughened wood bar.

"Nah. I know it's because people don't see past the surface. Show most folks a shiny new ornament and its tarnished and dented twin and they'll go for the shine like a moth to light. It doesn't even occur to them that the tarnished one might be more valuable. It has a history and holds stories they can't imagine. It has a heart." She sighed. "See that wall?"

"Yes," Hope said. She was also seeing that Brie wasn't just talking about ornaments or Bentley's. She hadn't read every plaque, but she had noticed the wall that held signed photographs.

"We've had famous people, politicians

and musicians come here over the years, but we're not good enough for everyone else." She whispered the last part so as not to offend the group walking out. "Bye! Thanks for coming!" She set a polished glass in place and picked up another, smile gone. "I had a college student do a great review a few weeks ago. No difference. You'd think all the adverts and effort would have negated anything that was said when Zoe died. You'd think that word of mouth would give us some chance against the newer chains."

"Brie, hang in there. Seasons change. You know…in Kenya, there is always an annual drought. It's tough, and many of the tribal farmers suffer and struggle to feed their families. But eventually the rainy season comes. Often with its own hardships, but it comes and life is renewed. We have a saying. 'There is no rain season without mosquitoes.'"

Brie cocked her head and repeated the words.

"Oh, my gosh, I love that, Hope. I'm going to put it on a sign in the back as a reminder. I may use it on Uncle Ralph, too. Or have a T-shirt made."

"Here," Hope said, reaching into her tote and pulling out a small bag. "This is for you."

"You didn't have to get me anything."

"I wanted to. You've become a good friend, in spite of the fact that you've added a few inches to my hips, but that's okay."

Brie laughed. Hope pushed the gift toward her. "It's not much, but it made me think of you."

Brie opened the small green velvet box and pulled out an ornament hand painted with giraffes, elephants and gazelle.

"It's Africa. It's gorgeous."

"I found it in a shop with international things. When we first met, you said that someday you wanted to go on a safari in Kenya. This will be your reminder that when you do, you have a friend there and she expects you to visit."

"Of course I would." Brie came around and gave Hope a big hug. "Thank you. I'm not risking this getting swiped. It's getting hung on my tree at home."

"Are you going to your uncle's after closing?"

"I don't know. They want me to, but I told them I might wait until tomorrow morning."

Brie took a deep breath and blinked. The tip of her nose turned pink, and she sniffed but held herself together. "It's just that I had imagined spending Christmas with Coop. I don't care if he goes blind. I wouldn't care if he'd lost his limbs. I feel as if we've always known each other. As though we were meant to be. Why isn't he feeling it, too?"

"I wish I could do something to help. If you want to come over, I'm sure the Harpers wouldn't mind at all. We'll be there for dinner."

"No. No. I'll be fine. You go and make your calls. I'm closing up and going home."

"You'll be okay?"

"Yeah," Brie said with a sad smile.

Hope walked to the door and started to pull it open, but it moved too easily. She stepped back. *Yes.*

"Hope." Cooper tipped his chin in greeting.

"Cooper." Hope's heart raced for her friend. Brie stood there trying her best to look stoic, but her fair skin gave her away. Wolf, who'd been lying down near the bar, sat at attention. Cooper limped a couple of steps closer to Brie. Hope gave a quick wave goodbye and wished them merry Christmas.

She walked outside and couldn't help overhearing them before the heavy door eased to a close.

"Hey, you."

"Brie—Brie, I'm scared."

HOPE LIFTED BABY Ryan in the air and wiggled her nose against his belly for the sixth time. His giggles and hiccups made him sound like a hyena. She'd joined the kids at their grandparents' after stopping to see Brie. Ben was supposed to meet them soon.

"An adorable, lovable baby hyena," she said out loud, and tickled him again and blew raspberries against his belly. "Okay, no more or you'll be hiccupping all night."

She put Ryan in the safe confines of a play yard. It was as if he'd gone from zero to sixty since that first crawl.

Eric came and sat down with a cookie. Hope sat next to him and snatched it right out of his hand. And took a bite.

"I can't believe you stole a cookie from a grandpa," he said. He looked over at the dining table where Maddie and Chad were coloring. "Did you see that, you two? Do I have witnesses?"

Maddie looked amused, and Chad poked his cheeks in with his forefingers and made a fish mouth.

"You're not exactly an *old* grandpa. How many of these have you eaten today?" Hope asked.

"A few," Eric said in a gruff voice. "It's not my fault she won't stop making them."

"Eric, get Nina out to do something. You're doing better. Go for a short walk with her. Take her with you to swim at that indoor pool where you exercise your knee. And when spring comes, get her in the habit of cycling with you. She's distracting herself with cooking and baking. It's up to you to break the cycle. Besides, you're going to give yourself diabetes if you don't stop eating these—" Hope took another bite "—and if you put on extra weight, it's not going to help your knees."

Eric made a face. He knew she was right.

"What about you, Hope? Is that a good example you're setting?"

"It's my very last one. I have to get on

track after this. I won't need as much will-power when I'm gone."

She noticed Maddie looking over and frowning.

"What's diabetes?" Chad asked, swinging his legs under the table.

"Diabetes is when sugar makes a person very, very sick," Hope explained. "Much worse than just a tummy ache. It can hurt your vision, your feet and everything in your body." Was that too scary? Chad slowly put down the cookie he was munching on as he colored.

She lowered her voice so the kids couldn't hear.

"Eric, I'm serious. Take care of yourself, for these kids and for your wife. And take care of her, too."

"You're being harsh," he said, his brow furrowing.

"Maybe, but I don't see you going in that kitchen and dragging her off dancing or to the movies. She devoted herself to helping you after surgery. Which, by the way, I know enough to know you milked your surgery a little longer than necessary."

He grimaced and gave her a sideways look.

"Don't go telling her that."

"Is surgery a cow?" Chad asked.

Maddie rolled her eyes at her brother.

"No, Chad. It's just an expression," Eric said.

"What expression are we talking about?" Nina asked, walking in from the kitchen and flopping onto the recliner next to their sofa. Hope tried to answer. She almost said something. But God help her, Chad beat her to it.

"I saw Daddy kissing Miss Hope."

BEN HURRIED IN through the Harpers' door. He needed to get the kids and Hope home. He'd taken Cooper to consult with a low-vision specialist to see if there was anything that would help him cope on a daily basis. The clinic had been eye-opening, so to speak. There were patients wearing headgear with special lenses, special computer screens that magnified words per the need of individual patients…even telephones with extralarge numbers on them for patients who couldn't function with standard phones. If there was a way to help someone visually disabled function better, those docs were gonna find it.

Brie had shown up with Wolf while he was

waiting. She'd insisted that her uncle was working the morning so she could stay and take Coop home. Ben had had a feeling Coop would rather have her stick around.

And that meant Ben could pick up the kids and get home to answer his emails. He'd gotten a reply that he was able to read on his phone, but he didn't want to respond from it. He needed to sit down at his laptop and be focused on work, not driving around. He also didn't want to drive them home after dark, it being Christmas Eve. He wanted a quiet night at home.

Ben found Nina in the kitchen, cleaning up.

"You're back early," she said.

What was with women? First Hope saying he'd left early and now Nina wondering why he was back early?

"I'm right on time, if you ask me."

"How's your friend?" she asked, packing tins of baked goods into paper bags to deliver to the local homeless shelter.

"It'll be a long road, but I think he'll be okay, emotionally, at least. Where is everyone?" He opened the fridge and grabbed a bottle of water. There was an odd whirring sound coming through the walls.

Nina sniffed and kept packaging without looking up.

"Eric went upstairs to burn off some steam. He actually raised his voice at me. Told me to get rid of all this—" she waved at the bags of goodies "—then stormed off. Would you believe he pulled his shirts that needed ironing off that exercise bike in our room and he's actually using it? And Hope is hiding out with the kids to the back bedroom."

Eric yelling and Hope hiding? Ben didn't like the warning burn in his gut.

"What happened here, Nina?"

She pushed aside a bag and cooled her palms against the countertop. She finally looked up.

"Something Chad said about seeing you and Hope kissing."

Ben inhaled long and slow, then recapped his water bottle and set it down. No secrets around little mouths. Little kids were like parental paparazzi. Chad in particular.

"It happened," Ben said, digging his thumbs into the pads of his fingers.

Nina nodded and went to the sink.

"What do you want me to say?" Ben asked. "What do you expect from me, Nina?"

"I have no clue. I'm not sure how I feel about it. Eric obviously didn't take it well."

Ben paced a few steps.

"Zoe's never coming back," he said. A part of him needed to hear the words, too.

"I know that," Nina whispered.

"I respect you both, but whatever is happening with Hope really isn't any of your business. It was a kiss. That's all. I'm human. The bottom line is, what I do personally or otherwise with the rest of my life isn't anyone's business but mine."

Nina didn't respond. He knew he was harsh. He needed to be. Every one of them, him included, needed a figurative slap across the face to snap them out of this purgatory they were in. Not dead like Zoe, but not living freely and fully.

Ben left the kitchen and went straight for the bedroom the kids used whenever they stayed over or took naps. Zoe's old room. A song that was definitely not the whir of Eric's stationary bike carried through the door. A fairy-tale melody. He knew it was Hope singing. He recognized her voice. It washed through him like the warmth of her kisses and hot chocolate blended to perfection.

He slowed his step, listening. The door was cracked open enough that he could see through the gap along the hinge. Ryan sat in Hope's lap, his eyes fluttering closed as he gnawed at his thumb. Maddie sat on the floor next to her, leaning on one hand while stroking the bottom of Ryan's tiny socked foot with the other, and Chad was curled on his side with his favorite pillow and naptime blanket. They all circled Hope, who sat in the "big comfy chair," as Zoe used to call it. All three looked lost in her voice and in the story it told.

And then everything shifted. Everything changed. Hope hit an off-key note but recovered and kept singing, her eyes directly on Maddie. There was no mistaking the sound of harmony. First humming, then soft words sung to her little brother. Sung *with* Hope.

Everything inside Ben caught in his throat. He couldn't breathe, afraid that if he startled her, she'd stop. Afraid he'd mess up again. He moved slowly, carefully, so that he could watch from the opening of the door. He needed to see Maddie's lips move and her sweet voice coming through them. He needed that memory.

Hope saw him. Her fingers kept strumming Ryan's hair as she rocked, but her voice hitched. She looked at him and blinked. A signal to let him know it was real. Tears rolled down her cheeks. Ben covered his mouth to stop his chin from shaking. His little girl was singing.

Maddie was singing.

The song ended.

"Maddie, honey," Hope said, her voice hushed. "That was beautiful. You're brothers are the luckiest boys in the world for having a big sister like you who can sing them to sleep."

Maddie got up and stood close to Hope.

"Do you think so?" Maddie whispered.

"I know so," Hope said. Maddie wrapped her arms around Hope's neck and began to cry. Cry the way she'd needed to all those months ago. A cry that Ben had no power against. He let the tears fall for his little girl. He pushed the door open the rest of the way and got down on his knees.

"Mads?"

Hope smoothed Maddie's hair and kissed

her head. She turned her gently so she could see and hear her daddy through her sobbing.

"Maddie, can I give you a hug?" Ben reached his arms out, and Maddie ran to him.

He held her tight.

"I love you, baby. I'm here for you."

CHAPTER SIXTEEN

Dear Diary,
My head is hurting me. My words came back and I told Daddy it was all my fault that Mommy died. She wanted to make something different for dinner the day he came home. She had already bought groceries, but I said no. It had to be his favorite burger because it was our tradition and we knew it made him happy and we didn't want him to go away again. She said that traditions can change and she wanted to start a new, special one. If I had listened to her, she would still be here. He said it wasn't my fault and that he loves me. I think he was just trying to make me feel better, but part of me believes it. I want us to start a new tradition this year with Hope.

HOPE CLOSED THE door to Ryan's room at the same time Ben emerged from Chad's. They both listened outside Maddie's door. No sound was heard, so Hope went ahead and opened the door.

"She's sound asleep," Hope said a minute later.

"She wiped herself out crying."

Ben had, too, and watching him fall apart over what Maddie had confessed—realizing why she'd retreated into silence and how deep the inner turmoil she'd suffered ran—had shredded Hope to pieces. They were all spent. Drained beyond reserves, yet relieved that she'd finally opened up. No child should have to carry that kind of burden or feel that level of guilt. No child.

Hope went to turn on the closet light as Ben turned off his daughter's bedside lamp. He pulled the covers up to Maddie's shoulders and tucked her stuffed monkey next to her. They left the room, feet dragging.

"I wonder if she'll sleep better or worse tonight," Hope said, heading into the kitchen. She'd told Ben about finding Maddie next to her in Chad's room.

"I think she'll sleep soundly, out of sheer

exhaustion, if anything. Her teacher was right. I don't think she's been sleeping well. Hope, I'll never be able to repay you for what you've done for her. For all of us," Ben said. Hope angled her head at him, then began filling the electric water kettle.

"Please, don't ever mention it again," she said. "I haven't done anything. There are so many factors in something like this. Perhaps the new psychologist is working, or it just happened because it was the right time for her." She set the kettle to boil and leaned back against the counter. "I desperately need a cup of tea. Would you like one? Or decaf coffee?" She held up the instant decaf she'd found in a cabinet.

"Sure. I'll have the decaf," he said, collapsing into a chair at the table. He put his elbows on the table and hung his head in his hands.

Hope put a teabag and spoon of instant coffee into two separate mugs. The electric water boiler clicked, and she filled the mugs and carried them over.

"What if she wakes up and she's not speaking again?" Ben said, lifting his face. If Hope had seen worry lines before, there were a thousand more now. She came around his chair and ran her hands over the broad line of his shoulders, then began to gently knead away his tension. She ran her thumbs along his neck. His muscles felt like iron rods with no give or take.

"You can't know. You can't predict," she said. "Morning will come soon enough, and you can give her therapist a call and see what she says."

"I don't think the office is open tomorrow, for Christmas Day," Ben said.

Hope stopped massaging. Maddie had spoken on Christmas Eve. With the excitement over Maddie speaking, she'd forgotten what day it was.

"It's okay," she said, running her hands down his thick upper arms. "Tomorrow she'll have fun opening presents. And then soon it'll be a new year. Remind her of that. A fresh start. It can be a new beginning for her. For all of you," she said, patting his shoulder and then sitting next to him and taking a sip of tea.

"Ben, I know it's none of my business, but did you talk to someone after Zoe died?"

Ben stared at the wisps of steam swirling from his mug. Maybe it wasn't her business, but she wanted to know. They were more than just friends, and if she was supposed to trust what was happening, she had to know how much healing he'd done.

"I did," he said. "For a short time. Then I stopped because I needed to focus on caring for the kids, and some of Maddie's sessions involved all of us anyway. Plus, I knew the steps of mourning. I'd read about them in college. I'd seen a campus counselor a few times back when my mom passed away. A single mom who'd dedicated her life to providing for me. And here I am now, her son, a single dad."

He shrugged. "I didn't want to talk about Zoe's death anymore. I got so tired of everyone trying to tell me it wasn't my fault when it was so obvious to me that it was. It had to be. I'd spent over a decade surrounded by death on a daily basis. Watching its horrible face. Knowing it could take me any second. And right when I come home…

"She was the one who was supposed to be here doing what she'd always done. I was the one who should have died. I was the high risk. I was ready for it. I should have been the one to go pick up dinner. But Zoe was right.

I was out of my element being alone with the kids…with a newborn. She insisted that I stay because of that. Just like you insisted I go to get a tree alone with them." He grimaced. "Man, I sound like Maddie, blaming myself, don't I? But in my case it's true. I let my guard down. I was tired and let it down, and I let her have the last word. I ignored the voice in my head that told me she was tired, too, that I should go. And that was all it took." He closed his eyes and held his head.

Hope scooted closer to him. She put her hand on his back and rubbed small circles.

"You *can't* blame yourself. Everyone who told you that is right. You can't live by what-ifs. That accident was a heartbreaking tragedy. I saw how it devastated Jack. I only knew of Zoe through him and Anna, and even so it tore me up. I know it had to have been a million times worse for you and the children. I *see* that it was. But you're the one who's living. You're the one who's here for them now. At this point, all you can do is honor her, cherish her memory and care for her children the way she would have wanted."

He looked up at her.

"I know I'm not the perfect father, but I *will* do whatever it takes to provide for them."

Hope reached out and took his hand, her soft fingers laced through his callused ones. That was what she was afraid of. He'd forget that what they really wanted was him.

She went over to the tree and brought him the gift she'd had made.

"You should open this now, Ben."

He took the small box and ripped the wrapping. Inside was a pewter ornament that framed a collage of his family. One picture of him and Zoe together, then the faces of all three kids branching out. She'd managed to make him a family photo. Something he'd thought was impossible, since Zoe had died before they could have one made with Ryan in it.

He closed his eyes briefly, overcome by her thoughtfulness.

"Thank you, Hope. This is the nicest gift I've ever received."

He got up, wrapped his arms around her and kissed the top of her head. Then he went and hung the ornament on "Zoe's tree." Hope had given him his family back. And he couldn't help but feel she was now a part of it.

THE NEXT FEW DAYS were spent mostly at home, enjoying all the games and toys they'd unwrapped under the tree and playing in the backyard. Just normal family stuff, and it felt good.

Ben couldn't believe New Year's was already here. A series of blasts and pops ambushed the air. Ben jerked his head up, then visibly relaxed. He ran his hand back across his head.

"Midnight fireworks," he said.

Hope got up and went to the front window. Sure enough, the sky beyond his neighbor's house lit up. The fireworks were a bit distant from the direction of the university, but it was the perfect vantage point.

"Come on," she said. "I'm stepping outside for a minute." She grabbed the afghan off the chair and slipped on her shoes.

It was freezing cold outside, and magical and brilliant. She sat on the front step, and Ben joined her, sitting one step above and behind her.

He wrapped a wool scarf around her neck and cradled her from behind. His warmth and scent caressed her back. Several more fireworks lit the sky. He jolted at the bigger explosions.

She turned suddenly. "Ben, I'm sorry," she said, turning her face up to him. "Let's go inside if this bothers you. I wasn't thinking about your past."

"It does bother me…a little…but I don't want to go inside. You being here helps."

Hope's pulse raced. Their breath swirled in a fog of want and need. Of honor and gratitude. Of understanding and acceptance. He ran his fingers along her cheeks, then held her face as if he'd discovered something too precious to release. She reached up and held his wrists. "Happy New Year, Hope Alwanga."

"Happy New Year, Ben."

He kissed her tenderly, and she kissed him back until the sky covered them in dark silence. She shivered and put her fingertips to her lips.

Maybe she didn't have to return to Kenya.

Maybe her destiny was here.

BEN WOKE UP earlier than usual. The anticipation of hearing Maddie say good-morning had kept him from a deep sleep. That and sleeping in an only half-reclined position. He'd forgo sleep for the rest of his life if it was the trade-off for Mads staying okay and getting to wake up every morning with Hope's face nestled in his shoulder.

They'd come inside last night—or really, early morning of the New Year—and he'd thrown a couple of logs in the fireplace to warm her up. Then they'd sat there, staring at the flame in comfortable silence until they had both fell asleep.

He sat now at the breakfast table scanning emails. Hope stirred on the sofa. She stretched her legs from the fetal position she'd curled into when he left her, and rubbed the side of her neck. She wasn't quite awake yet.

He looked back at his email list and found what he was looking for. He clicked on it. *Finally*. He read through it. He had interviews at two more major military contract companies in DC.

Hope opened her eyes and yawned, rubbing her neck again.

Ben closed his laptop.

"Sleep okay?" he asked.

Hope craned her neck to see over the

counter to the table. He had the height advantage.

"Good morning," she said. "Tell me you brewed coffee."

"It's waiting for you."

She stood and padded across the room.

"I'll be right back," she said.

Ben got up, poured out the black ink that had formed at the bottom of the pot he'd brewed a few hours ago and started a fresh pot.

As soon as the kids woke up and ate, they'd all head back to Grandma and Grandpa's house—assuming that Maddie was okay when she arose.

He put his laptop back in its drawer and grabbed the sheet of paper and jotted down reminders of what he wanted to bring up at the next therapy visit. If he ended up getting the job in DC, he'd want to talk to his kids about it during a counseling session. Not only did he not want to upset Maddie and have her retreat again, he'd want advice on what would be best: leaving the kids in the environment they grew up in, with Nina and Eric...or uprooting them completely. Now that Maddie was recovering, the latter option might be a possibility. He folded the paper and stuffed it into his pocket.

What about Hope? She'd become such an integral part of their lives. A part of their family. But she was leaving. They both knew it. She had a life and a career. He couldn't take that away from her. He *had* learned that lesson. He'd let Zoe sacrifice her dreams for him. He wasn't going to let Hope do that, too. And she was younger than him. She had so much to offer. So many ways she could make a difference in the world.

Hope reentered the kitchen.

He handed her a mug of coffee.

"Bless you." She sighed. "I'll stop seeing two of you once I drink this."

"Two of me, huh? Must be nice. Here, give me that mug back before you're only left with one of me."

"Ha, no, you don't." She laughed, holding her cup away from him. "I can barely handle *one*."

"Good morning."

Ben and Hope both spun around.

Oh, that sweet, sweet voice. Maddie stood at the door to the hallway. Her tangled hair was sprawled against a backdrop of flannel snowmen.

"Morning, Mads," Ben said. "How'd you sleep?"

"Good."

"Are you hungry?" Hope asked.

Maddie nodded. She still looked as though she needed a second to wake up. She rubbed her eyes.

Ben went over and put his hand on her back and guided her to a chair.

"Which cereal do you want?"

"All mixed up," she said.

"I like that idea," Hope said. "The breakfast of a creative genius."

Maddie's mouth spread into a smile, and she waggled her eyebrows.

Hope and Ben burst out laughing.

JANUARY HAD FLOWN BY. Hope wiped Ryan's face with a wet paper towel and coaxed him to take another bite of jarred chicken in between the cubes of sweet potato he was managing on his own. He pushed his tongue against his lips, and beige sludge oozed out of his mouth.

"I don't blame you," Hope said.

She wiped him up again and gave up on the jar. He wasn't feeding himself the diced cooked carrots on his tray, either, although he was having fun throwing them on the floor. She peeled one strip back on a banana, got a new spoon and scraped the edge along the fruit. Instant mash filled the spoon and disappeared readily into his mouth.

Maddie was at school, and Ben had taken Chad to his very first half day of preschool. The mere idea of going to school like his big sister had him acting at least a few months older and 25 percent calmer. He was a smart kid, and preschool gave his brain an outlet, as well as taught him to deal with schedules and rules. Preschool was going to do wonders for him.

She pretended to pop a carrot cube in her mouth and made yummy noises. Then tried it again on Ryan. Not happening. He'd developed a sweet tooth, albeit for mashed fruit, before getting used to cereals and vegetables.

"Little man, I feel your addiction. I do. But I swear if you eat one spoon from your jar I'll kiss your slobbery cheek and play crawl races with you." Medical training did not a parent make. Nothing beat experience when it came to things like raising babies. She couldn't help but feel as though Ryan was her first baby.

She sat back and let him play with the mess on his tray. A few months ago, if anyone had told her to consider pediatrics, she'd have laughed. In her life, she'd been the child patient and the family baby. And then as an adult, she'd seen other children suffer and hated it. But she had never considered that she could speak up and tell her parents that joining their practice was not what she wanted. That if they cared about her happiness, they'd understand and let her pursue her own path with their blessings.

And, boy, did she now understand, firsthand, that a parent wants nothing more than happiness and health for their child. She wasn't Maddie, Chad and Ryan's mother— no one would ever take Zoe's place as the woman who had given them life—but she felt as if she was in her heart. She wished she could figure out how to be in two halves of the world at once.

Because falling in love with Ben's children and watching Maddie suffer and heal made her realize she wanted, needed, to help as many children as possible. Telling herself that there were too many needy children—like that Masai child who'd died from lack of care—for one person like herself to make a difference was nothing but cowardice. She'd wanted to believe that she couldn't help. That it would be a futile effort. Convincing herself of that meant that she wouldn't have to face her parents and tell them she wanted to change the life they'd laid out for her. It would have meant facing times when she didn't succeed and having to experience the pain of witnessing child suffering or death. Pure cowardice. And she saw that now. Both Maddie and Ben had made her see the power of courage.

But she also knew that making a difference meant returning home. She had to figure out a way to make sure medical care got to all. Children too rural and distant from hospitals. Children like Chuki's sister who needed regular care but who couldn't afford what was available even close to home.

Home.

How could such a simple word become so loaded? Home had become two places. Two impossible places.

She let Ryan wrap his chubby fingers around hers, and she kissed his hand. She didn't care that it was sticky with the banana from reaching into his mouth to chew on a finger while he ate. She would have kissed it with jarred chicken. Ryan made a face, as if he could hear her thoughts.

"Okay, maybe not with chicken, but I do love you that much," she said. "I'm going to miss you all."

CHAPTER SEVENTEEN

Dear Diary,
I heard Grandma and Grandpa fighting over Miss Hope. If she heard them, too, and goes away, I'll never speak to them again. Instead, I'll say all those words Daddy says that I'm not supposed to say.

HOPE SAT WITH Ben in his car in the Harpers' driveway. Dawn was just breaking, and the ash and oak trees that towered over Nina and Eric's house were silhouetted against streaks of pink and purple. February snow had been plowed into muddy piles along the roads, melting into slush and then refreezing nightly. The Harpers had been spending more and more time with them. They had even shown up at Ben's on Valentine's Day, no doubt to strip the romance out of it.

Ben had an early flight to catch to DC and

looked sharp in his suit and trench coat. He had three days' worth of interviews scheduled and wouldn't be here when she left tomorrow. She'd be staying at the Harpers', so that when she left, the kids could remain until Ben's return. She worried about how Maddie would take it.

"Is this it?" she said. "Just like that? As if nothing has happened between us?"

Ben sat staring straight ahead.

"Hope," he finally said. "There's absolutely no denying that this…thing between us is powerful, but you can't let it cloud your judgment, and neither can I. I can't in good conscience stop you from pursuing your career. We have responsibilities. My family is here. I could be moving with or without them because I need to earn a living, but at least I'll be in the same hemisphere. And your job isn't the kind a person can walk away from. It's too important, Hope. And what you told me about going back and helping kids…" He shook his head. "You need to do that. I've been enough places to have seen the kind of desperation and lack of care you're talking about. Knowing that you're going to be over there, dedicating your life to providing that care, makes me think you're even more incredible and amazing than I already knew."

Hope closed her eyes.

"Thank you for thinking that," she whispered, putting her hand over his.

After a moment, she put her hand back into her lap and looked across the front yard at the snowman she'd built days ago with the kids after they had coaxed her into watching a cartoon movie about Frosty. Frosty looked right at her, and she could almost hear him warning her that seasons change. Moments pass. And what we let ourselves believe is real can melt away so very easily.

"What if I was willing to walk away from Kenya and medicine and all of it? Wouldn't it be my decision?"

"Hope, I can't answer that," he said, rubbing his eyes. "I can't be responsible for that. For you having regrets ten or twenty or thirty years down the road. I can't do that to you. It wouldn't be fair. I did that to Zoe, and I can't feel that kind of guilt again. I don't want you to ever look back and think you'd made a wrong decision."

BEN DIDN'T WANT to hurt her. But whatever pain she felt now would eventually pass. Distance would help her forget. How could she know he was worth losing everything for? She'd spent her entire adult life working toward becoming a doctor. Even if it turned out that she had another calling, it wasn't his place to change her path. She couldn't go after what she was meant to do if he stood in the way or she became the instant mother of three. He knew more than anyone how sudden, unexpected parenthood could send your life in another direction.

Hope licked her lips and looked outside.

"Ask me to stay, Ben."

"I can't."

She looked the other way and covered her mouth. Her chin trembled, and he wanted to hold her and tell her it would all work out. But he couldn't lie.

"Then, we're done," she said. "Whatever was going on here wasn't meant to be. If you can't bring yourself to ask me to stay or at least tell me that you wish I could, then at least tell me you won't move away from the children. Please promise me that."

"You don't understand. I can't promise that, either."

HOPE WENT TO say her goodbyes to Brie right after Ben left. She and Brie cried so much, Cooper had to leave the room.

But they were going to stay in touch, and Brie promised to bring Wolf to see the kids again, and any future puppies, too, once Wolf moved on to the next stage of his training.

Hope wanted to see Wolf pass his tests and move on, but another part hated to see him separated from Cooper. At least seeing how much Cooper and Brie meant to each other saved a drop of her belief that good things happen.

That night, Hope didn't mean to eavesdrop, but when it happened, she couldn't tear herself away. The thin walls of Nina and Eric's home were hopeless as a sound barrier, and the vent overhead funneled voices and made them even clearer. Lying on her bed, she hugged her knees to her chest and listened, tears filling her eyes.

"Eric, I'm telling you she's meant to be a part of his life," Nina was saying. "The kids' lives. She's brought joy back into that home. I didn't want to accept it at first, either, but I see it now."

"What would Zoe think?" Eric's voice now.

"Our daughter, Nina. What would she think if she knew Ben wanted to share his life with someone else? I'm sorry, but I can't accept that. What kind of father would I be to let that happen? Zoe trusted me, trusted us to look out for her. She was so giving. She did so much to keep her family together when he was gone. She doesn't deserve this kind of betrayal."

"But she's gone!" Nina's cry exploded in Hope's chest, and a sob escaped. Hope pressed her hand against her mouth and closed her eyes.

"Our girl is the one who is gone now, Eric. Only she's not coming back. We have to accept that. I know my daughter. She would have wanted us to look out for her family... for our grandchildren. If there was ever a loving, giving, unselfish soul on this planet, it was our Zoe, and she wouldn't have wanted Ben to live out his life alone. She would have wanted him to find someone who'd love him and her children the way she did. She wanted so badly for him to come home to stay. To be with his children. Safe. Hope granted her that wish. I could see the signs, Eric. I think somehow Zoe brought them together. Like an angel."

"Dear God. Now you've really lost your mind."

"How can you say that? Don't you believe in fate?" Nina asked.

"Fate? You mean the fate that killed my daughter?"

A haunting silence followed. Hope covered her face with both hands, dropping them to her waist when Eric spoke again.

"I have nothing against Hope. I agree that she's a special person, and I really like her, but that doesn't mean she's supposed to take Zoe's place. She'll hurt him. She's a career woman. She has a life on the other side of this planet. And if she gets any closer to him or the kids than she already has, she'll break their hearts. The kids are already going to suffer when she leaves. If she and Ben tried to do some sort of long-distance relationship, eventually they'd see it won't work, and the kids would get hurt all over again."

There was a pause, then Hope heard Eric continue, "Ben's still mourning my daughter. At least he'd better be. He couldn't possibly know what he wants. He's clinging to the first woman he can trust with those kids, just so that he can return to his career."

Hope pushed her hair back and felt a wave of tears and a sob rising in her chest. That was what her parents would have said, too. That he was disrespecting her by having her go from highly educated to an instant mother for his convenience. She refused to believe that about Ben. He'd said he didn't want that. But had it been an excuse? Maybe in the end he wasn't ready to move on. Not with her, at least. Maybe the three months of her help had felt good to them both, but in the end, he'd wanted out and gave the best, most honorable reason he could for his escape. He'd needed a way out and had let her down as easily as he could.

"You stubborn man!" Nina responded. "Think about Ben. After all he has risked to support his family. After all he has sacrificed for his country. Did he deserve to lose his wife? Is he supposed to suffer, alone, for the rest of his life? He's only thirty-one. You're sixty-one. Could you imagine not having had me around to share your days with for the past thirty years?"

At last the house fell silent again, and Hope

sank farther into her bed and curled into a
fetal position. Fatigue consumed her. Disappointment drained her. She was so naive. *Stupid girl*. She pressed the heels of her palms
against her eyes and held her breath to slow
her breathing, but it didn't work. Her lungs
heaved. Her head spun. And the scar that had
sealed the hole she'd once had in her heart felt
as though it'd come undone. Ben had never
really wanted her. Not badly enough.

A TAXI HAD BEEN called in the morning, and
the Harpers and Corallises stood near the
door, looking as though the world was coming to an end.

Hope cradled Ryan and inhaled his scent.
She kissed him, letting her lips linger against
his temple, and put him back in Nina's arms.
You'll always be my baby.

Then she knelt down and rubbed Chad's
arms.

"You're the handsomest four-year-old
young man I know. And you, just like your
daddy, are going to have a lot of fun with
your little brother, but always remember that
you're his protector. Okay? Take care of him
for me."

"Okay."

"Give me a hug," she said, then held him tight and kissed his cheek. "I miss you already," she said.

"I miss you already, too," Chad said.

Then Hope turned to Maddie, who stood quietly by the steps.

"I'm going to miss you so much, Maddie. I want you to promise me that if you need someone to talk to, you'll call me. Call your uncle Jack, if that's easier. He'll find me for you. Or have your daddy show you how to email me. Just promise me," she said, taking Maddie's hands in hers, "that you'll stay in touch. It would mean the universe to me."

Fresh tears welled up in Maddie's eyes. She nodded, and Hope's stomach sank, thinking Ben's being gone and her leaving had caused Maddie to retreat again into silence.

But then Maddie squeezed her hands and said, "Okay. I promise."

Hope slipped the last bangle off her wrist and put it on Maddie's.

"Try to remember this. 'When you wear one, good things come your way. When you wear two, happy memories will stay. And the magic of three is, it sets your heart free.' Always remember that I love you," Hope said.

Maddie flung her arms around her and cried, "But you're supposed to stay. I know you are. You belong with us. I don't care what Grandma and Grandpa said!"

Hope glanced up at Nina and Eric and, despite the hurtful things she'd overheard—and apparently Maddie had, too—their looks of embarrassment made her feel awful for them. She focused on Maddie.

"My sweet Maddie, I want to stay with you, but I can't—there are things I have to do in Kenya. But I promise we'll see each other again someday. You could come and visit your uncle Jack, auntie Anna and Pippa and all the crazy animals they have. And you can take a zillion pictures when you're there. You'd like that, wouldn't you?"

Maddie nodded, her cheeks damp with tears. "I love you," she said.

"I love you, too." Hope fought hard not to fall apart in front of her. "Do me a favor, okay? Take care of your brothers and your dad and grandparents. And if anyone needs something, you let me know."

"I will." Maddie sniffed, then wiped her

nose on her sleeve. Hope gave her another hug, then went to her grandparents.

"Nina, Eric—"

"Hope, I'm sorry that—"

"Eric, please don't apologize. It was meant to be a private conversation." She looked from him to Nina and back again. "Know that I will cherish every moment I spent with you two. I can see why Jack loves you so much. Leaving would be so much harder if I didn't know Maddie, Chad and Ryan have such wonderful grandparents to make sure they're okay. And, please…please, take care of Ben, too."

Eric gave her a hug, and then Nina wrapped her in her arms. "Please come back and visit us. We're going to miss you," Nina said.

"Me, too. Do me a favor, Nina. I left a bag of the winter clothes, the jacket and such, in the bedroom. Please donate them to a shelter for me."

"I will." Nina hugged her again. Hope waved to the children and hurried out to the taxi before she lost all control. She got in and shut the door on the life, the family, that felt like her own, just as her tears began to flow.

Life hurt. Love hurt. That was what her

parents had been protecting her from all along. Why her life had been laid out for her, why their walls of protection had no doors, why they worried. There were never guarantees, only better choices to make and cleaner paths to take.

She fished in her tote for a packet of tissues and saw a bright pink envelope she knew wasn't her ticket. She opened it and gasped.

Photographs that Maddie had taken. Mostly from the day they went to the tree farm and a few candids from around the house. Ryan rocking on all fours while staring at their Christmas tree. Chad— She looked closer. The little devil caught red-handed. Chad peeling the end of a present to peek inside. Ben— She felt a lump rise in her throat. Ben sitting in a chair with Ryan and Chad on his lap and reading to them. She and Ben standing close, facing each other as they held their morning mugs of coffee, talking about something she couldn't remember. But in the photo, nothing seemed to matter but each other. It didn't look as though any of the subjects knew their pictures were being taken. Hope flipped through again. There were none of

Maddie. Just as there'd been so few of Zoe on their shelves in the living room.

Maddie had been the one behind the camera. She'd inherited a gift from her mother. An ability to capture the moment, the emotion and life, before it disappeared again. Maddie already understood an important lesson Hope wished she hadn't had to learn so young.

Nothing lasted forever.

It was time to go home.

CHAPTER EIGHTEEN

Dear Hope,
I raised my hand in school today and answered a question in science. It was about metamorphosis and Ms. Serval told the class that I was the only one who got it right. It felt good. And Sara sat next to me at lunch and was being really nice. She invited me to play at her house. She has a puppy, two cats and a chameleon. I'm definitely going. Chad tried to kiss a girl in preschool and then he asked her to marry him. He's such a dork! I have my big-sister work cut out for me. Especially since Ryan walked for the first time today. I took a lot of pictures but I didn't download them yet. I know you just left yesterday, but I miss you. I'll send pictures next time.
Love,
Maddie

HOPE SHIELDED HER eyes from the brilliant Kenyan sun and searched for her ride. She covered her mouth and coughed when an old Fiat swerved from the lane near her and sent a puff of exhaust fumes into her face. The sounds of Kiswahili, Kikuyu, Luo and even English blended together with many more in a chaotic rhythm she would have taken for granted only a few months ago.

From the grating sounds of traffic to the barefoot drummer on the side of the road, and from the swish of an expatriate's skirt to the tribal beads clicking against the chest of the woman they adorned, all the sights and sounds filled her. All of it bound and lifted her senses and the air around her. This was all a part of her. This was her life.

She turned toward the double honk to her left. Jamal pulled up in his large black sedan and jumped out to get the pile of luggage she guarded.

"*Jambo*, Hope. It is so good to see you again. Dalila can't wait."

"*Jambo*, Jamal. It's wonderful to be home."

Hope took two carry-ons and climbed into the backseat. She leaned back, closed her eyes and sighed. She was here now. She needed to accept that there wasn't anything else out there in the world. Nothing else in store for her. She'd had her getaway, her break, her time to decompress. That was all it was supposed to have been. Only now, a part of her felt worse than when she'd first left Kenya.

"Jamal, can we stop at Chuki's? Or are Mama and Baba already home?"

"We have time," he said, switching lanes.

Hope let the vibrations of the car soothe her stiff muscles. The flight had been awful. Crowded and turbulent and suffocating. They passed the hotel where Anna and Jack stayed during supply trips into Nairobi. She couldn't wait to see them. She'd see Jack sooner because of the lab. She couldn't wait to fill him in on how wonderful his parents were and how they were doing. And on Chad and Ryan's antics. Especially on Maddie's recovery.

She'd definitely have to be selective in what she said about Ben. How impossible it had been not to fall for him. How impossible it was to keep him from her mind. She'd leave those details out.

What she felt for Ben would be her secret. Her regret.

Her chin quivered like Maddie's had when she'd said goodbye. Hope scratched her chin, so that if Jamal saw her through the rearview mirror, he would think it was merely an itch.

They passed a small grassy park where a man was showing off a caged monkey to a group of tourists. Anna would have a fit if she were here. Maddie, too. Funny how alike the two were.

Jamal finally turned down the street that had become sort of an art district for locals. Very few tourists knew about it. Chuki's family lived at the first corner, on the upper level of the small café they owned. Nothing fancy. Old blue metal chairs, tile floors and chipped paint. But the place had character. It reminded her of how Brie felt about her family pub.

"I'll be right back."

Hope jumped out of the car and ran in. Chuki's twelve-year-old sister, Ita, saw her and came running.

"Hope! I didn't know you were back."

"I just arrived and came straight here. See how important you are? Tell me, are you still okay with your medicine or are you running out?"

"I'm okay for now. Your brother came to check on me at least five times."

Five times? Simba? He'd promised to help out, but Ita didn't usually need refills that often in three months, even when Hope was around.

"Did he take you to see a doctor?"

"He said he'd try to set something up, but it's not for a few weeks. I think he just kept coming to irritate Chuki. They argue a lot, and when he leaves, she tells me he's irritating and full of himself. What's that mean?"

"It means he's lion headed," Hope said, laughing. It sounded like Simba.

"Chuki told me you were going to come back Americanized. Are you?"

Hope closed her eyes briefly. "Chuki has a wild imagination. I'm the same Hope you last saw." *Only heartbroken, and this time no surgery in the world can fix me.*

"Hope? Eek!" Chuki screamed loud enough to announce her arrival to the whole street. Hope embraced her friend. "I want to hear everything. How did it go? What was it like? Did you meet any Hollywood stars? Did you fall in love?" Chuki fluttered her eyes and fanned her face.

"It was beautiful, especially the seasons, and the people were wonderful. And no, no movie stars or falling in love," she lied. It was good to see her again. "Come sit. Ita, go bring her a Stoney."

Oh, she'd missed her favorite soda, Stoney Tangawizi. Ginger perfection. An American company made it, yet she couldn't find it there. She sat across from Chuki.

"Ita said that Simba came by a few times?"

"He did," Chuki said, her cheeks flushing. Very interesting.

"It was good of him," Chuki went on. "And now, of course, he won't have to because you're back." She smiled. "I'm so glad you're here." She wiped the mouth of the bottle Ita brought with a clean paper napkin and passed it to Hope.

Hope stayed at Chuki's long enough to finish her drink and satisfy her friend with general details of her trip. Then she gave Chuki a kiss on both cheeks and headed to the car.

What could be more grounding than seeing her friend again, checking on Ita, sitting in a café that had Nairobi in everything about it, down to the mismatched clay pots decorating the counter near the register? Yet it was as though she was still floating over the ocean, lost. Everything felt different.

"Home?" Jamal asked, looking at her in the rearview mirror. That loaded word. She wasn't sure what defined it anymore.

"Yes. Home."

BEN SET HIS carry-on by the door and took a minute to just listen. He'd called Nina, and she'd told him that she'd bring the kids over and get them ready for bed to save him the trouble of picking them up at their place. He could hear rustling through the monitor, but no babbles. He met her coming out of the hallway.

"Welcome home," Nina said.

"Thanks for watching the kids." He went into the kitchen to grab a glass of water.

"How did it go?" Nina asked, picking up her purse and keys.

He took a swig. "It went well. Very well."

Nina sat down at the table. Her face fell, but he knew she wasn't wishing that he'd blown the interviews. Like him, she was just wishing the decision didn't have to involve a sacrifice.

"What are you going to do?" she asked. "I

don't know if I can handle not seeing these kids as much as I do if you decide to take them with you. I'd miss them so much."

The way he missed Hope. It was unbearable. Their last conversation, just before he'd left for DC, had left him lost. Mentally and emotionally lost. He'd used every ounce of his marine discipline and focus to get him through those interviews because he couldn't get her out of his head. One company had had him scheduled for a mandatory lie detector test on the same day he'd arrived, since he was from out of town, and they wouldn't even consider talking to him if he failed.

He'd passed.

Only because they hadn't asked him about Hope.

If he'd been hooked up to the detector when she'd begged him to ask her to stay, when she'd made her feelings so clear and he'd acted like a brick wall, and if they'd asked him questions like, "Do you love Hope Alwanga? Do you want to spend the rest of your life with her?" he would have failed had he said no.

"I know, Nina. Trust me, I've thought about that. I know how much a part of their lives you've been and how much you've been there for me. But the past three days just about killed me. I don't know what's happened to me. I used to spend the majority of a year away from them, and all I could think about in my hotel room at night was how did I do it? I tried to remember what I'd done to harden myself and I couldn't. So trust me, I get it. But I don't know if I can be away from them, either."

A six-figure job in DC, practically in the palm of his hand. His if he wanted it. All he had to do was accept and they'd start the ball rolling. Their words.

And then there was Hope's last request. The same request Zoe had once made. Both of them had asked him not to leave the kids. To put them first.

"I'm going to go look in on them," he said.

"I should get back to Eric anyway." Nina put her hand on his arm. "I used to reassure Zoe—every time she had to make a big decision on her own because you were overseas—that she'd be okay. To just listen to her heart, and everything would make more sense."

Ben locked the door behind Nina when

she left. He knew how to listen to his gut. Wasn't listening to your heart the same thing? Mostly? All "making sense" meant was that you'd finally figured out the answers. The problem was, this time, there weren't any.

RYAN AND CHAD were sound asleep.

Ben walked by Maddie's room and could hear her talking, her words too soft to make out clearly. The door was ajar, and he peeked inside. She was holding a photograph of Zoe. She was talking to her mom—out loud.

Hearing her voice still felt like a privilege he could lose so easily. What if she wasn't okay and those therapy sessions weren't keeping her emotionally strong? He entered the room and sat on the edge of her bed. He took the framed picture of Zoe from Maddie and set it back on her nightstand.

"What were you thanking Mommy for?"

Maddie turned to her side and made herself comfortable against her pillow, but tilted her face toward him.

"For listening. I asked her to help you be okay and to keep us together as a family. And she answered."

Ben swallowed hard. He cleared his throat, but his voice still cracked.

"She answered? How?"

"She gave us Hope. Even if Hope didn't get to stay forever. You're here."

Dear God. The day Hope had given her the first bracelet. No wonder she'd been so attached to it at school. It'd been a sign, in its way, that her mom was still there, listening to her when he didn't even know what to listen for. And now she had three hanging on a hook over her bed.

She caught him looking at them.

"I know what she told me the bracelets mean, but I just think of them as me, Mommy and Hope."

Ben pulled the covers up for her and kissed the top of her head.

He wasn't the only one missing Hope.

HOPE HAD BEEN BACK for three weeks now, and drowning herself in her old routine had failed to make anything feel right. Nothing here was normal anymore.

She'd spent all of yesterday through today seeing patients in the emergency room, and was already wiped out. Any rest she'd gotten had been negated. She flopped onto a stool in Simba's lab and waited for him to nag about her sandals. To her surprise, he pulled up a stool and sat.

"What happened over there, Hope? What's going on with you?"

"Like what? I'm doing everything I ever did before."

"Exactly. You're miserable. That wasn't the point of your trip away."

"Oh? Perhaps you wanted to get rid of me so that you'd have an excuse to go visiting Chuki." She bit her lips to hide a smile.

Simba shook his head as if she was going to make him lose it.

"I don't know what you're talking about. I kept an eye on her just as I promised. Actually, I think she hates me."

"Ah, yes. My brother has finally run into a woman who doesn't melt at his feet." This had potential.

"Stop changing the subject and talk to me. I'm your brother. All I wanted was to give you a chance to grow up. I don't mean academically or chronologically. I mean, you know… Let you reach your genetic potential."

Wow. So emotional, Simba. No wonder you irritated Chuki.

"Didn't you learn anything in getting away from here?"

Like how painful it is to find love and lose it?

"Yes." She grabbed a tissue from her pocket and wiped her nose. "I figured out what I *don't* want. I don't want to die like this. I don't want to walk out that door to go home and get hit by some random car and die, leaving nothing that was truly me behind to be remembered by."

He didn't speak. He probably knew what was coming from.

Hope dried her eyes. "I love you, Simba. I know I promised Mama and Baba, but the thought of joining their practice makes me want to *throw* myself in front of a car."

Simba scratched his forehead and chuckled. "Well, it's about time, Hope."

Jack walked into the lab with a bounce in his step and went for a box of sterile gloves.

"Hi, Hope, Simba."

"Did you hurt your foot or something?" Simba asked, teasing. "You're walking funny."

"No. I just have news. Anna's pregnant."

Hope gasped and stood up to hug him.

"Oh, I'm so happy for you!" she said.

"Congratulations, man," Simba added.

The phone rang, and Jack ripped off a glove to answer it.

"Maddie, my girl! How's my favorite niece?"

Hope rubbed her hands against her hips and stood waiting, anxious to hear Maddie's voice. She'd gotten her letter shortly after she'd returned to Kenya. It was handwritten because Maddie had said she was getting extra credit at school for writing a letter to a pen pal in another country. But nothing could come close to talking to her.

"No kidding," Jack continued. "Cool. Okay. Great. Is Grandma or Grandpa there? Let me say hello. Take care, Maddie." Jack finished listening to Nina, then hung up.

"Wait. Didn't Maddie ask to talk to me? Didn't you see me waiting?" Hope asked.

Jack shrugged.

"She didn't say so, and I got distracted. Sorry, Hope. Next time."

Hope's insides sank into her sneakers.

Jack waved a finger at her brother.

"David, I forgot about something I was supposed to tell you. It's about a shipment we're getting. You hanging out here, Hope? We could all grab lunch later."

"No. I'm going home," Hope said. "I'm done."

DINNER LAST NIGHT had been pivotal. Her parents had been talking nonstop about their latest patient. Some potential Olympian. And about the new timeline for Hope's degree now that she was back. It wasn't until Hope had raised her voice and demanded they be quiet that they'd stopped and listened to her. She'd changed, she told them. She'd always be their little girl, but she was also an adult who was accomplished and had ideas and had the right to make herself happy.

She'd taken them by surprise, but instead of coming down hard on her, they'd listened. She'd spoken, and they'd listened, and no one had expressed disappointment in her. They all still loved her.

And now, the next day, for all her so-called freedom, Hope stood in her family's lush courtyard next to a fig tree, bracing herself for one of her parents' boring, professional dinners and feeling utterly empty.

She thought about leaving and escaping to Chuki's, but Simba told her that Zamir was coming to this dinner, too. She was prepared to tell him, once and for all, to just back off in terms of his personal interest, but really he wasn't a bad guy. He was stable. They shared careers, and he respected her.

She grabbed a fig leaf and crushed it in her hand, not caring if the milky sap from the stem irritated her skin. There she was, trying to fit herself into a round hole again. Who said she needed anyone? Who cared if her parents assumed she'd marry someday? She didn't have to.

She was going to devote herself to studying pediatrics, as well as public health. She wanted to found an organization dedicated to raising global awareness of the basic medical needs for underprivileged families, particularly children, and to raise funds to support getting supplies and care out to those, even in remote areas, who wouldn't otherwise have it. Not just mobile clinics, but more permanent setups.

She didn't have all the details figured out

yet, but the ideas kept coming. They made her feel fired up. Energized. Both Ben and Simba had been right. If she discovered what she was passionate about, she'd never tire of doing it.

Like a parent who never tires of their children, no matter how demanding or exhausting they can be.

She looked at her watch. The guests would be arriving any second now.

"That poor tree looks like it could use some medical care."

She froze, only moving her fingers to release the leaf she'd crushed into the pile she'd formed at her feet.

Only one man had that voice. Only one voice had the power to awaken every cell, every atom, in her body. She didn't dare turn around. What if her ears were playing tricks on her? It couldn't be him.

"The tree will survive. It has strong roots," she said, still facing away and biting her lip till it hurt.

"What if it had its roots dug up and got transplanted?" This time she could feel his breath on the back of her neck. It brushed her ear. "What would its chances of survival be?"

She closed her eyes. Dare she hope?

"All it would need," she said, "is some nurturing and love. If it has what it needs, it'll grow." She almost choked on her last words. Unwilling to believe he was really here.

She felt warm hands on her shoulders, and she gasped. He turned her around and she gazed at him. It was really him. Here. In Kenya. Looking at her. Touching her.

"Ben?" Her chest heaved. She put her hands on his chest, spreading her trembling fingers, needing to be sure he was real. "What are you doing here? This…this is Africa."

He scratched his head, and the corner of his mouth quirked the way it always did when he smiled. "Africa? Really? I wonder how I got here without knowing that?"

A small laugh escaped her, and she put her head against his chest. She wanted to wrap her arms around him and kiss him. But she knew her family was watching. And just because he was here didn't mean that he was staying. Maybe he'd taken a trip to see Jack. Maybe he had brought the kids to see their cousins.

"You cut your hair," he said.

She reached up self-consciously and touched her tightly cropped hair. It had been part of the new her. Symbolic of discovering her true self. No chemicals. No dyes. Just the real her.

"Yes, I did."

"I like it," he said, tilting his head and gazing at her. "You're so beautiful."

Her cheeks heated, and she fidgeted with one of her hoop earrings, ones that reminded her of the bracelets she'd given Maddie.

"Are the children with you?"

"No. I didn't have the paperwork ready, and I couldn't wait to come see you."

To see me.

"Ben. The last time we spoke—"

"The last time we spoke, I was confused. I'm not confused anymore."

"You're not?" She tried to read his face, his eyes. "Was Jack in on this?" she asked, recalling his comment to Simba about a "shipment," and not letting her speak to Maddie.

"Of course. He and Simba picked me up at the airport. I already met your parents, too. And I'm still alive." He grinned.

"And you came across the world to tell me that you're not confused?"

He took her face in his hands.

"Hope, I haven't changed my mind about not wanting you to give up your career. I told you that I couldn't ask you to stay in America, and I meant it. But I don't want to be without you. We all miss you, and nothing has been the same since you left. We love you, Hope Alwanga. I love you. You're part of our family, and we can't let you go."

Hope couldn't hold back the tears. A curtain fluttered off the living room, and Hope saw her parents before they closed it to give her privacy. That had to mean they approved. But she knew no one could stop her. No one could keep her from loving someone and wanting to be with him for the rest of her life. No one could cheat destiny or fate.

"Oh, Ben. I love you, too, and the kids. I've been miserable without all of you. But how? You went off to DC and—"

"We'll make it work. The kids are young. If there's a good time for them to experience living abroad, it's now."

Her eyes widened. Was he saying…?

"I've spoken to a few companies that have foreign locations. I'm also looking into potential work with the American embassy here. I want to move here, Hope, with the kids, to be with you. And we can take vacations back to the States to visit Nina and Eric. There are no rules, Hope. We'll do what it takes to make this work. There's only one thing you have to do."

"What? Anything."

"Ask me to stay, Hope."

She swallowed back tears. She'd asked him that very question in America and he'd turned her down.

"Ben, I want you to stay. Please stay. You and the kids. I want us to be together."

He frowned. "I don't know. That depends."

She frowned back and slapped his arm.

"You just want to mess with me," she said.

"I just want to marry you."

She licked her lips and took a shaky breath.

"Hope Alwanga, will you marry me? And Maddie? And Chad? Although I hear he's spoken for. And Ryan?"

"Yes. Absolutely, yes."

"Does kissing you in plain sight of that curtain that keeps opening and closing mean that I'll have to face a lion's wrath from your overprotective brother?"

Hope laughed. "That's a chance you'll have to take."

"Consider it taken," he said, then he sealed their future with a kiss.

* * * * *

LARGER-PRINT BOOKS!

GET 2 FREE LARGER-PRINT NOVELS PLUS 2 FREE MYSTERY GIFTS

Love Inspired

Larger-print novels are now available...

REQUEST YOUR FREE BOOKS!
2 FREE RIVETING INSPIRATIONAL NOVELS
PLUS 2 FREE MYSTERY GIFTS

Love Inspired.
SUSPENSE

YES! Please send me 2 FREE Love Inspired® Suspense novels and my 2 FREE mystery gifts (gifts are worth about $10). After receiving them, if I don't wish to receive any more books, I can return the shipping statement marked "cancel." If I don't cancel, I will receive 4 brand-new novels every month and be billed just $4.74 per book in the U.S. or $5.24 per book in Canada. That's a savings of at least 21% off the cover price. It's quite a bargain! Shipping and handling is just 50¢ per book in the U.S. and 75¢ per book in Canada.* I understand that accepting the 2 free books and gifts places me under no obligation to buy anything. I can always return a shipment and cancel at any time. Even if I never buy another book, the two free books and gifts are mine to keep forever.

123/323 IDN F5AN

Name	(PLEASE PRINT)	
Address		Apt. #
City	State/Prov.	Zip/Postal Code

Signature (if under 18, a parent or guardian must sign)

Mail to the **Harlequin® Reader Service:**
IN U.S.A.: P.O. Box 1867, Buffalo, NY 14240-1867
IN CANADA: P.O. Box 609, Fort Erie, Ontario L2A 5X3

**Are you a current subscriber to Love Inspired Suspense books
and want to receive the larger-print edition?
Call 1-800-873-8635 or visit www.ReaderService.com.**

* Terms and prices subject to change without notice. Prices do not include applicable taxes. Sales tax applicable in N.Y. Canadian residents will be charged applicable taxes. Offer not valid in Quebec. This offer is limited to one order per household. Not valid for current subscribers to Love Inspired Suspense books. All orders subject to credit approval. Credit or debit balances in a customer's account(s) may be offset by any other outstanding balance owed by or to the customer. Please allow 4 to 6 weeks for delivery. Offer available while quantities last.

Your Privacy—The Harlequin® Reader Service is committed to protecting your privacy. Our Privacy Policy is available online at www.ReaderService.com or upon request from the Harlequin Reader Service.
We make a portion of our mailing list available to reputable third parties that offer products we believe may interest you. If you prefer that we not exchange your name with third parties, or if you wish to clarify or modify your communication preferences, please visit us at www.ReaderService.com/consumerchoice or write to us at Harlequin Reader Service Preference Service, P.O. Box 9062, Buffalo, NY 14269. Include your complete name and address.

LISDIR13R